GALWAY STORIES: 2020

Edited by Alan McMonagle & Lisa Frank

Doire Press

First published in 2020

Doire Press
Aille, Inverin, Co. Galway
www.doirepress.com

Layout & design: Lisa Frank
Photos: Róisín Flaherty
Map and icon design: Tríona Walsh
Alan McMonagle photo: Fionnuala Hanlon
Lisa Frank photo: Apple Photo Booth

Printed by Clódóirí CL, Casla, Co. na Gaillimhe

ISBN 978-1-907682-73-5

We gratefully acknowledge the assistance of both The Arts Council / An Chomhairle Ealaíon and Galway 2020 European Capital of Culture as part of the Small Towns Big Ideas programme.

CONTENTS

GALWAY COUNTY:

INTRODUCTION

I have begun these lines on one of those gravestone-grey, late-November Galway mornings. It's already cold and damp, the rain has made fast friends with a barbaric breeze that seems to have it within its powers to turn the rain around so that as soon as it lands, it starts falling upwards—pretty much in keeping with how it was when I first arrived in Galway twenty or thirty or forty years ago.

I've been living in Galway on and off since I did my Leaving Cert. On four separate occasions I have legged it for stints abroad and every time, upon my return, I have sought out Galway as a place to quell my pervading restlessness. I've long since lost count of the number of different addresses, but I can easily recall the locales I have inhabited. Whitestrand. Newcastle. Shantalla. Rahoon. Castlelawn. Forster Court. Tirellan Heights. Dangan Heights. Mary Street. College Road. Cemetery Cross. New Dock Road. Clybaun. And though very much a blow-in, I have it on good authority that I was conceived in Galway—

lower Salthill to be exact, not far from the sight of the much-missed Claddagh Palace cinema. And so, there too, I stake my claim.

This is an anthology of and about place. Thematically speaking, all the usual suspects—love, loss, grief, aspiration, despair, coming-of-age, survival, madness—have been rounded up; the narrative registers run the well-trodden though always welcome gauntlet of joy and lament; hope and regret; fear and uncertainty; courage and perseverance; the antic and the absurd. But this is first and foremost an anthology suffused with the tang and essence of a small city and far-reaching county on Ireland's western seaboard.

The stories make trips far and wide. To Clifden and Killary. To Rosscahill and Barna. To the bowels of Conamara and to that sturdy bastion of East Galway, Ballinasloe—a place I used to visit on the first Saturday of every month in order to show off my doggerel poems. We even leave the mainland—at Cleggan Pier to be precise—traversing twenty minutes of gibbering Atlantic as far as the mystical island of Inisbofin, home to the five a.m. *swalking* corncrake and habitual host to many's the solace-seeking artist. Stories rock up in the outlying neighbourhoods of Salthill, Knocknacarra and Roscam. And of course we find ourselves very much in the thick of it, deep within the alley-wide bars, the ghostly building sites, the resolute nightclubs and rinky-dink cafés, and numerous other getting-stranger-by-the-minute emporiums of the arts, trade and commerce that grace the intricate streets and waterways of the city itself.

Because Galway—city and county—is all the time theatre and song and dance and music; it is stage and screen; painting and poem; it is buskers and traders; blink-and-you'll-miss-it tricksters and never-want-to-wake-up dreamers; it is a white swan emerging from the darkness of a Claddagh night; it is not one but two fig trees along the banks of Middle River (though I have been told fig trees are not native to these parts). It is definitely too much traffic. It is river and lake and roiling sea; cloud-mountain and boggy-field; whistling-wind valley and white-sand shoreline. It is Maam Trasna. Coral Beach. Sky Road.

Sinking River. Rosmuc. Gort. Bullaun. Recess. Cnoc Breac. Killimor. Lackagh. Glinsk. Portumna. Tuam. Glennamaddy. And a place I can never find goes by the name of Cappataggle. It is wild and various and contradictory; it can hoodwink and charm; big you up and cut you down; it is a rugged, brooding, at times infuriating, swing-high swing-low, dreamtime amalgam of the wondrous, the nonsensical and the chaotic; it is drop-dead gorgeous. Most of all, as far as I'm concerned, it is a never-the-dull-moment performance space, peopled by a cast of thousands, each and every one of whom has a story to tell.

And so it was that Lisa Frank (another blow-in) from Doire Press pitched me her latest project—a follow-up of sorts, but very much its own thing—and invited me to be a part of this anthology. Along with her co-publisher and partner, John Walsh, she is to be commended, lauded, indeed feted both for her unflappable dedication to the cause and for her ongoing contribution to Galway's literary adventure. Long may it continue.

Galway. It is north, south, east, and west; past and future; here and now. And as of right now—that gravestone-grey of earlier in the week having yielded to a crisp-clear, blue-sky Sunday afternoon—I am on the Prom in Salthill, perched on my rock, looking out into the much-sung-about bay, marvelling at the sundown light. It is the first of December; almost time, then, to say goodbye to another year and hello to a new one.

Welcome to Galway, 2020. Here are some of its stories.

Alan McMonagle
November 26 / December 1 2019

GALWAY CITY

The Claddagh.

City Centre

The Farmers' Market outside St Nicholas' Church.

Galway has often been called 'the lilting capital of the west'. Its medieval city centre is made up of narrow streets and even narrower lanes; it borders the sea and is sectioned by a complex waterways system, all of which combine to give it great charm. In 1984 the city underwent a makeover when it celebrated its Quincentennial, 500 years a city since it first received a royal charter in 1484. It was a year-long party during which people became a lot more aware of their heritage, culture and history. It energised creativity and imagination and helped bring the arts to new levels. The face of the city changed as old buildings were tidied up and a significant amount of new construction took place.

Galway is a young person's town, full of energy and street enter-tainment; the former City of the Tribes has evolved into The City of the Vibes. A city of festivals, it has the major benefit of a rich Irish-language tradition, and in the recent past, the arrival of so many different nationalities, which have added considerably to the rich multicultural tapestry. You rarely hear, *Howsa go-ann, Luveen* on the street anymore.

The Latin Quarter.

The Docks.

Pádraic Ó Conaire Statue, Eyre Square.

The West End.

Aoibheann McCann

THE BLOW-IN'S GUIDE TO GALWAY

You have only been in Galway for a few weeks, but Claire has been here for a few months, so she teaches you all she knows. You came here to get a job and she came here to do a secretarial class at the technical college. You can't picture it when she tells you this, you imagine her split-ended hennaed hair would get tangled in the typewriters.

The grey skyline is thronged with cranes and the air shudders with the reverberation of rock-breakers in the daytime, so you stay in bed until six o'clock every evening except on Wednesdays. On Wednesdays you go with Claire to collect your dole, then do your weekly shopping in the Londis on Father Griffin Road, where butter vouchers are treated like cash. You buy the cheapest cuts of chicken, run the gamut of the cross-eyed butcher and his leering about thighs and legs. He'll throw in a few wings if you laugh along with him, though you roll up your eyes and give him the finger when he turns to weigh them. On the way to the till you stand with your back to Claire to provide cover for the jars of Dolmio sauce and the tins of sardines that vanish into her velvet patchwork bag.

Claire got the bag from the Cerebral Palsy charity shop, where you buy a leopard-skin coat for £5 to go with the leggings and the vest top and the red bra from Penneys. All bottomed off with your faithful black Doc Martens.

In the evenings, you and Claire spend hours putting on the make-up that she shoplifts from upstairs in Roches Stores. You listen to The Red Hot Chilli Peppers or The Prodigy, smoking joints and drinking cans. You keep a towel by the window that you wrap around your hair before you stick your head out if someone rings the doorbell. If they look like they might wreck your head, you say you are in the shower and slam down the sash before the smoke escapes or they hear the music.

Then it's off to Mixers or The King's Head or Cullinane's, where you and Claire flirt with the middle-aged men who might buy you drinks, and then set the bouncers on them if they come on too strong. Then out to Salthill where it's free into The Castle or The Warwick after one in the morning. You dance beside the speaker and your hands join in communion with the strobe lights. As the crowd is herded out the door, you finish off the best of the discarded drinks. Then out onto the street for the banter and the fights until the last of the clubbers have left in taxis. You laugh at the girls in high heels, the only time you have to get a cab is if you are so gasping for cigarettes in the night that you have to go to the twenty-four-hour Esso off the dual carriageway.

You wait near Mighty Macs for the leftover food they throw out the back. Then home between the edge of the prom and the marsh, where you rob a clothesline or two and pick up a few bits to go with the coats you take from the clubs, or just sheets and towels to save you from paying for the launderette.

Pat, the old security guard, shines a torch in your face when the two of you are at the back of a building site one night looking for scrap wood for the fire. You screech to distract him from his suspicions by pretending Claire is peeing. You end up in the hut where he is stuck alone all night. There are maps on the wall, and you are reminded of a film where the detective turns up and asks questions about the body that has been uncovered by the excavators.

Pat is added to your routine, with his dirty teacups that he uses to share a tartan flask of warm whiskey. He never touches you and has Woodbine cigarettes that he lets you smoke. You don't know what you talk to him about, maybe the changes in the city, maybe where he is from and you aren't, or maybe the new apartments that he is supposed to be looking after and the people who will live in them after they are complete.

You decide to leave the clubs alone for a while because the bouncers start following you around after one girl says Claire is wearing her hoodie and another says you took her bag. You start smoking a joint in bed because the fear is waking you up early. You wish you had some more of those yellow tablets, as your nerves have been shot since you dropped that Superman acid and went mad decorating the flat with tinsel and fairy lights from the pound shop, though it is months until Christmas. But the doctor has told Claire he's not having any more of it, so it has to be the hash, though for the last few months it has been laced with diesel and gives you a headache. You get it in The Canal or The Hibernian or The Galway Shawl, empty apart from the denimed men with badly repaired noses, who sell bad deals by the pool tables.

Sometimes you walk up past the Rahoon Flats, where the fields multiply unceasingly until the orange glow of the city meets the salmon sunrise, and you look across the bay to The Burren and, although you are on a farmer's land, it's not the same as the countryside where you were brought up; you don't feel watched here. And you wander for hours in the mist, your boots soaked with dew, your pockets full of magic mushrooms, and everything is real but not real, and there is no right and no wrong, this is just how it is done.

The girls downstairs used to be good craic but now they just bang on the ceiling, so you and Claire turn up the music. They move out. Your landlord is a countryman with a big flat face, he gives rent receipts and doesn't seem to care who lives there as long as they don't complain about the state of the place.

Linda and Kevin move in, you can't remember where you met them first, maybe in the Community Welfare Office in Shantalla, where you collect your rent allowance once a month, or maybe on the street drinking. You drink in Eyre Square now, as it's cheaper and there are no bars left that will serve you.

You feel sorry for Kevin; Linda says that he was made homeless because of his father's gambling, or a sectarian house fire. Or that he was made leave West Belfast by men in balaclavas when he was caught joyriding. Kevin gets his dole on a Tuesday. Linda buys a ten-kilo bag of potatoes in Silkes on Munster Avenue that they bake, boil or mash for dinner every day, and then fry up the leftovers at night when they come back from drinking. Linda has fled Ballymena to escape glue-sniffing, post-natal depression or child abuse charges, depending on the day or how much cider she has drunk. She has the hair of a forty-year-old housewife and the tracksuit of a thirteen-year-old.

When they tell you they are getting married you make a pot of mushroom tea and bring it downstairs in its tea cosy, a knitted one, yellow and mauve, that you stole from a bin-bag outside the Simon shop early one morning. You can't remember what you wear to the church but there are flowers in Claire's hair, white flowers. Linda and Kevin are holding hands and smiling at each other at the altar. Linda wears a white lacy top and white trousers and white court shoes. Kevin wears a black suit flecked with purple, a red rose in the buttonhole. You are not sure who takes the photographs as all the pews are empty.

After you leave the Augustinian Church, you go to McDonaghs on Quay Street for fish and chips. Linda and Kevin buy themselves a Manchester United mirror to celebrate.

The next day Linda and Kevin tell the St Vincent De Paul they can't cope on the dole and soon the white-haired women with the pioneer pins visit; they purse their lips and ask questions about The North. But the following Friday, and every Friday after that, a large bag of coal is delivered to stoke the fireplaces in the sitting room and the bedroom. Some of the heat drifts upstairs through the cracks in the ceiling. You go to the office on Augustine Street and ask for a visit from the women, but only get Dunnes Stores' vouchers that have 'No Alcohol, No Cigarettes' stamped on the back in firm black letters. They can only be used out in Terryland and it is too far to walk. But you and Claire go back to the basement, where the EU surplus corned beef and stewing steak are given out for free in white-papered tins. Linda adds it to the mash that you eat before you go back up to Eyre Square.

When you and Claire walk towards the hut in the night—this is all that's left of your old routine now—you speculate about Pat's life: he lives with his mother, he was in the army, he is secretly gay. One night he shows you around the show apartment; it is warm even though it is the middle of the night. He invites you out to his house; he says he'll get a big bottle of whiskey to celebrate. You don't recognise the address so he offers to pick you up, but you say no. You pretend you have a car, that you have boyfriends.

You don't know why you take Linda, maybe Kevin talks you into it. You get a cab past the outskirts of the city, past the red and white of the twenty-four-hour Esso.

Pat is waiting by the gate, you follow him around the back and into a green and white caravan that is not much different to the hut. He sits in front of the brown paisley curtains, his thick glasses glinting in the dim light as he pours a bottle of Jameson into what he says are Galway Crystal tumblers. Linda sits beside him and talks incessantly about the bonfires and the RUC and the time her father tried to kill her mother. You stare out the window at the dark void of the dilapidated house Pat tells you he's having renovated.

Pat says who is going to give me a kiss and Linda says me, so you and Claire drink more than your share of the whiskey while their silhouettes join in the half-light. Then they stop and act as if it never happened, and when you begin to think about it, maybe it didn't. But you understand now that Linda has spoiled it all. Though Claire will try to convince you otherwise, you're going to have to move out of the flat and leave them all behind.

As Claire starts rolling a joint for the road, you imagine your life two or three years down the line—you'll have made new friends with highlights in their hair, friends with jobs and boyfriends who'll go for a few drinks in O'Connell's on a Friday night before they go to The Bentley for a quick bop. You'll be living in one of the new apartments, up early every morning to put on your nylon uniform and your name badge, staring at the storage heaters while you eat your cereal, bringing the bin-bags out to the shed where the hut used to be.

James Martyn Joyce

ANGEL HANDS

It was Race Week and Galway was tippled. And here we were, downstairs in a backstreet food place off Shop Street, well over towards the river. A pile 'em high but grease 'em first sort of a place, a sheen of weepsweat on the orange walls, no natural light worth noticing and the overheated waitresses under the eye of the surly cashier bustling plates with a vengeance bordering on hatred.

There were twelve of us in all, me and Kevin and ten young fellas, my own son, Tomás, included. They were all decked out in their best tracksuits with the club initials on the back. Last year's models, fair enough, but I'd picked them up cheap. We had to try.

Half of the team were bruised and one or two battered as well. One lad was sucking back gobs of dark slug-blood 'cos his nose wouldn't stop seeping and might even be broken.

But it was all good, they were boxers after all; pain was inevitable, and we'd just won a serious boxing challenge by seven bouts to three.

Even the boys who'd lost were buzzing and Kevin and myself were buzzing too.

Not for the first time I'd been pressured into a bet with the trainer of the city club, a deathly silent, winner takes all kinda bet and, as a result, we were very close to meeting the full cost of a load of new gym equipment. A heavy bag for a start, something not weighed down with decades of spit, stale sweat, stiffened snot and faded knuckle blood. Something solid for the lads to wallop chunks out of on the dark winter nights ahead in the breezeblock shed I'd built onto the house years before and called it a boxing club.

Even worse, Mellett, the city trainer, had pushed his fat face in mine when we arrived at their clubhouse and whispered a further challenge.

'How about you and me adding a little extra sweetener here, Colm. Say, two, three hundred, just to make it interesting?' I could smell the bastard's smugness, like he knew I had no option, like he knew he'd already won. 'Just between you and me, mind, nothing to do with the other stuff,' he winked. The other stuff already amounted to a thousand Euros, no small thing in itself. I wasn't sure, but he had me in a corner, working my ribs, what could I do?

It was the wrong time of the year for a challenge like this, mid-summer, with the city bursting at the seams, piling on festival after festival, flaunting themed event after themed event until you could barely guess what was going to happen next. A boiling pot, I'd call it, where the serious holiday people rolled in to grease their axles in one way or another. The plush hotels were knee-deep in big spenders, half-horse, half-human types, singular betting addicts and middle-aged businessmen with disappointed wives. Some punters were festooned in an array of 'dick-the-biggest' racecourse badges, flapping cardboard disks with God knows what written on them. But they still screamed exclusivity. 'Look at me,' they purred, 'I belong.'

The cheaper hotels and short lets were bursting too. No exclusive badges here, just a flood of unfortunate suits and peaky caps. Lads in chesty waistcoats and tight, head-lice haircuts, thin-faced shapers and poor-dieters hoping to make it big, but with folding money all the same, thin pinches of it.

And everyone had a tip, some four-legged goldmine, quivering nervously in a stable somewhere, that would romp home at a hundred to one. 'Romping' was a word that got used a lot during Race Week; others included, 'hammered', 'pissed' and 'buckled'. Even 'blathered' was making a comeback, and I'd just added 'tippled' myself.

Boxing is an all-year-round sport, with the serious tournaments in the winter and spring, but we'd taken the challenge when it arrived. The city boys were sure of easy pickings; just like always, free money for The Galway Races off our Connemara, mountainy backs. But they'd reckoned without Kevin, my trainer, my new secret weapon.

I watched him from the end of the cobbled-together stretch of tables where we were sitting, the lads ploughing into mountains of chips, razoring the welts of clammy mince, nibbling at the brittle, thawed-out buns and talking with their mouths full. He had come out of nowhere. Himself and a thin woman, some said a wife, and they'd taken the Guiney's old house down beside the pier. Rural Regeneration and Resettlement, someone had called it and, sure enough, they'd settled in. The thin woman made little shell sculptures from the pickings of the shore and painted delicate flower designs on weathered beach stones which she sold to the local shop. Kevin signed on like most of us, did odd jobs where he found them and spent the rest of his time beating back the years of salty briars behind the house, downhill towards the tide.

One night he showed up at the clubhouse door and stood there, watching. Big Joseph was working the old bag, body shots, hooks and crosses, laying into it, welting it, bustling it away to meet it coming back. There was a healthy steam rising off him, his muscle grunts filling the busy space.

Kevin had stood there for a while, his shoulder to the jamb. He caught my eye and nodded. I left him so, figuring he'd move when he was ready. Then he stepped forward and showed Joseph how to crouch, how to set his feet right and put his weight where it counted, how to work his punches up into the belly of the bag. Big Joseph had blanked his advice, told him to fuck off, asking what a badger like him would know about boxing, a cut at his greying temples. Kevin had paused, blinked like Big Joseph was a sad surprise to him, nodded to the ring and held up two fingers.

'Hit me once in two minutes, big man, and I'll do as you say. I'll fuck off. Deal?' His accent was way north and Joseph had laughed, his toothy smile promising blood and pain. 'But if you don't, and you won't, will you listen then?' Big Joseph nodded, and Kevin turned to me, made a bow. He hung his jacket on the ring post and ducked through. I moved to the gong, got my stopwatch ready and asked if he wanted gloves.

'Naw, I won't be hitting the big man.'

I clocked the gong and watched the second hand crawl forward. And Joseph didn't touch him once in the two minutes. He came out shuffling, quartering the ring, cutting off the avenues and then started to swing. Except Kevin wasn't there. He barely moved, I can swear to that, but by the time Big Joseph realised he'd missed, Kevin had melted across the ring, wraith-like, feet moving, soundless on the worn canvas.

And that was how it went, Big Joseph winding up, ponderous, and Kevin never there when the leather telegram arrived. The other lads urged Joseph on, but I doubt if any two, or possibly three of them together, would have done much better.

After two minutes I clocked the gong again and Big Joseph hunched over, sucking air. Kevin stood before him, his hands at his sides. I bollocked Joseph about it afterwards, but I could do nothing to stop his wild punch. He straightened and launched an uppercut at Kevin's jaw.

Everyone in the room heard the dull sound. Joseph's punch sailed on its way skywards, but the older man barely moved. Most of the lads swore they never saw it. Kevin's liver shot only travelled about six inches, but it made a sickening, fleshy crack. Big Joseph's body seemed to lose track of itself, did a kinda Bambi shuffle, doe-like, before he sank to his knees, his crying intake of breath a wail for mercy, but way too late.

'Unworthy.' That was all Kevin said to the hunched-over Joseph before stepping through the ropes and introducing himself to me. He stayed late that night, doing as he'd promised. Big Joseph broadsided the heavy bag until I thought he'd drop. Kevin kept him at it, the other lads gathered close, flurries of punches rocking the mottled leather, Joseph's grunts bouncing off the walls.

Kevin showed up regularly after that. I was a part-time trainer, always had been. I was carrying weight and what with drifting past fifty as well, all help was welcome. By day I was still driving the school bus for Conroy, a cash job, trundling across the hills, morning and afternoon to Clifden, where most of the parish kids did their learning. There was no problem getting young lads who wanted to fight, and I'd taken them a distance. But we were never going to make the Nationals. I knew where my knowledge ended, and probably the lads did too.

'Ah, I used to box in Belfast years ago and I trained in London for a while.' That was all Kevin said when I asked him. Bare information but I didn't press him. A man has his business and it's always his own. He'd tell me more or he wouldn't, and he never did.

But he worked magic with the lads. They became a unit, did the road work together, the skipping and the bag work, the speed ball, the heavy pads. Kevin would pattern the ring, his hands held before him, the lads shifting their attacks, high to low, low to high, jabs to crosses, rationing the exuberant uppercuts. And yet, he was never fully there, always moving, sapping the power from their best shots, shadowman, making them work.

Every man has hopes for his son and I'm no different. Tomás is a good lad. I'd recruited him early, baby gloves and tiny boots for Christmas, and he'd started on the bag when he could barely reach it. And he had talent, I could see that early on. But with time he improved less and less. I tried everything, training videos, extra time with me, individual gym work. But he just seemed to settle, like he was happy with a certain level. I couldn't push him harder; I loved him too much.

But Kevin saw the potential in Tomás' fast hands, his nimble movement, his eye for the punch, and he worked on that. Before I knew it I had a fighter on my hands. Tomás came through from the kitchen one morning, a towel on his shoulder, his tracksuit blotched with sweat, and told me he'd been running on the shore. After that, he trained before school every morning and got better and better.

I studied Kevin down the table where he was sitting, his head close to my son's, talking. I knew it was boxing; he feinted, doing the angel hands, shaped a move and Tomás nodded, his eyes all glint and focus.

Angel hands are called angel hands because they guard and protect you, they keep the danger away and Tomás' opponent earlier had barely touched him. A Southpaw, he should have been difficult for Tomás, but not so. My son was all movement and economy in that fight, skipping across the fresh canvas, jabbing, weaving, making his opponent miss, and scoring points on the turn with his clean shots. And he would have been happy with a points' decision; we could all see it, until the town's lad, tired of clipping air, had muttered something under his breath about inbreds.

A look passed between my son and Kevin, barely a nod, but a

licence to hurt all the same, and Tomás changed. He turned cold, slowed down to speed up, a calculated cut to his punches, more zip in his feet, razor combinations, his hands a painful blur, his chin tucked well in.

Left-handed or not, Southpaw grew confused, speed-blinded, tried to parry, tried to skip away, tried to cover up. Tomás' rib shots had a brutality to them, a sapping hollowness, a groan factor. That's what you don't hear in a fight on TV, the crowds and the microphones sanitise it. But there, on the ring apron, we heard the slow grunts, the rasping intakes, the sad pleas a body makes because it has no choice, until Southpaw dropped to one knee and the referee waved Tomás away.

All credit, the lad got up at the count of eight and the referee dusted his gloves off to give him a few seconds more. But everyone knew that something inevitable had slipped through the ropes; it perched there on my son's shoulder. Tomás moved in and his first shot almost folded the lad in half, his downward chop catching Southpaw along the jaw, the head-guard useless, and that was that.

'That young lad of yours will do well at the Nationals.' Mellett was complimentary afterwards, but I'm shy of veiled praise, a gloss for the sake of civility. We both knew what we thought of each other. He saw us as country fools from Connemara, easy pickings, a chance to put one over. Like he'd done before.

This time we could both feel it, the shift that had come about. Five matches in and we were ahead four to one. After the final fight, when Big Joseph had retired their heavyweight, Mellett shook my hand, a grudging clasp, but one he'd never proffered before.

'That new trainer of yours, there's something about him,' was all he said, and I wondered what he meant. I nodded and let it go. To tell the truth, there was something about Kevin that I'd started to wonder about myself.

The thing was, the lads loved Kevin. Even Big Joseph had moved from noncommittal to full fan. I saw how the team were around him, and they were a team now, he'd made them a unit. Most nights after training Kevin would stand there in the tight dressing room, the lads towelling off, pointing out individual moves, faking shimmies, insisting on diet, always offering advice. Sitting there at the table, I watched the way Tomás listened, their heads close together, Kevin's hands moving, flurries of speed, how Tomás smiled, taking it in.

'Let's do it if you have the cash. We need the new equipment.' Kevin's voice had been upbeat after the quiet offer of the bet from the Galway club. I was reluctant, there would be trouble if we were ever found out, and we'd been skinned before, a hundred here, a few there. And this time was different; Mellett was talking a thousand, a lot of cash, enough for a heavy bag, a proper weights bench, new headguards, punch pads with all the stuffing still in them, a speed ball, maybe two, whatever the money ran to.

'But what if we lose?' I looked at Kevin.

'We won't lose.' He sounded so sure.

'And if we do? What about the equipment then, the new kit?' I knew I was nervous.

'But we won't lose.' So we went for it. After all, it was Race Week.

And now I knew I'd never forget the look on Mellett's face when he handed me the fat roll of fifties, the pinched choke of his, 'Well done'.

Our desserts arrived and the lads' laughter carried through the room. They might be the hardest table here, but the sight of chocolate and whipped cream could still bring out the boys in them. Kevin spooned some of the cream-covered mess into his mouth and someone cleared their throat and gravely mentioned diet. He took another mouthful to cheers from the lads and Big Joseph dabbed his creamy spoon to Kevin's nose. The laughter exploded but Kevin took it well, touched his own spoon to Tomás' nose and another cheer followed.

I saw how Tomás blushed, how Kevin held his eye for an extra blinktime, a breath-held pulse of anticipation almost, as the creamy baptism, spoon by spoon, continued on around the table. As sure as a straight left, I knew what was nagging me. I'd seen how Kevin had looked at Tomás, the fleeting hunger in his face. I thought of the way he lingered in the dressing room while the lads dressed. I thought of why a top-class boxing trainer might show up in a country village, as far west as sunset, away from everything, no one with him but a thin wife. I thought of our surprise win, the pinched face of the city club's trainer, his rictal smile as he handed the money over, the way he'd said, 'There's something about that new trainer of yours.' How I knew he'd never tell me.

But we were getting the new equipment, we were going to the Nationals in February, two, and maybe three fighters, and for the first time ever. I'd mind the lads. I'd keep an eye on Kevin. I'd look out for Tomás. I felt the weight of the fat roll of notes close to my heart. It would all work out.

Caoilinn Hughes

I ATE IT ALL AND I REALLY THOUGHT
I WOULDN'T

It's the soggy kind of wind that undoes all the hair-dos on the west coast of Ireland; that makes broken tents of nice new outfits, and shouting matches of good wishes:

I'll love you and leave you. What, love? Love me and leave me. I'll let you go. Have a good life! Indeed it is. Fine a day as any for blowing off cobwebs. A northerly with wet spells. Where has the day gone? We lost track of ourselves.

It'll be quiet in the shop today. What harm. Marjorie finds the work involved in customers to be quite annoying. She prefers to watch them come in and twirl around. If they slip their wallets from their back pockets, better's the view. But framing their wedding shots and family portraits and homeopathic diplomas smacks too much of taxidermy. And the business, she can gladly do without.

This Dominic Street property — sandwiched between cafés —

was part of last year's divorce settlement, along with the three-bedroom house, its contents, two and a half empty beds, their cars, their pug-terrier Michael Flatley, and her ex-husband's golf club set. Balls and all. The shop has no website and if it has word-of-mouth, the words are French. It wouldn't behove Marjorie to sell it anyway, as the country is unkinkily spank-bang in the middle of a recession. It was Brendan's architecture start-up premises back in the 90s when Marjorie's inheritance became his seed fund (well, one of them); back when he was still astonished that his wife built his desk for him, and his closet. The closet, alas, didn't stay shut. After a twelve-year largely platonic marriage, he asked for a divorce on the same weepy breath as coming out to her. 'Who are you crying for?' she'd said, flaunting the dry whites of her eyes at him like hankies. All the same, it felt as though they were tilting down the farside of a twelve-metre wave— one that would deposit them oceans apart, differently wounded. She dragged her suitcase from beneath the bed for the passage. 'Leave it,' he'd said. 'I'll go. You stay. Keep everything.' Marjorie's face glazed suddenly, as if an eggy brush had been wiped across it. '*Everything*?' Brendan's teeth chattered. He shivered in his spectral flag. Horrible, yes, to stand before a loved one, in shreds… for them not to hold their arms out to collect you. She glanced from the mole on his nose to the one disappearing into his crimped chin to the scar on his hairline; she could inch her way around him blindfolded. But he her? Not a hope. *How* she'd never connected the dots… Brendan had clutched his moisturised elbows then and, as a witness claiming guilt, said: 'You're my best friend. I never didn't love you. It's my fault. I'm… I wanted to give you everything.' It was the new millennium before Marjorie understood her deeper grief: that the closet she'd built for herself had been locked from outside and in. She'd *wanted* every-thing.

She should be in the back room now, cutting glass and mounts to size, but she's not in the mood. Her Topman Hawaiian shirt is blanched in dust from the workshop this morning, where she'd been making a custom frame — the only such order this month. 'Do you think a recliner chair would suit the place?' she asks her new colleague, who hums, as if sounding out the faxed information: that the boss plans to make napping at work more comfortable.

Bróna is cleaning the windows, having insisted that windows are the *frames* by which their expertise is assessed. Up and along the rivered glass she swans, with her lemony-white cremnitz skin, her bachelor's degree in Art History, her Picasso sketch eyeliner and, cubistically, Marjorie's eyes all over her. On the crescent scar that lends a smile line to her pussy face, on the shadowy ulnar bones of her wrists, her angular palette knife arms, the slant fact of her waist, the firm hold she has of herself, of that shammy. From the register, Marjorie clears her throat, which has the satisfying effect of making Bróna twist around. With her in profile, the composition is particularly consoling.

Possibly because of the recession or possibly because of the general drain-ward motion of society, Bróna has taken it upon herself to be *concerned* about the business's viability. 'Let's hope that wet wind makes it looks cosy in here. Hygge!' she says, keeping her ear close to the glass as if listening for the squeaking counterfactual: the fine crack in the reality of this permanent, salaried job, with sick days and — for the love of god — retirement contributions.

'*Hooga*. Is how the Danes say it.' Marjorie DJs the scalp behind her ear rhythmically. 'But you know... I think your higgy sounds cosier.'

The tone had been set at the interview stage a month back and, since no complaint was made, Marjorie took it as understood that one mustn't resent what libido is left in a forty-five-year-old woman. Lechery is nicer to be around than bitterness. And their taste in music has a sizeable overlap — Talking Heads, Oscar Peterson, the *Schindler's List* soundtrack. Bróna had said as much. 'The *noise* that would be on in SuperValu!' (where one of her college friends has wound up). 'The factory din of Medtronic!' (one of the only employers taking people on in the county). 'The TV operatics that would be on at home!' (that is, in Bróna's parents' house) to overpower the vibrato of their negative equity: the passive-aggressive *Say Yes to The Dress*, the colonialism-nostalgic *Antiques Roadshow*, the tongue-clicking misconstruing of *this new generation*. Bróna doesn't quite know what to make of her own generation. *She* hadn't remortgaged a home willy-nilly when it had magically doubled in value, as her parents had. And if *she* had ever driven a brand-new 2007 Audi A4 Quattro out of a dealership, it would have been to test drive it to Lidl for discount korma. But then, she *had* come into shops like this, as people under thirty-five tended to do, to fawn over the merchandise, photograph the desired product furtively, and to abscond and buy it online from China, via the neighbour's wireless on mam's MasterCard. She'd admitted all this to Marjorie, demonstrating the 'candid and open nature' her C.V. had listed as a Key Skill. Reading through her contract, she'd been shocked to see no mention of commissions. And how does that even work thermodynamically — that business can cool off and its employees are retained all the while? She voiced an interest in part-time diplomas in business to wrap her head around it, which Marjorie immediately offered to fund *if* Bróna would only keep her profit-ability aspirations to herself.

Bróna sidles up to the Staff Wanted sign still up on the window and, with the tweezer precision of an art conversationist, frees a fly from its Sellotape frame. Scrupulously, she cleans the glass all around it, to no avail. Marjorie doesn't tell her to take it down. When no more wishes can be genie'd from the glass, Bróna moves on to dusting. Right into the bevels of the display frames. The little bell above the door. Lest she arrive at the cash register altogether, Marjorie sends her into the back office to boil the kettle. Meanwhile, a couple arrive in making a fuss of an umbrella that was protecting the woman's painting. The man is clad in cycling Lycras and high-toe shoes — the opposite of high heels, but with the same clenched-arse result. Marjorie had described to Bróna this classic customer type:

the middle-class couple with a pramful of—lo and behold—hobbies. 'You'd want a lilo to get around in that,' the woman declares, eyeing up her husband's wet t-shirt rigout.

'A submarine, more like,' Marjorie says. 'But it doesn't bother himself on the bike?'

'Ah no,' the man does his own answering. 'The wind dries you off as you go, sure.'

Marjorie glances from his treaded-tire face to his knuckular groin. 'The more you cycle, the worse they swim. Is that true, or is it only a myth?'

'What's that?' the man angles his helmet-strapped ear toward her.

Embarrassed now that she can see some of the expert drawings leaning against the walls awaiting pick-up, the woman cradles her painting to her chest and glances around as if lost—TK Maxx would do her, surely. Idly, she goes to the wall to rifle through the frames that are in a poster-like flickthrough display. The metal ones tick. The wood ones tock. The man gets her to lay her painting on the huge table so they can see what they're working with. He thinks of it as an equivalent to opening a fitness metre app post-ride to see one's form laid bare: one's personal best. When she sets it down—a muddy Connemara pony in a Kenyany sunset—the man awaits commentary from the vendor. Surely this is how they earn their margin, his Elvis lip cues. But Marjorie's eyes are trained away from the painting as from Medusa. Bróna arrives with a cup of tea for her boss and beams at the customers. A dozen recommendations sputter at her lips, so desperately yearning The Close.

'I haven't a clue,' the woman replies when asked what she's after. 'I mean... I don't know. Do you normally have glass on top of an oil painting?' The woman shifts her weight from one Croc to the other.

'Not *typically*,' Marjorie says, 'but, you know, we can do whatever we like.'

The woman looks to her husband—his wedding band is hidden

by cycling gloves, despite the nude fingers. She doesn't *want* to do what she likes: she wants to do what's *right* to do. Without causing hassle: hassle is for the rest of life; not for hobbies. The way she's breathing, it's clear the let-down will be sore: she mightn't paint again; that's how fragile her generosity is towards herself.

Squaring up with Marjorie, the man removes his windshield glasses. What kind of a doctor's appointment is this, where self-diagnosis is both frowned upon and required? 'How would this be *professionally* framed, if you *yourself* were to do the choosing. Would it have a mount around it? Or what about those hover frames with the gap around the sides? I've seen them with can-vases. What's the *perfect custom frame solution* for this, no matter the price?'

'Oh god, Raymond, stop, I'm... it matters, the price. It's not worth some fancy frame, not —'

'Claire.' Raymond grips his wife by her fatty upper arms, im-printing bike oil on her shawl-like cardigan. 'Your painting deserves a *good* frame, and no two words about it.'

The woman tucks her chin to her chest and smiles like the bash-ful seventh dwarf, who could have been the sixth dwarf if it weren't for shame. The man stamps a kiss onto her forehead before clicking from his cleated advantage over to the wall, arrowed in display frames — their cut-off corners V-ing to the ceiling like poorly-painted geese. Marjorie responds to their questions evenly, even though there's an enormous price difference between the frames they're considering and the off-the-shelf ones that can be easily bought online. Bróna gushes almost pornily when the couple handle an art-deco silver gilt-inlaid frame, even though it would render the painting ridiculous. Finally, the woman decides upon something humble and asks what time the shop is open until — they might come back later. 'Grand,' Marjorie says, blowing on her tea.

Bróna stands with her arms suspended several inches from her sides, making a peace sign of her body. 'You could leave your painting here, till then… if you like?' The pitch of her voice might shatter the windows, after all her shining work. 'We could frame it for you, and have it ready to collect? And if you don't love it, we can just change it.'

The woman shimmies now — her hormones dancing a jig they're not at all fit for. And in Crocs! Knowing well this perimenopausal urinary urgency, Marjorie helps her out: 'They're a labour charge for framing it.' Conspiratorially, she adds: 'You could equally take it home and do it yerselves.'

'Ah sure look,' Raymond says, holding the door. 'I could whack it in no bother.'

'You surely could,' Marjorie nods. 'And if in doubt, there's instructive videos online.'

At that, the couple takes off, pretending to have forgotten to leave the painting there for safekeeping. In the rush, they've left their umbrella instead. Bróna's eyes go to it. A baton? The drizzle has eased, so they may not bother returning for it. A dripping profit margin. While Bróna is immobilised by thought, Marjorie has advanced to prying staples from a linen-covered frame, and the playlist has advanced to that iconic cello fifth that would bring the shop to a standstill weren't it stoodstill already. 'The good thing about the Schindler record,' Marjorie addresses her plyers, 'is that it lends perspective to the minor tragedies.' Bróna takes the umbrella hostage to the back room, in case they return for it. The phone rings and Bróna actually runs to pick it up. 'Eh… yes. Hegarty? Yes. It's been ready now for two months… Of course, Miss Hegarty… Till six. Okay — oh sorry, just, just one sec, Miss Hegarty. Just one moment, please.' Marjorie had been gesturing to Bróna and, now that the phone is pressed against her chest, Marjorie stares at the phone and tells Bróna to inform Miss Hegarty that their insurance doesn't cover paintings stored beyond a fortnight — certainly not ones bought at auction. They are not a storage facility. 'Looting is on the up now, tell her. On account of the recession, and a very good batch of methamphetamines in from Longford.' A laugh bursts from Bróna's lips and she lowers her eyelids at Marjorie. She puts the phone back to her ear and tells Miss Hegarty that it would be much-appreciated if she could pick it up because they're very short on space in the shop. Profuse thanks. With the trace of a smile, Bróna takes up the iPod shuffle. 'Can I put on something else?

'Oh do. Slip on something more comfortable.'

Bróna clears her throat and says: 'It's a friend's band. It's kind of... trad electronica. They were on at the Róisín last week. They're really good.'

'We'll find out, so we will,' Marjorie says. But she doesn't get to find out because two people enter the shop simultaneously. One carries the cardboard-cylinder evidence of an ill-advised Monetprint.com purchase, for which there is no frame suitably cheap; the other is a Colin Farrell-looking thirty-something interviewee Marjorie was expecting four minutes ago. His shirt and jeans give a 3D-printed impression; he has a raincoat bunched in one fist, and a backpack held like a briefcase in the other. Le Coq Sportif. In dismay, Bróna watches Marjorie place her hand on the interviewee's lower back to lead him to the office. 'You'll hold the fort?' Marjorie asks rhetorically, then glances back at the unfurled *Water Lilies* print and tells its owner: 'Fair *play* to you! Gorgeous colour palette on that.' The office door shuts and it stays shut until their bellies begin to grumble.

During this time, Marjorie has managed to extort such information from the lad as he didn't know he had in him. Which way he voted in the Twenty-eighth Amendment Treaty of Lisbon referendum. Whether he prefers savoury food for breakfast or sweet or neutral — for example porridge. What he made of *Inglourious Basterds* altogether if not a pile of American self-flattery, with some good lines in it, albeit. 'The eye-talian scene in particular. *3 Idiots* I thought was superb. And *Mr. Nobody*. Did you see that?' The interviewee doesn't bother with humming sounds at this stage. He twitches his face in the negative. 'And, you know... *Transformers: Revenge of the Fallen...*

it got an awful hard time but I quite enjoyed it. Shia LaBeouf and Megan Fox, sure, they're worth six stars before they open their divine gobs.'

One of the interviewee's caterpillar eyebrows tries to climb over the other one. There's a knock on the door and Bróna sticks her head in. 'Sorry to interrupt, but... will I go on my lunch-break now, or—?

'Do that,' Marjorie says, 'and leave the door wide there so I know if there's a customer but it's unlikely.'

'Sure. Sorry...' Bróna says with throat-frayed deference, tilting her head at the interviewee. 'Were we in NUIG together? Art History?'

The interviewee cocks up his chin. 'I went to Trinity.'

A brushtip's worth of red marbles the white of Bróna's face. 'Sorry, I thought I recognised you. But...' She backs out, then stalls and surges forward. 'What did you do, at Trinity?'

Good on her, Marjorie thinks. Promoting herself to co-interviewer! *That's* how it's done. Marjorie thumps the five-page C.V. on the desk before her. 'He has a 2:2 in Film Studies and History, which would complement your art expertise and my carpentry beautifully, not to mention his impressive experience in furniture removal, as well as retail, but... alas...' Marjorie taps her fingers twice on the C.V., 'the challenge is in the job-seekers' pool being so full, and us being further along in the interview process with two others. Women.' Marjorie takes a lavish pause here, and Bróna eventually drops her shoulders sympathetically.

'O...kay?' The guy stretches the two syllables like udders. 'Why d'you call me in then? Why didn't you cancel the interview?'

'Oh believe you me,' Marjorie warns, 'my mind's not made up. I want to be fair and equitable. I take great pleasure out of equally considering all options on the table.' Marjorie stands to reveal her embodied impartiality—her very shape, unresolved. She extends an even hand, stating: 'You're hot mail.'

When he responds with the word *what*, it is packed with enough vehemence to blow out a set of birthday candles.

'Pee underscore nethaway at hot-mail dot com?'

Copping on to the implication, he demotes his briefcase now to its backpack state.

'Grand. We have that memorised, so we do.' Marjorie smiles so completely that the metal crescents of her crown bondings are on display as a full set of filthy nails. She offers him his C.V. back because she's into sustainability. It's the only thing that's ever come into fashion that's actually suited her, besides a knee-high boot. 'Do you know the way? You go around in it, and you feel a million dollars. Or a quarter of a million euros. It makes you *look* and *feel* good. Recycling and a knee-high boot.' Her pleasantries carry on at his retreating back like surplus credits. 'There we have it. Grand. Now. Alright. Thanking you.' Though he's letting himself out, she follows him through the shop so as to show him the way all the same. 'Ah look: she's dried up for you! Just in time.' He utters no parting thanks, only side-eyes the Staff Wanted sign as he sulks off down Dominic Street, shoulders umbrella'd to the wind.

Marjorie spins around on the heel of her wide-fit trainers and tells Bróna: 'I never lost it really... but I've bloody well found my appetite. Would I be a mean tease of a boss to take my lunch-break before you?' Bróna crosses her arms, which Marjorie didn't know she was able to do—that the planed, carved limbs could be bendy.

Here is the window that needs cleaning: a small window to pose the qualifying questions. 'Sure,' Bróna says. 'But... Marjorie?'

Will she come out with them, finally? Her questions: It isn't a twist on the sexual harassment cocktail, is it? Or—hardly—a generational vendetta? If the shop doesn't need to be profitable, surely there's something *else* it could accomplish? There are plenty of other values it could have.

'Marj, *please*. You say Marjorie as if you want to spread me on toast.'

'I'd like to experiment with the set-up while you're gone,' Bróna says, firm as cold butter. 'I have some ideas.'

Marjorie collects her coat and wicker bag from the back of the chair behind the counter. 'So you do. Whereas himself had only notions. And resting bitchy face.' Marjorie grins at Bróna and holds it. Then says: 'I must admit, Bróna, I admire your initiative. As well as a lot of other things about you. Be sure to enjoy yourself. And regale me with all you get up to afterwards.'

Nothing less than a picnic on the riverside grass by the Spanish arch would do Marjorie. For lunch, she ordered a large fish-and-chip supper at McDonagh's. She had lived so many years eating appropriate meals at appropriate hours.

She lays her windbreaker coat on the damp grass and plonks herself down with a jolt to the sit-bone. No one is around to hear her yelp but one fisherman on the far bank, gulls describing the wind with Renaissance overkill, passersby on the road aways behind her, and patient fuckers at a bus-stop. A yellow box containing a life-ring interrupts the view of the River Corrib, gushing rightward. It is a castratingly cold Jacuzzi, the colour of manky denim with white spray all along it, like used shaving foam. Beyond it: the vibrant green algal slime of the stone riverbank; a row of mixum-gatherum townhouses of yellows, burgundies, blues; a grey convent-looking erection; and, an inch above that, cloud—like the surface of the ocean seen from underwater. Marjorie smacks her throat to feel for gills.

Her neck had begun to thicken in her late thirties, without any children to impugn. 'I'm getting more and more grotesque,' she'd told Brendan on her fortieth birthday, to which he'd responded with a wicked smile: 'You're getting more and more like Marlon Brando!' They'd gone out for a walk in Barna Woods before a four-course meal back in town so neither of them would have to be designated driver. Marjorie stopped walking and stood there, quizzing her husband's face, which had gone funny. His gaze darted from her one eye to the other and his lips were pursed, as though he were the one awaiting a defence or apology. After a long moment, Marjorie said: 'In *On the Waterfront*... or *Apocalypse Now*?' Brendan coughed out a laugh, as if he'd been holding his breath. He looked off behind her and said that forty was when things got interesting; that forty couldn't give two fucks about pretty, slender necks. 'No, that's right,' Marjorie said. 'I give *one* fuck now. By forty-five, I'll be down to no fucks.' Brendan grabbed her by the hand then and marched her off the track between shivering trees and clicks of his tongue. Who he was scolding, she didn't know. She found his outdoor sex kink to be far too effortful, but it was an effort she made, if only to dig a well in their dust-dry acreage. He was the full five inches shorter than her, so — given it was *her* birthday — he let himself be pressed against a tree; the bark making of his vanilla arse a twin-cone with chocolate sprinkles. The sky had darkened and, under the canopy, the particularities of their bodies were homogenisable. Still, she could make out Brendan's closed eyes. The wince of his cheeks, like the torn page of a journal that's been scrunched up in self-disgust, then ironed out with the warm heel of a palm. He cut out anagram-wheels from newspapers to bring home to her; she consulted on his hiring of employees based on their ample laurels; he primed and varnished her headboards on sunny weekends; they droopily enacted scenes from films with malty, late-night breath. All that time, she thought she had everything.

'*On the Waterfront*,' Marjorie tells herself now, unbagging the polystyrene container and salivating at the gluggy tartar sauce vomited over three fillets of battered cod and five spuds' worth of chips. She prongs a mess of cod onto the plastic fork and shovels it into her: salty, temporary fullness. Hygge. Gulls trapeze through the air, screaming. They, too, can be grotesque, but they do not repulse their feathered husbands. They go wild on one another — out in the open, wings spread — and, afterwards, they slope around the town for munchies. Their eyes are open and red-rimmed all the time, and no one pities them.

Her mastication pronounces blue veins travelling from her throat up onto her cheeks so that she resembles a dark clown who hasn't properly cleaned off her paint, post-show. It's his fault this habit formed: of seeing herself from the outside. To try to reason the unengorgement, and to locate the pitied feeling. Whose feeling was whose? Enough now. Enough flagellation. Moping. Look forward. Ah yes, the fisherman on the far riverbank. Or is it only a wanker? The two hands are held before his crotch and there is no equipment at all. No rod, no wire, no coolly-box for the catch. The scrawny man is barely clad: he has on a long-sleeved striped t-shirt, a cap, and... gloves. It's a mime artist, she realises. Performing for no one. For no fish supper. Marjorie's phone buzzes in her pocket and she jumps exaggeratedly, so that it counts as exercise. She sets the supper down beside her and roots out the device. It's a text from Bróna.

> 'Trinity just posted a bunch of vitriol
> about you and the shop online. 1 star
> reviews all over the place.'

It takes Marjorie a moment to realise that Bróna means the interviewee. 'Ha!' she proclaims, and looks around for acknow-ledgement. Deep in concentration, the mime artist is either fitting imaginary bait onto a fly lure or inspecting his foreskin for a hook— real or imaginary. Another text ignites the phone:

> 'I took down the staff wanted sign.
> Hope you don't mind. If I'm a bad hire,
> Marjorie, please let me know and I'll
> try harder or quit. But for now at least I
> need to know it's not a scam. And that
> I actually got the job! Thank you so
> much for understanding.'

Then, after a few seconds, a postscript:

'I'll boo all his reviews.'

Marjorie is concocting a witty riposte when she sees the ellipsis still pulsing on her screen. The girl's lovely thrumming fingers. The new hire has more ideas to impart, so she does. Marjorie waits awhile, blinking at the dots, catching herself ensnared like the youngsters by four puny inches when there is so much content around the pixels: so many people, unintroduced; such landscapes, light on history. And there: a mime artist, casting out expertly; turning on his sit-bone as the current tugs the unseen line downriver. There is no one in the vicinity to throw him a euro or a plastic fish. Marjorie will duck in that way heading back to the shop soon enough. Tuck a tenner under his beret, or give him the coat off her back. Well, from beneath her arse, but sure it'll be nice and warm for him. She has heat in her yet, to transfer.

The phone buzzes again and she really fucking jumps this time. Thirty calories at least in the lep, she's out of breath at all the action, and the college graduate essay showing up on her screen.

'I really love this job btw. I'm grateful for it and I badly want to keep it. It's impossible to find a job at all, much less one that doesn't involve signing away your conscience. There's just one problem I should flag. Sometimes there's a mildly inappropriate tone sometimes that makes me uncomfortable. I really don't want any awkwardness to develop in terms of sexual misconduct or anything like that and of course there's been Nothing of the sort so far. And I

understand it's just your cracking sense
of humour which I love. But I can't tell
you how much I want to keep this job,
so it's more I'm just thinking about
long term sustainability and establish-
ing really good frank relations between
us. Can I draw the line on 5 innuendos
a day Marjorie?!!! I hope this is all okay
to lay out. I've just found that I get less
anxiety if I air greivances or concerns
early on before they become something I should never have let them
become. It's preventative. Because the
job's worth protecting. I can see myself
here in 5 years, if I'm lucky. I've locked
up for lunch because it's half two and
I'm starving!! (I guess you're napping
in a recliner chair shop, testing merch!)
Thanks for hearing me out.'

A fine drizzle congests the wind and Marjorie squints at the
air before her, as if she's about to sneeze. She presses the phone
uncomfortably into her pocket. 'Well,' she says, neither question nor
statement. Searching for the punchline that had been the line too
far, she can only call to mind scenes of herself preparing quotes and
timescales, packing and completing orders, feeling up the furniture
with a damp cloth, closing out the till. She cannot even see herself in
her workshop, or visualise anyone alongside her, or hear any words
close to the truth that had been uttered — let alone too close. Then
again, going through the motions is hardly blameless. Was his
heart ever in it — even once — pumping to the point of arrhythmia;
flushing the skin beneath his chest-hair like parched soil in a
sudden downpour? Marjorie wipes the mist gruffly from her face,

and still the blue veins don't wash off. 'You came out in the wrong season!' she shouts at the mime artist, empty-handed. The artist's gaze is devoted to the line, which he is reeling in, dutiful to himself; reverent to the motions. The river is boisterous between them in its unflagging, forthright, littery youth: the wet fucking youth of it! 'But you!' she calls out ineffectually. 'You'd have gone back for the umbrella. Wouldn't you?' She didn't mean the physical thing, but the gesture of it. And in a similar gesture of collection, a colossal white gull swoops down for Marjorie's mushy cod remains. The gesture comes first—a batting motion of smacking the dust from a hung rug—then a scream wrangles from her throat. Sitting, she is useless against the gull. The motion of pushing herself up to her feet suffices as a fitness regimen, so many muscles does it use. There is more to the routine, too: Marjorie tears fistfuls of grass from the ground and flings them skyward. 'Fuck off! Fuck off!' She remembers the catapult she had once carved, for something to do with her hands the evenings she and Brendan sat on the couch. He didn't like fingers in his hair. When he asked what she was making, she said a rape alarm. They'd had to pause the film, Brendan laughed so uncontrollably. To him, it was the multi-layered joke only his amazing wife was capable of.

She's ripped out so many bits of earth, her picnic area looks like the Celtic Tiger's cleaned its claws there. No one comes running to the gulls' rescue, because they will be fine and dandy. There is ample detritus strewn about the city. Besides, they are unpitiable. The mime artist has stressfully packed up his things, and clears off. The bus-stop is deserted. Buses must arrive these days, now that all the leased Audis have had to be returned! There is a new petrol bellyful to the sky, but Marjorie doesn't pay it any heed. She collects the cold tissuey dregs of her supper and gobbles every spec. It tastes of mime, she thinks... of salty mime. But it hadn't done before—there had been flesh involved—she had seen it, from the outside. Pacing the patch of grass, she wonders if she'll be sick. But then, there is Bróna, who isn't yet trained to close out the till. What possession that young, fuckable woman has of herself: how easy and urgent she found it to state her truth, in writing — to formalise the complaint. But Marjorie needn't channel such discipline. The nausea has already passed. 'T'was only a wobble.' She is sweating, but it is a hot flush. Her cool will come back to her momentarily. She inspects the polystyrene container with satisfaction: so well polished it could be recycled. She moves a finger against its slippery skin, pushing the rain around.

Soon, there is enough rain that *it* moves around her. Even the gulls have absconded to some eave to dry off. Hump their feathers light again. Marjorie collects her handbag and tucks the strap up onto her neck-shoulder amalgam. She marches riverward, smacks the polystyrene container flat and frisbees it into the water. A floaty... lest anyone jump in, and then change their mind. What use is the life-ring for a U-turn, and it boxed up on dry ground? Well... dryish. Marjorie snorts to herself. So sapped a nation is it that even the metaphors don't work! Now that she's standing on the bank, she can see that the mime artist hadn't left; he'd only taken shelter in the convent. In its portico — across the body of water — he is on his mobile phone... calling some authority, maybe, to come and fine her?

'You think *that's* litter?' Marjorie yells across to him, dripping; her eyes wide to the elements. 'That's nothing! Wait'll you see! That's only to keep the youth employed.'

Celeste Augé

DEEDEE AND THE SORROWS

At the back of the Róisín Dubh, the door is not a door; it's a curtain, a heavy black one that makes Deirdre think of grand hotels and magic shows. Stephen (her manager/ex-boyfriend) pulls it aside and she follows him into the venue. Small tables look as though they could be pulled over to one side of the room to clear a space for dancing. But they're bolted down, with spindly chairs and wooden stools clustered around them. The room is cold.

What was she thinking, going on the road around Ireland in mid-November? It had seemed like a good idea back in front of a gas fire in Dublin. Just get to work, don't think about it. Set up and sound-check.

Deirdre's pink fleece pyjama bottoms snag on the end of a guitar stand and she nearly topples the entire pile. Three hours trapped in a van with five guys and she's about ready to kick someone. Owen tries to yank down her bottoms. She tells him to eff off out to the van with the other guys and help bring in the gear while she hunts down the house sound engineer. Owen's thirty, only four years younger than her, but sometimes she feels as though the age gap turns her into a handy version of his mother. One more prank like that and she might not be able to have sex with him anymore.

There's no sign of the sound guy, so she digs her phone out of her bag. Lily should be getting into bed soon. She misses her daughter; though less now that she's at the venue, now that she has had some time to recover the scattered bits of herself, glue her idea of who she is back together without the umbilical pull of Lily's four-year-old stream of questions.

'Mama, where does money come from? Who makes it? Why do you need it?' And on she goes. Deirdre mock-whispers goodnight, two kisses into the phone and then two more, asks her to put her dad back on the phone, she wants to talk to him.

'Bout what?' Lily asks.

'Stuff,' Deirdre says, not in the mood for more long-winded explanations that will only lead to more questions. 'Just give him the phone, sweetie.' She can hear Pete in the background saying something similar, and she misses Lily even less. 'Did you give her both inhalers?'

'Yep.'

'And her tonic?'

'Yes.' His voice gets tense over this one syllable, but Deirdre can't help herself.

'Don't forget she needs to have a poo before bedtime or else she'll be up at 4am with a pain in her belly.'

This time he doesn't try to hide the sigh. 'We'll be fine, stop fussing. Besides, my mum's here to help me out.'

Deirdre wishes him good luck, and disconnects. Thank God he wants to help raise Lily. And that they broke up early on. He doesn't question her itchy feet: she's lucky she can take five days and head out on the road, feel the tug of a Lily-shaped gap inside of her.

She pulls out the set list, a fresh sheet of paper from her notebook and a black marker. Gig number three. Galway on a Tuesday night. In the damp cold. In a recession. Still, it's supposed to be a party town and the manager claims this is a student pub on weekdays. Move the cover of 'Girls Just Wanna Have Fun' from her encore set to the top. 'Fishbowl' and her other songs can wait till three songs in when she is warmed up, and the crowd is warmed up.

Deirdre walks around the room, tries to get a feel for the place, pretends to help the boys as they load in the gear and scatter it in front of the low stage. Pacing calms her down, gets her ready for the gig. The house lights are up and she can see too much: the beer stains on the tabletops, the bits of silver gaffe tape left on the walls long after whatever decorations they'd once held up are gone, blobs of chewing gum and other things worn into the black wooden floor. Venues without punters are gloomy places.

A clang startles her; the stage is filling up with cases of different sizes and shapes, holding drums, guitars, keyboards. Owen steps onto the stage, hoists her handbag over his head. 'Where do you want this monster?'

It's the bag that can fit everything: a spare T-shirt, her scrapbook of random magazine clippings, an original Sony Walkman, the kind that takes cassettes. Deirdre doesn't have an MP3 player—she's the only musician she knows who doesn't—but she has an extensive back catalogue in her head and a good cassette collection. She likes the hiss of tape, the ghost-prints of other songs on tapes that haven't been played for years.

'Lob it over to me,' she says, but Owen knows better and reaches down to hand it to her. There are too many distractions up by the stage. She avoids Van's outstretched legs—he's grabbing some shuteye to recover after the crappy drive from Monaghan—and aims for the back of the venue, figuring she can hide out behind the sound desk, get some space.

Back when the lovely girls were learning to write thank-you notes and to make suitable conversation, Deirdre chased love and the unexpected. The nuns warned her that she would end up living a life of sin, that she would end up a single mother without a penny to her name or a steady job, and on the whole, they were right.

She spots a poster for tonight's gig next to the black curtain. *Tuesday Night Special: DeeDee and The Sorrows, 9pm till late, No Support.* So she's one of the Tuesday Night Specials. Sounds like a dodgy tribute band.

Deirdre tries out the first verse of 'Fishbowl', slowly, to make sure her voice is still working. Way back when she was in school, the nuns used to stick her at the very edge of the choir, towards the back, claiming her voice would put off the rest of the girls. One nun in particular — Sister Alphonsus, a square-shaped hag — used to make her stand beside the piano and practise the songs on her own, telling the other girls that they were to listen quietly and make sure that they never sang like Deirdre. Her range is good, but she sounds raspy, though she doesn't smoke.

'Well howya, now there's a voice I haven't heard in years,' booms a voice she had finally stripped out of her head.

She turns around, face tense, shoulders tense in her old T-shirt, and sure enough, it's Liam Rynne. Last time she'd heard, he was in the Canaries, playing pub covers.

'Liam,' she says and nods. Six years. Keep it cool. He broke up with her after three intense years together, dumped her by text message on the first mobile phone she had ever owned. It took a fling with Sunbear's bass player and an unplanned pregnancy to get over him. Plus six months of writing nasty (but mostly true) things about him in black permanent marker in the toilets of any pub she went to.

'Deirdre, gorgeous,' he says and walks right by her, pats her on the shoulder on his way over to the sound desk. 'Sorry I'm late, had to run out for a spare lead.' He holds up an Ethernet cable. Still a lazy tech nerd: surfing emergency.

Great timing. She looks down at her fuzzy pyjama bottoms. Forget clean underwear in case you get into an accident, you should always wear your best jeans when travelling in case you run into the man who stole pieces of you. It's way too late for her to change bottoms — it's time for the sound check with her band of borrowed musicians: friends who have agreed to come on the road for a five day world tour of Ireland for peanuts, who have left their girlfriends and wives and crap jobs and bands to play backup to promote her first ever solo CD. On her own independent label, IndoBabe. The album that took four Lily years to make, between nappy changes and feeding times and part-time temp jobs and too many romantic mishaps.

He's just one man, that's all, just one man. Breathe in and out and forget he's in the room.

She can easily think of at least three bad choices in her recent past — not bad men, Liam is the only one of those she has risked — but men who expected that deep down she is like the other women they know: itching to take their lives in hand, fill up the gaps that emerged once they left home. Imagining she'd be domesticated.

Forget him. Forget them all. Deirdre takes a deep breath and stands up on stage in front of the mic. Slings her bass strap over her shoulder. Waits while the guys tune and twang and plug in the bits that need plugging. Liam signals her to test the mic.

'One-two. One-two.' Eff you, eff you. She sings the first verse of 'Your Cheatin Heart', hopes the message will get through to him. Sticks her chin out.

The band is as ready as they are ever going to be, but Deirdre wants to try 'Blame it on Breakfast' without the keyboards. Just to hear how it would sound, raw.

Owen is down on his knees in the middle of the small stage, his Nord keyboard balanced across two low pub stools, the laptop open behind it on a third stool. They lost the keyboard stand while they were loading up the van, or at least it hasn't made it to Galway with them. 'It'll sound stupid, that's how it'll sound,' he says, and Deirdre isn't in the mood for another row, so she gets him to come in on the last verse. She wishes she hadn't had the bright idea to bring her boyfriend on tour with her; she wishes that for one week she could be free from every kind of love.

*

Outside the Róisín, the street glistens in the rain, an uneven sprinkle of mismatched buildings providing some shelter from the wind. *Dominick Street Upper*, it says on the tiny sign across from the Pizza Cabin. Beside it, the vintage *Ideal Drapery* sign has lost a d and l and has become *Idea rapery*. Deirdre counts at least three pubs on this short winding street, along with a few restaurants and takeaways. In the time the band spent sound checking, doormen—standard-issue size and weight, serious-faced, dressed in regulation black— have taken up position in front of the pubs, the adult club and the casino. People are huddled outside a place called Monroe's, the other venue at the top of the road. Deirdre shivers with the damp but tries to fit in with the general buzz: young, all the time in the world, out for a laugh. The pavement narrows until the lads have to walk in single file. Locals step out of their way onto the road, walk past the front door of the Róisín, looking for somewhere else.

Deirdre steps back into the venue and the song 'Horses' unfurls in her mind. When she first heard Patti Smith's voice, she decided she would become a singer, no matter what the nuns said. Life always comes back to the music, especially the music she loves. Eighties girl-pop (Banarama, The Bangles, Cyndi Lauper, The Go-Go's) and the depressive men (Tom Waits, Leonard Cohen, Nick Cave, Hank Williams, Vic Chestnutt). When she couldn't get enough of the kind of music she wanted to hear, songs started to write themselves in her head.

She can still smell the garlic on her breath from the cardboard pizza they ate after the sound check. She doesn't mind smelling of garlic, but when she is on the road surrounded by men in black T-shirts—hefting amplifiers and favourite guitars in and out of venues, testosterone on display wherever she turns — the strong odour leaking through her pores makes her feel like she is turning into one of them.

In the blank glare of the ladies' toilets, she pulls on her denim mini-skirt, the one she made out of an old pair of jeans an ex-boyfriend had left behind, and her superhero boots: calf-high blue boxing boots with deep red toes and bright yellow laces running all the way to the top. She leaves The Bangles T-shirt on; she figures she needs whatever moral support she can get, even if it is screen-printed.

Two minutes to nine o'clock and the venue is barren. It could probably fit a hundred-odd punters on a good night.

From the stage, the room looks even emptier. The black walls and floor suck in the light, so that the round wooden tables clustered in front of the stage seem to float up toward her. Tuesday Night Special at The Venue. Even the poster — she should have known her band would be bigger than the audience.

There are three of them sitting out there: Van, who drove them down here in spite of the cast on his right arm, Stephen her manager/ ex, and a teenage girl in a fifties-style dress who looks as if she must have a really good fake ID. She's the only one who scares Deirdre. She has been reading a book of poetry, which she carefully bookmarks and places beside her pint of Guinness the moment the band walks on stage. And Deirdre can see her lean forward out of the green shadow pooling around the pillar behind her, into the yellow lamplight that covers the front of the stage, her stage, the one she has just stepped onto, carefully picking her way around Eddie and his two back-up Telecasters, past Owen squatting down in front of a pub stool trying not to press the keys too hard in case the keyboard goes flying off its makeshift stand, and the tangle of cables Van and Stephen helped string around the stage, connecting each instrument to its amplifier, each amp to its power source, micing up every one of them — even

John hiding behind his drums—so they can join her in the first chorus.

The room is still cold—only the spotlight gives her any heat—and the small round stools are still tidily gathered around the empty tables. She frets the note on the neck of her battered pale blue Danelectro bass.

Deirdre doesn't feel the sound.

John calls out time, and the band is off, playing without her. Deirdre tries to catch up, she's never missed an intro before, and when she should be singing her voice cracks. Stage death, and her life flashes in front of her eyes. Boyfriends, bills, too many different jobs, one shock pregnancy and one near-miss, pop soundtracks and Leonard's 'Hallelujah'.

She steps back from the microphone. 'Right, stop,' she calls and takes off her bass. She can't do it.

Deirdre knows this is the choice: sing now, to a near-empty room, for the one member of the audience who has paid the cover charge, or drop the bass guitar, let it break and go back to her temping data entry job, aim for permanence, a deposit for a house, singing in the shower, holidays and nice things because she is going to be thirty-five years old in March and this is not going to get any easier, the empty room and the stage alchemy.

'Give me three minutes.' But instead of charging off she stands in front of her microphone, whispers something that no one else can hear, and summons back her younger self—her shiny-eyed dreamer, the part of her that can do this gig—and summons back the music, the magic part of the world.

'Pass me your guitar,' she says to Eddie, and he hands it over, carefully, though he looks as though he would rather not.

Her voice relaxes open and she starts off unaccompanied on the opening lines of 'Bird on the Wire', the first song she ever learnt on the guitar. Then she goes for it—hammering out power chords on the borrowed guitar.

The music is taut. Deirdre's body is electric with what she sees when she looks out into the black room: the face of her daughter Lily—four years old and convinced she will one day rule the world—her own face at age four singing into a hairbrush, and at fourteen tearing her T-shirts, and at twenty-four with bright orange hair, ready to take on the world with music and poetry and the contents of her soul, and now she sings for the part of her that still chases butterflies around the balcony of their third-floor flat, for her little girl who thinks a song can make a midnight monster go away, she sings for the crap she has been through and the fed-up days yet to come, she sings as though her life depends on it.

Alan Caden

SOCRATES, IN HIS LATER YEARS

Nobody I've ever seen had the shakes like Socrates. He stood at the old, chipped marble counter of the bar, unaware that I was watching him with the fascinated guilt of a dealer about to make a sale. It was eleven and I had just opened. He had already had his customary free coffee, followed by a glass of water to wash down the daily cocktail of pills, followed by his customary refill and his customary morning bowel movement. Now it was time for a pint. His hand emerged from the stinking black trench coat, rattling change like he was about to throw craps on the bar. He began to count it out and I stopped him, unable to observe any longer his pitiful efforts.

'Put it down there and I'll count it.'

Short twenty cent.

I said nothing. He picked up yesterday's *Mirror* with the special on the Races and began to look through the form for the day. I went to pull off half a pint to clear the lines and he piped up, 'Here now, you're not going to give me the first one, are you?'

'Well, I can hardly give you the second or the third, can I?' I snapped back, then softened. 'Course I'm going to pull a bit off first, Socrates, relax.'

'Good man. You are the Prime Mover, after all,' he said, more to himself than to me, and returned to the paper. 'Nothing can come into being without...' He trailed off, picking a bookie's pen out of his pocket and circling something in the 1.25 at Sandown.

I had heard that Socrates used to study philosophy. It didn't gel with me at first, his habits and appearance, but ever since then the image of that man has come to define my perception of philosophers. If I hear a reference to Nietzsche or Hume or Plato, it is Socrates' unshaven face and frame that I see in my mind's eye, his trench coat and oscillating hands. No one seemed to know his real name, but I imagine it must have been Trevor or Valentine or something like that, something that would have caused him to be happier with Socrates than the one he was born with.

The first pint of the day is the first brush-stroke on the canvas. It must be carefully done. Unhurried. I selected a chilled glass from the half-dozen I had placed in the fridge; a nonic, not a tulip. Socrates was old school. I introduced the glass to the tap at a sixty-five-degree angle and gently pulled the tap. I let it settle, not counting, but waiting patiently until harvest time, when I filled the remainder with a backpour. I presented him with the pint and he assessed its slightly overtopping head, its brown swirls as they mixed towards the spectrum of black. With his trembling thumb, he wiped the condensation from the outside of the glass, top to bottom, turning the glass for each wipe like a window-cleaner, shaking the droplets from his thumb after each go. I had to admire his willpower. He wanted it. I know he knew he wanted it, but he held back. His first brush-stroke of the day.

He made that first pint last for nearly an hour. He sat quietly on his usual stool, hunched over in his rancid coat despite the mild weather. Mild, but wet. Sometimes I think that God mustn't approve of the Galway Races. Most every year he mandates rain upon the country-people, the shapers, the milliners, the raucous groups of lads, the non-tipping millionaires, the upper-class women who urinate on the street and, of course, the poor horses.

Socrates' eyes wandered plaintively towards the door and the old stained glass as shadows passed along Upper Dominic Street outside. But no one came. None of the regulars had so much as poked their heads in this morning. His sip-to-minute ratio fell dramatically as the next pint began to appear in doubt. I busied myself at the other end of the bar and put the music on loud but reasonable. It was quite a comfortable silence between us. I knew he wasn't up for talking yet, not until he had a couple more in him, the soothing unguent which, when applied to the shell, can make it disappear.

I snorted into my coffee, having my own hangover to worry about. I considered the feats in front of me. Wipe a cloth over the counter. Open all doors to dilute the odour of a thousand sessions. Slop a mop around the jacks. Add a little more cocaine-preventing WD 40 to the cisterns. Avoid at all costs the antediluvian muck accumulated on the beer-lines under the counter. Light some incense. Spray the shit out of the fruit flies who had a commune down the back bar. My time-worn tradition of doing the minimum possible, a trait which defines the Irish, and is particularly evident in sports, a great thermometer for the character of a nation.

So I kept myself busy.

I made a rollie and then saw Socrates glancing hungrily my way, so I made him one too. What am I, I thought, the dole? We went out the front to have a look at the passing street. It was just gone lunchtime and the teenage language-school students were strutting along, munching on sunflower seeds or paninis, pushing each other around and gesticulating loudly. Cars rolled slowly along the narrow street. Residents strolled confidently in front of them. Across the road, they were putting the finishing touches to the paintwork on the signage of the Adult Shop, Galway's first, and I wondered briefly whether I'd get flashers and perverts in the pub when it opened. Rumours had it a lap-dancing club was sniffing around the street as well. I could just hear some of the locals now — 'What the hell would ye know about lap-dancin'! Sure yer not even from Lapland, heh, heh.' A proper red-light district for the town that imagined itself into a city. From up the street, we could hear a boisterous early crowd in Monroe's. To the right, the Pump-house had not opened yet, and further up Sea Road, the staff of Strano's and the Blue Note still had another few hours rest before their night began again. As for the Old Forge, who knows what was going on behind that opaque exterior? Perhaps the same level of excitement as here in Taylor's.

Socrates smiled at me amiably and began to chat about horses, enlivened by the pint and the fresh air. 'That young lad, Dean, he's doing well, rode a winner yesterday so he did.'

'At the Races?' I asked, feigning interest.

'No. Kempton.'

'That racetrack's five miles long. So I hear,' I said, smirking.

'Ara go 'way, will ya! Anyway, wasn't Dean home a few weeks ago, he was up in McAlinden's, and he bought the whole lot of us a pint. Two, he got me! Sound ould shkin. Magnanimous.'

His word-choice was peculiar. Not perfect, but then whose is? Regardless, it wasn't every day you heard a word like that and, my curiosity piqued, I couldn't resist probing a little.

'Is it true that you used to be a professor up in the university, Socrates? Is that where you got the name?'

'Hah! A professor of shite, maybe. Who told you that?'

'Seamas.' Seamas was the manager, my boss and friend. He had no time for the bullshit the regulars regularly spouted, and no time for shitehawks of any kind. He had a bark on him that'd cow any piss-artist and he neither minced words nor tolerated seafóid of any description. But he liked Socrates, and this intrigued me.

'Mulligan, hah! No,' he said, pulling on the rollie and pondering its tip. 'I was never a professor. I was doing a postgrad there. Gave some tutorials, that's about the height of it. Wild times.'

'And did you ever work in… in philosophy?'

'Are you fuckin joking me! Sure what do you think I'm up to every day in here!' He laughed till he coughed and he coughed till I got him a drink of water. He wiped his mouth. 'No. Things didn't end well up there. Wild times.'

I was about to drum up the brazenness to ask him what had happened, but he switched the conversation, taking advantage of our little heart to heart. 'Emm — I wouldn't ask you if I wasn't stuck, you know, would there be any chance of…'

Just as he had me nearly impaled on his spear of guilt, Gerry the Yank swerved around the corner by the hostel and I shouted a hearty hello. I took the opportunity to open the door for Gerry. I looked across at Socrates and saw his face light up unselfconsciously, like a child whose best friend has returned to school after being out sick. He had someone to play with now. Maybe alcoholics are just kids who refuse to grow up and toe the line, who pay the price and become helpless as a result of their efforts to drink from the fountain. Maybe all of us drinkers are like that.

Gerry was American and one of the loudest men I've ever met. When you heard his voice booming from the doorway you knew you were in for an earful. Pubs tend towards extremes, towards totalities and you notice it when you work in one for any length of time. They are the catwalk of stereotypes, where characters who are larger than life seek refuge from it. The pub allows people to assume the mantle and character they wish for themselves. They reinvent themselves here, or at least they emphasise the part of their character they like best. And Taylor's had its fair share of characters.

Gerry took a seat, and from the excruciatingly smug good-humour of him, he had obviously got a touch. He proceeded to explain to us exactly how this came to pass,

'I was walking into town earlier, and I was looking at all the gawdamn traffic, SUVs, Japanese cars, Opel Astras... and I thought to myself, *Man, not a single American car in sight here. Not one Cadillac or a Chevy or a Ford...*'

'Will ya get on with it ta fuck, Gerry!' said Socrates.

Gerry didn't take offence. 'Anyway, I went into Boyle Sports...'

'On Eyre Square?'

'You got it, Soco.'

'Decent sandwiches, so they have.'

'They sure do. So I walk in, I look at the first race of the day, I got a score in my pocket, that's all I got, and the first race in Deptford there's a horse called Buick Whaley in it. Buick, can you believe it! So that was the first of my Yankee. Then I got one placed in the 12.30 in Sandown, then another in, I think, Doncaster. Bim bam bim,' he tapped out the simplicity of it on the bar.

Socrates thought for a minute. 'Buick Whaley?' he said.

'Ah-hah.'

'Buck Whaley, ya feckin eejit! Buck!' He passed the newspaper to Gerry, who put on his glasses and squinted at the page.

'Well whaddaya know. Ain't that something.'

Socrates shook his head. 'Jesus wept. Only you, Gerry.'

Gerry shrugged. 'A pint of that beautiful gawd-damn black stuff you guys got here. And one for my buddy, Socrates.'

Socrates failed to disguise his eagerness and once Gerry had gone to the jacks, he nearly fell off his chair describing what a great guy Gerry was, despite his undeserved luck. His eyes watched the settling pints until they appeared to get lost in the ebb-and-flow of the dark brown liquid. He muttered something to himself. He was too proud to ask me to top it up early but I knew he wanted me to.

'Cheers.'

'Sláinte.'

Between the two of them and their banter, they kept me from boredom and the morning passed. A rolling stone gathers no moss, but a piss-up certainly does and they developed into an amorphous cluster of every-day regulars, break-out boozers and complete randoms. There'd constantly be one of them out at the bookies, or going to the pass machine, or looking for someone who owed them a few bob down at another pub. In this way, they managed to keep going all day, and I would've been bored and the till empty if it wasn't for them. The craic was mighty and Socrates sat there in his usual corner, on his usual stool, lapping up the attention and reminiscing about the old times, becoming increasingly loquacious and playful in his banter. He was as happy as a pig in shite and could anyone blame him?

At one point, when Socrates went to the toilet, I took advantage of his absence to ask the others, 'So lads, do ye know where Socrates got his name from?'

'Some sort of philosophy thing, I guess,' said Gerry.

'Yeah, but what?'

Welsh Mark piped up. 'I heard he drove a car through the wall of the Philosophy Department. Some argument with a lecturer. He was standing there, bolloxed yeah, looking at the car when the police came, and they asked him what he knew about it and you know what he fucking said? 'All I know is that I know nothing.' Classic. Then they kicked him out.'

'Sure what would you know? It was 'cos he was bringing the first years on all-day benders,' said Tall Gerry.

'I heard he just didn't finish his studies. Too much of this,' said Gerry the Yank, holding up his pint. Socrates had exited the bathroom at this stage and was certainly within earshot, but if he heard anything he gave no indication. He sat on his stool and acknowledged the new pint in front of him with the tiniest trace of a smile. He raised the glass to me, then to Gerry and the others and took a sip.

'The thing about Galway,' he said, 'is that it knows how to get dolled up. It knows how to make itself look like a city, even though by Chinese terms it's barely even a fucking village. We have our festivals, we have our races, we have our "Orts and Culcha" and so on,' he said, with a foppish flourish of his steady hand. 'Oh, we do. The likes of Neachtain's are full of people talking about the book they're going to write, the masterpiece they're going to paint, the one-act surrealist installation they're going to put on. But at the end of the day, it's the City of the Tribes. Always was, and still is, a merchant city, and when the festival season's done and the races are run; when the students' rent for the year is paid; when the buskers have fucked off back to Bristol or Berlin or the Costa Brava; when the boxes of flowers have been returned to whatever fucking nursery they're rented from, whose pockets are going to be fatter? The publicans and the landlords and the merchants, that's who. The Tribes. The rest of us...? Well, we might as well be shadows dancing on a wall.'

Seamas arrived to check the stocks before he sent out the Guinness order. He had a look at the lads and exchanged a few words in Irish with Tall Gerry. 'Alright?' he asked me, half-smiling and winking at the company. I nodded.

Gerry told a rambling story about growing up in the Bronx. Seamas told a joke a about the Inis Mór ferry, a bull and a stevedore. Socrates threw out a few conundrums about which European country begins and ends with the same letter, which five parts of Dublin end with 'o', and on it went. I had to change the keg. A young lad came in with an accordion, an old lad with a guitar. Someone tried to steal a photo from the wall. Eimear came on to start her shift for the overlapping two hours.

Then Socrates' phone rang. I hadn't even been aware that he had one. I had imagined, rather hopefully, that some bastion of tradition was still holding out against the shock-troops of the future. He looked at it, held it at arms' length from his face so he could see it better, while all the time it kept ringing out a digital rendition of 'The Ketchup Song'.

'Gawd-damn it, Socrates, will ya answer the damn thing! Here, show me!'

Gerry grabbed the Nokia off Socrates without so much as a by-your-leave and answered it, talked for a minute, having the laugh with whoever was on the phone. He must have known them. Everybody started talking again.

'Socrates, it's your daughter. My Gawd, she's got a beautiful voice — are you sure she's yours... ha ha ha!'

Socrates shot him a look that'd curdle a pint and took the phone off him. He walked to the front bar, to the other side of the partition, but he spoke as loudly as though his daughter were out on the street.

'Oh, you're just leaving now? Yeah... yeah... No, I'm just having a pint with the lads... just my second, actually... No, I know, sure of course I know that, I know what he said... Yes, I will be there... amn't I just after sayin' to ya it's only just my second... No, sorry, of course... just a half an hour, like... No, sure I've no money to be going in there, you know that. Anyway, how are you, love?... Good, good... What?... But I've nearly a full one in front of me here... yeah, I know that... You're right... OK, so... right, right... See ya in a...'

He prodded the end-call button viciously and slipped the phone back into one of his voluminous pockets, then straightened his shoulders and let out a sigh that wouldn't have been amiss in a French art-house film. He looked at his pint, gauging the remaining millilitres or perhaps sizing up his opponent. Then he looked at me. And he knew that I had been listening. I turned away, embarrassed, to move a few stacks of pint glasses from one end of the bar to the other and when I came back the pint was sitting there, empty save for the customary black and white line at the bottom. But Socrates had arisen from his seat.

A horn beeped outside and he jerked his head up. He looked at me for a stay of execution.

'Wish me luck,' he said and shook my hand across that old marble counter.

'Good luck, Socrates,' I said, and I had never meant it as much.

He said not a word to the rest of them, who were absorbed in other talk and had no time for ship-leaving rats, and out the door he went. I never saw him again, neither in there nor anywhere else around the town-city. Taylor's closed down later that year, only to reopen some months later in another incarnation altogether.

I had always meant to go back, not for the dancers, or for the goings-on that were rumoured to occur in the old rooms up the stairs, but to see whether the long-legged Eastern Europeans were dancing on my marble counter, the marble counter that was preserved along with the rest of the pub as the result of a Heritage order, the locals' final revenge. For whatever reason, though I passed it several times a week, I never did.

Now, fifteen years later, I have come back. I walk down Dominic Street, Upper and Lower. Restaurants everywhere. McAlinden's is O'Carroll's now and they have a double-decker pizza bus out the back. I cross over the canal and look up its length towards the lock and the water cascading down and on back to the river and thence towards the Claddagh. The hostel at the corner looks closed, derelict. Monroe's is under new ownership, old ownership or some sort of different ownership. The Pumphouse is the Bierhaus. Strano's is Nova cocktail bar. The Old Forge is a hipster pub. The sex shop is still there, though I still haven't caught anyone in the act of entering or exiting it. And Taylor's is back, re-opened two months now under different ownership!

I push on the same brass handle, walk in the same door and along by the same counter, hoping perhaps to see some old faces, scattered in the Flight.

I sit at the bar while the barman extracts a series of wails and groans from a coffee machine. Taking a handful of change from my pocket, I try to steady the one hand with the other, wondering whatever become of poor Socrates.

Patrick McCabe

THE GALWAY SPIKE

T
U
B
U
L
A
R

B
E
L
L
S

bing

                    bang

bong

weren't they playing
amn't I telling you
ag bualadh-*barang*
ringing out loud and clear
don chéad lá d'fhág mé
the sunny quartz glow
of Carna
i gConamara
mise, Bartle Conneely
at last bidding slán
to the low walls
of its rock-fields
and the red quarter strand
with its neat white
wind-whipped stones
yes, saying farewell
to my birth-country without trees
leaving Conamara
for good
chun dul go dtí Albain
long ago in the seventies
and me with me heart in
me mouth, God help us
is féidir Dia logh dom má
imirt i breagach agat

        may
        God
        forgive
        me
        if
        I
        should
        play
        you
        false
        this
        night.

Can you hear them?

Can you hear the bells?

That's the sound that the gruagach
makes
Pazuzu they call him
here and there
yes, the demon Pazuzu
that'd be his name
and I ought to know
for I seen him at work
in that very first place
that I laid my head
beyant in London
on that strange feather-bed.

'O, I love the hashish,'
said the colleen
'from your water-pipe puffing it
until I seen me soul.'
That's what she said, Tanya
bright-eyed, sweet and slim
pretty little *girseach* that she was
in her patchwork britches
and multicoloured jacket
as the lightshow's patterns
formed chemically-enhanced
dance shapes that merged
with the pulsating blobs and drips
of the lightshow oils
as she swayed, delirious,
ecstatic, exotic
with brown eyeballs rolling.
'Yes, I'm a lover of peace
an inner traveller
a psychic cosmonaut
who's going to change the world.
Yes, my sisters and brothers
here in this beautiful commune
we are going to... we are going to...
we are going to...'

Before backing away
with such imní in her eyes

pointing and squealing
help me help me
as around and around
and around it went
yes, an cheirnín, an dtuigeann tú
a bhí ag seinm ag an am sin
leis an mbanna cheoil Budgie

she scraked and her
shaking
aye, trimmling, God help her
before she could bear it no more

taking a tumble out the
window
and turning into
cailín bhocht gan éadaí
for hadn't she gone and torn them all
off of herself in her extremity
and landed on the cobbles of the
courtyard far below, leaving the outline
of her body behind
imprinted on the
overhanging glass roof
supported by rusted iron pillars
coming in to land.
God help her
directly beneath an fhuinneog
twitching and hoarsely breathing.
'Help me help me
can anyone help me
what made me do it?
I didn't want to die
I know something
or someone
made me die.
I could see him smiling
this is what he wanted,'
her very last words

aye, and me, Bartle, quaking
never in all me days, having
seen the like before
and such an amount of screeching
and wailing
which had never been experienced
all along the length of the Kilburn
High Road
not far from Queen's Park
in the long long ago
where I lived in a commune
that was going to change the world
and where

T
U
B
U
L
A
R

B
E
L
L
S

had chimed and chimed
the whole of the day
and all night long
with you not being fit
to tell one from the other
as Pazuzu in his Chinook
he swooped again and
swung in for the kill
high above the flames
and they devouring Saigon.

*

In the course of me travellings
I came to
The Spike in Galway
a home to lay me weary and auld
tired head
never again, pray God, meet the devil.

The Spike, you'd have found it
in the middle of Dominic Street
Not far, a short spit, from Mick Taylor's
teach tábhairne cáiliúil
public house without compare.

Dammit sowl
it's true and I won't deny it
that I'd had me a skinful
and divil the bit I care
who knows or hears about it
as in I clattered
aye, right through the door
not that I'm about to pretend
or let on
that me poor auld *ceann*
was right or natural
as I pulled out my fiddle
and started to *nyaah*
before sweeping the bow
in one mighty delirious curve
just like I used to and me
ag dul ar na bóithre
landing, as they say, in every
bit of a Spike atwixt here and
heaven
just like I tault them
I intended to do here
i nGaillimh
every bit as supple and me swerving
with the wild violin playing
aching as I lifted and repeated
the arrangement acting
as a kind of springboard

soloing away
as the sound with
sharp and lilting phrases
along with me butties'
syncopated handclaps
striving for ecstasy.
Then I bashed my boots
till someone went got the old
bodhrán and away we all went:

There was an auld man down by Killiburn Brae
Riteful, titeful, tiddy folday
There was an auld man down by Killiburn Brae
had a curse of a wife with him most of his days!
With me foldoraol dol, titty fol ol
Foldol dol dolda dolder olday!

The divil he says I have come for your wife
Riteful titeful titty folday
The divil he says I have come for your wife
For I hear she's the curse and the bane of your life
With me foldoraol dol,titty fol ol
Foldol dol dolda dolder olday!

So the divil he hoisted her up on his back
Riteful, titeful titty fol day
So the divil he hoisted her up on his back
And away off to hell with her he did pack
With me foldoraol dol, titty fol ol
Foldol dol dolda dolder olday!

And when they came back to Killiburn Brae
Ritfeul, titeful, titty folday
And when they came back to Killiburn Brae
Well the divil he capered and shouted hooray!

It was then the Connie spoke up.

'Are you looking at me?'
he says and he all ablaze.

'No,' I says, 'as the Christ that rose once
may swear
on Calvary, nail me if I speak a
word of a lie.'

'Well that's all right,' he says
and sits down
and doesn't he commence it, the telling
of his story
aye, his *scéal*
in the very same bar as the girls
did the dancing.

'There was this fellow, do you see,'
he began, slow and even,
'in a little town that they call Kilcash
in the very dark deep and quiet part of
Ireland, in the South.'

'See,' he said
'there was this fellow living there
who thought himself all the
big modern-type go-ahead
this would have been, oh, in 1923
when the pictures and the cinema
was only just getting started
and when, after the Civil War and all
that style of thing there, there wouldn't
have been all that much to be doing
in Kilcash
only maybe counting your spits
at the crossroads
or tugging on your *peist*
late at night under the covers
so this bookil, didn't he get thinking
sure amn't I the sort who as aisy as
falling arse over tit off a log
could turn my hand to anything
that I please
so why not establish my own personal
amharclann

my own private cinema in Kilcash
where there are the double of husks walking
that seem to be dead already
for the want of a wee bit of
entertainin'.

So off he went on the bus, aye to Cork
where he knew of a theatre and it the
wonder of the whole of the South of Ireland
called The Alhambra, do you see
and it being the pride of Tom Twomey
who liked a drink
and would often be known to scarper
and layve come cans of film in the hallway
which he did this particular night
yes, one two three four five cans
of film
of which he only took two
Laurel and Hardy
ah sure how would they not love them
he said
as back he went to his old home town
and to Mattie Mc Larnon's granary
indeed
which, as far as being an amharclann
goes
it was a very long way
from The Tivoli or The Luxor or indeed
The Alhambra
with the only means of access or exit
being the crockeddy old ladder
hanging down from the upper door.

O what a show it was going to be
the play of the century
with Stan Laurel and Oliver Hardy.
Well what a sad and maybe foolish
idea it might seem to us all in the new days
now
with not one or two but
twenty

thirty
forty
fifty
yes, actually fifty-five people
paying their ticket as they
wrung their hands in excitable glee
one by one ascending the old
ricketty rail
which was then pulled up
and the door heavily bolted.
With not divil a one ever
to show their faces
whether in Kilcash or the world
cé go tapaidh
nitrate film
can burn
given the right
— or wrong —
conditions.
'Tis said that yet
they can still be heard
the screeches
that night
that rung out
in the loft.

'What a mistake that was,'
said the Connie
from Ros Muc
except, as I'm telling you
that it was no longer the Connie
from Ros Muc or anywhere else
because, you see, when I looked
the walls weren't they gone
and the roof that they'd supported
yes, it along with them
spirited away
to reveal not a lockeen of stars
but a hape
gone
just like Mick Taylor's aye and Dominic

Street and all of the world that had
been the place I'd landed
Galway City that Winter's night
with nothing remaining only
the mark of The Spike.

I stood there as it poured
aye, punished, so it did
the hard rain of Gaillimh
the rain of Galway
and all its sorrow
forming the outline
of a dead cailín, a girl
right there in front
of me on the road
a sight, and all the recollections
that it brought with it
which saw me tumbling
back inside
to get me bags and all of me
belongings
with once more Bartle
setting forth on his journey
with bing bang bong, them same old bells
barang!, and they like before
ringing out above the Claddagh
never to be seen in The Spike again.

May
God
forgive
me
this
night
should
I
play
you
false.

Niamh Boyce

THE DOTEEN

On a street in Galway city, there's a shop that most people miss; just walk on by without noticing. It's in the Latin Quarter, down where Shop Street meets Quay street and Quay street becomes a quay.

It has a narrow front, painted midnight blue. A window guarded by a spike railing. The first sign that someone inside might be finicky, might not appreciate loungers on their sill, gobbling vinegar-soaked chips, attracting gulls and their screeches and shit.

Nearby, tourists feed the swans in the Claddagh. A young girl dances old steps on the cobbles. A helicopter passes overhead, and somewhere in Galway a woman is being held by the neck.

That window.

It's curtained like a theatre whose actors are vintage dolls. They're arranged by height, similar to children in a school photograph— smallest to the front, tallest at the back.

There's a bell over the door, which seldom rings.

And then, it does.

For the first time in months.

Maria charges into the shop. Breathless, carrying a wreath, of all things. White carnations, baby's breath, a red rose. The bell swings back and forth, delirious with shock.

The Shopkeeper looks up and nods before turning his attention back to the head on his worktop. It's pink-cheeked and ceramic with a crack from mouth to ear. He wears a waistcoat but no shirt. His arms are muscled, his weathered hands are elegant and silver-ringed.

Maria shuts the door behind her, moves towards the back of the shop, out of view of the window.

They had been on their way to the grave when he started... muttered those things into her ear. Gripping the back of her neck, squeezing as he hissed. *Why were you looking at him like that?*

A young one, barely fifteen — still in school uniform — stopped and gawked. She had a high bun and hooped earrings.

'Leave her alone,' she roared.

'Stupid bitch,' Kevin said, but dropped his hand.

So he could stop, if he wanted to. Just like that.

'It's over,' Maria said to him. 'For good this time.' And she walked away. And then she started to run.

She raced down Prospect Hill, across Eyre Square, Shop Street, Quay Street. Weaving through the tourists. He was behind her, calling her name. *Maria. Maria. Maria, love!*

Love, so that anyone that heard might imagine he had some good, polite reason for chasing his girlfriend across the city.

Maria glances at the shop window. It has started raining. Kevin can't be far; he saw her veer onto this street. She looks about her — sees the place properly, the rows of dolls, the confusion of frills, ringlets, the faces: heart-shaped and round. All those eyes in the semi-darkness.

'They come alive at night,' the Keeper jokes. Oh, what a nice voice he has. Maria smiles back. He was beautiful once, she imagines—those brown eyes, high cheekbones, olive skin and dark shorn hair.

'Feel free to look around,' he says and she moves about the shop to please him, to play for time.

A tall doll with long blonde hair and a puffy pink dress stands on a pedestal. A crescent fringe frames her porcelain face.

'She's the first-ever talking doll,' the Keeper says, coming over. 'I call her Angela.' There's a ripe spice to him, as if he has slept in his clothes. He lifts the doll's skirts to reveal a metal torso, a chest ventilated like an old-style radio. He winds the hand crank at her back. And then the voice comes — crackling and faint as if from a scratched record. The plummy accent sounds distant and mildly hysterical.

The tinny haranguing voice recites a song. *Twinkle! Twinkle! Little Star!* The doll's mouth is crimson, its cheeks full. She has a gorged predatory expression — as if she's been eating spoon-after-spoon of custard on a lawn during a midsummer murder.

How I wonder what you are!

'Please stop it,' Maria asks.

'It has to play out...'

'Please.'

'I'll put her in the back.'

He lifts the doll and takes her through a heavy red curtain at the back of the shop. Maria moves towards a lit cabinet with tiny relics. Teapots, combs, hand mirrors. Miniature accessories for miniature females.

Rain beats against the window. Kevin's out there; she knows he is. He was right behind her, yet he hasn't passed the window.

She met him at the after-party of an after-party. Recognising his smile, but not knowing from where. The newspapers — sports pages, as it turned out.

That was over a year ago. There was no First Time; just a series of almost harmless warnings. Tiny red flags that got bigger and bigger.

An arm pinch. A tug. *We're going home.* A shove. *Your friends don't really like you.* A fist against the wall. *You slut.* She tried to leave. He had gotten down on his knees, wrapped his arms around her waist. Begged. Wept. Declared that he loved her, and that she loved him.

'No,' she said, 'I don't.'

'Yes, yes, you do!' he tightened his grip.

She braced herself for what was coming.

She never struggled. There was no point. She just went numb and thought, *Never again, never again will he do this to me, never again, as soon as it's over — this time, this time I'm getting away.* She wasn't really there in her body; she wasn't there when he was doing it. There must be rips in her soul, she thought afterwards — tears from each time she left, each time she found herself hovering over her own body like a ghost.

The Keeper's back. He looks pointedly at the moonfaced grand-father clock, and then at Maria. It's almost six. He's going to ask her to leave.

She notices more dolls like Angela on a high shelf. She points to them.

'Are they talking dolls too?'

'Yes, hundreds were made, but sadly no one wanted them.'

'Why not?' She doesn't care, she can hardly think straight with fear. Her wreath is shedding petals all over his floor. Some flowers are missing. Maybe they lie scattered on the paths she ran earlier. Her mother is a year dead today; whatever happens, she must lay this wreath on her grave.

'The dolls' singing frightened the children. The recordings were made in a factory you see, by women in cubicles shouting into machines — it made their voices rather strained.'

She imagines being one of those women and the sound of all the others, shouting alongside her — reciting rhymes into recording machines.

How I wonder what you are!

The Keeper looks towards the door and frowns. She turns too.

It's Kevin, he's outside. Back to the window, hunched against the rain, looking towards the river. He said once that he would put her in that river.

She believed him.

The Keeper's holding up his keys. His key-ring is a brassy mermaid, with a curled tail. 'We're about to close.'

'I can't leave. That man out there…' She doesn't want to say it, but she has no choice. 'He'll hurt me.'

She never said it out loud before. The girls in work call him The Doteen, they think she's lucky. They call her a cradle snatcher, a cougar, they ask her what he's like in bed.

'He'll hurt me,' she says again. 'Please let me wait.'

The Keeper doesn't answer, doesn't react at all.

'I was in a window once,' she finds herself telling him. 'I was a mermaid with a tail and cockle shells. It was for a festival. I had…'

Kevin's turning around; he's about to see her. She races towards the back of the shop, steps between the curtains.

A giant security screen faces her. A low couch beside it. Red velvet. Worn. Angela is propped on a cushion, and on the screen is a view of the shop, the Keeper, the dolls.

She can see Kevin too. He's still outside. He's looking in the window, his hands making binoculars, as if searching out a rare bird.

Maria looks for somewhere to hide. A crammed shelf lines one wall — wooden limbs, ceramic hands, wigs, each item tagged. On the other side are a row of full-size mannequins. They wear old-fashioned clothes, sun-faded fringed shawls, wide-brimmed hats.

The curtains part and the Keeper appears.

'You shouldn't have come in here,' he says, 'it's private.'

She can't take her eyes off the screen. It's panning back towards the window. Kevin is no longer there.

'Please,' she says, 'promise that…' the bell jangles, and without promising anything, the Keeper goes out front.

She watches on the screen.

Kevin's inside the shop.

He's chatting to the Keeper as if he knows him. The Keeper might be a fan. He might be congratulating him on that goal he scored. Kevin throws his eyes up and grins. 'Women! What can you do, huh?' she imagines him saying.

Kevin scratches his arm as he talks. The tattoo is bothering him. He got it on that stag in Amsterdam—a Celtic band. Half the team got one. 'It must be septic,' she had told him. 'They're not meant to look like that.'

'How would you know? Have you been looking at some fucker's tattoos?'

She watches Kevin, so likable and boyish as he chats to the Keeper. He will kill her when he gets her home. He will make shite of her this time. She's tempted to run out through the shop and past him. She's still fast; Maria was always fast. Silver medals, never gold and never wanted it any different. Gold has to pose, gold has to give interviews, gold has to follow up. She flexes, rocks on her heels.

The Keeper's not smiling anymore—he's pointing Kevin towards the door, but Kevin won't go. Kevin is looking about the shop, Kevin is walking towards the curtain.

She steps in behind the mannequins. Closes her eyes and slows her breath—seven counts in, seven counts out... It's all she thinks of, standing in the shadows, her back to the wall. There's a scent, an old-style smell—like dried roses. She opens her eyes. Oh, fuck. Her wreath is on the couch.

Then he's here. Calvin Klein fills the room. *Eternity*. She tries not to look; he might feel her watching, but she can't not, she can't not look at Kevin. The air is dusty, nylon curls tease her nose. He circles the room, taking it in. The easy-going smile has slipped off.

There's a white door she hadn't noticed. He opens it—goes through. The Keeper has come in now, frowning; he follows Kevin.

She hears glass break.

She hears Kevin laughing.

She waits.

There's silence.

After an age has passed, the Keeper comes out.

He sits on the couch. There's a piece of rope in his hand. A loop, a stick. A noose is the word that comes to mind, but there's another one… one from her mother's crossword puzzles — what's the right word? She can't recall.

The Keeper stares at the screen as if hypnotised by the dolls. They are all so different, all so various in the slightest of ways. Some of them seem almost real; a soft mouth, a red-rimmed eye, a pale thread vein… the Keeper's face softens, he relaxes into the couch.

Maria slips out from hiding. The Keeper doesn't look up. She tiptoes towards the half-open door and peers in.

She sees tiles, black and white. Gleaming. A large glass case with a mannequin. Life-sized. Black hair. Beret. Round face. Hands together, clasped. A handbag hanging from her elbow. It's not a mannequin.

It's a woman.

Maria pushes the door further open.

The lower part of the case is broken. Kevin is on the floor, kneeling forward — his head turned as if looking over his shoulder. Mouth open, neck reddened.

Dead.

The Keeper's behind her now. He rests his hand on her shoulder. It's warm, heavy.

She must not go numb; she must stay alert. *Stay. Stay. Stay.*

She stares at the figure in the glass case. The woman was mummified, treated. Her face and hands are tanned a colour that has nothing to do with the sun. She wears a high collar shirt under a red suit. Her eyes are open, bright as a doll's.

'He laughed at her,' the Keeper says, 'and you can't do that.'

'No,' she agrees, 'you can't.'

He lifts his hand from her shoulder.

The Keeper hunkers down then, begins to sweep the shattered glass around Kevin's body into a dustpan.

Maria backs into the screen room. She collapses on the couch beside Angela. The doll tilts but does not fall over. The screen shows the shop, the rows of still faces. Maria picks up the wreath and puts it down again. Kevin is dead. She tries to feel something more compassionate than relief.

The rope is on the floor. She touches it with the toe of her shoe. Kevin is dead. It's hard to believe. She can't stop staring at the noose, the loop, the twist of rope that choked him to death. A shiver runs through her.

The Keeper stumbles in then, and without speaking, sits alongside Maria. After a time, he lays his head on her lap. She puts her hand on his hair. It feels just like pelt.

The tourists feed the swans at the Claddagh, a young girl dances old steps on the cobbles, a helicopter passes over the city, and somewhere in Galway a woman lays down a wreath.

Maria stands a while at the foot of the grave. It's so peaceful there. She slips her hand into her pocket and touches the shop keys, feels the sharp tail of the metal mermaid. Garotte. That was the word from her mother's crossword — the one she couldn't remember. *Garotte.*

Nearby, a school girl's smoking.

It looks like the girl from earlier, the one who had set Maria running. *Leave her alone!* Was that only today? It seems like years. Maria studies the girl. Yes, it's her — the same high bun, the same hoops in her ears. Just then, the girl notices Maria's stare, drops her cigarette and shoots her middle finger into the air.

Moya Roddy

POETIC JUSTICE

Fuckin' mad, Stacey thought, eyeing the crowd milling outside the theatre. Imagine goin' to hear poetry at this hour of the morning. Across the entrance of the large building opposite a red banner blazed: *Cúirt International Festival of Poetry and Literature.* The word *Cúirt* had a fada on the *u*. Stacey wondered what *Cúirt* meant. Something to do with courting? Isn't that what her granny called snogging? Having a good court, except she pronounced it *curt*. Not that Stacey could imagine her granny kissing anyone. Or anyone kissing her granny. Still she must have done, otherwise her ma wouldn't be here. And if her ma wasn't here, she wouldn't be standing outside a poxy courthouse waiting for her case to be called. Her granny shoulda kept her tongue to herself.

Stacey shook out a cigarette, lit up. It was mainly middle-aged women across the road, although there were a few girls her own age, one chatting to a gink with glasses. *What kind of poetry do you like?*

My arse! Going to a fuckin' poetry reading and she was up for stealing a bloody hair straightener. Top of the range though; she'd been hoping to sell it to her sister-in-law, whose hair frizzed if you sneezed near her. Would ye look at them, gab, gab, gab. Wonder why no one's talking this side? Except barristers and solicitors and they only talk shite.

I could be over there, Stacey suddenly thought, I used to like poetry at school. When I went. Fuck! I'll be feeling sorry for meself in a minute. Where the hell is Dennis — she scanned the foyer of the courthouse, saw him speeding towards her like a giant bat, hair and spit flying.

'Stacey, sorry, I got caught up in Court Two. You won't be called before 12.30. I had a word with the magistrate.'

'What am I supposed to do? Hang around this dump all morning?'

'You could go into town, I suppose.' He looked at her sharply. 'If you do any shopping, remember to pay for it!'

Stacey gave him the finger. Not that she minded Dennis. He was alright. Mostly.

'Fuck off.'

'Sorry. Have to go. 12.30. Here. Don't be late.'

'You sound like my mother.'

Stubbing out her fag, Stacey watched him rush back in, gown ballooning, documents slipping.

Asshole, she thought, tripping down the steps.

The poetry crowd had begun to drift in. As she crossed to the other side of the road, Stacey stiffened, certain they were watching her.

Relax, I'm not going to take your bag. Not today anyway.

Stupid cows, she liked the thought of putting the wind up them.

From inside the theatre a buzzer sounded. Stacey stopped, hovering at the bottom of the steps, awkward.

'It'll be starting soon,' a woman nudged her.

'I'm not going.'

'It might be good. It's free anyway.'

Stacey shrugged.

She watched the woman push open the doors, disappear inside. Out of the corner of her eye she noticed the traffic lights at the junction had turned green.

Cheaper than a cup of coffee, Stacey decided, attaching herself to the tail end of the queue, eyes glued to the ground. Anyway, she didn't want to risk bumping into Ryan uptown. Cunt. Didn't even turn up this morning, although she'd asked him. Told him she was up anyway. Just as well. Great impression he'd make on a judge.

The warmth hit her as she slid into a seat. It was next to the exit so she could do a runner if it was crap. Around her, mouths opened and shut like the goldfish in her granny's flat, only noisier. Her granny was going to kill her when she found out. Why had she done it? Just an impulse. A feeling of being able to. A crackling sound interrupted then a voice erupted from a large speaker. Stacey listened to the usual warnings about exits, entrances, not taking photos, turning off mobiles. When the announcements came to an end there was silence, a feeling of expectation. After a few minutes of nothing, a hippy-looking man ambled onto the stage.

'You're welcome,' he beamed, 'to this year's annual Cúirt Festival...'

Stacey's fingers tapped her thigh. She felt trapped sitting there. Like in a cell. Everyone clapped when the man finished, the sound increasing as a woman scuttled out from the wings. 'Thank you. Thank you. I'm delighted to be here,' she nodded. She was slight, nervous-looking, the papers in her hand trembling.

Just like that woman, Stacey thought. The one she'd robbed. Shook all over, she had, handing her the purse. Stacey hadn't meant to scream so loudly, it was the way she'd reacted made her.

She squinted up at the stage. What must it be like walking out there, having everyone clap. All those eyes looking, expecting something. She'd die. Probably like being in the school play, only worse. Not that she'd ever been in one. Never been asked.

The woman fumbled, began to read.

Stacey's mouth twisted into a sneer. Fuck, she hadn't even learned the poem. Stacey looked to see if anyone else minded but no one seemed bothered. Signs on, she'd never had Sister Agnes for English. She wouldn't have stood for that. Ye got a real bollicking if you couldn't say it off. The poem was over in a flash and when only a few people applauded, Stacey felt sorry for the woman. As soon as she began a second poem, Stacey realised she hadn't heard a word of the first one. She couldn't listen.

Slumping in the seat, Stacey closed her eyes. The woman's voice had a kind of rhythm or maybe it was the words; half-listening she felt her body relax, settle, the rush of blood slow. God, she was tired. Tired, fucking tired. The voice grew fainter and fainter, finally vanished.

Stacey woke with a start. People were standing, pulling on coats and jackets. Fuck, the time! She pulled out her mobile. Twelve twenty-five, she was alright. The people leaving had gathered in front of the theatre and ducking out from behind them Stacey saw Dennis pacing up and down outside the courthouse. Spotting her, his eyebrows shot up.

'Didn't know you liked poetry,' he commented as she hurried up the steps to join him.

'I don't. Are we going in?"

'We've got another few minutes. Wasn't the reading any good?'

'I fell asleep.'

He looked at her, the way guards do when they want you to

incriminate yourself.

'Okay, I used like poetry at school. One poem anyway. Can't remember, something about going into a wood.' She knew the whole thing off by heart—Sister Agnes had made sure of that—but she wasn't going to tell him.

'You mean Yeats? "The Song of the Wandering Aengus"?'

Stacey shrugged.

'"I went into a hazel wood, because a fire was in my head—"'

'Yeah, that's it, so,' Stacey interrupted. She didn't like the idea of him knowing it. Spoiling it.

'What did you like about it?'

'Nothin', I dunno. It's how I feel sometimes. There a fuckin' like fire in me head.'

She shouldn't be telling him this either. Told him too much.

'What do you mean?'

'Ah fuck. Listen, you gotta get me off. I can't go down. It'll kill my mother and my granny. You won't see me here again. I promise. Cross my heart.'

'You said that last time. You know it won't be easy. There's your previous.'

'I didn't mean it when I said it before. I do now. I've got a boyfriend. We're gonna like get a place together.'

'Tell me about the poem? The fire in your head.'

'What for? It's like, nothin', like seeing red...' Stacey shuts up. It's embarrassing talking like this.

'Is that what happens,' he pursued, 'before you take something, you see red?'

'Maybe. Dunno. Sometimes. You'll get me off, won't ye?'

'I'll try. Behave yourself in there. No temper.'

Stacey listened to the proceedings, trying not to catch the judge's eye. Fuckin' woman magistrate, the worst. Feel they have to punish you.

At the end of his plea, Dennis sat down then seemed to change his mind.

'Might I request this case be adjourned for reports?' he asked, standing up again.

The magistrate sniffed. 'I don't think I see any need for reports. Young lady, I meet your kind far too often in my court, you're a disgrace.'

'Your Honour, I think... My client gave me some new information... which may have some bearing.

'What sort of information?'

'What I'm proposing is a psychiatric report. You see my client told me before she commits a crime, that, as she put it, her head goes on fire, she sees red—'

'What the fuck—' Stacey screamed, jumping to her feet.

'Young lady, one more word out of you—'

'That was private, dickhead! What are ye doing telling the whole world?' Stacey's heart was thumping, the room spinning.

The magistrate banged the table. 'I warned you.'

'I'm not fuckin' mad, I'd rather go to fuckin' prison.'

'That's precisely where you are going. I sentence Stacey O'Connor to six months. Leave to appeal withheld.'

'Bastard,' Stacey shouted at Dennis as they led her away. 'Fuckin' bastard.'

E.M. Reapy

RAINWORDS

I'd been holed up in the flat for months at this point, staring at my laptop. Sometimes, I'd take down a notebook, hoping on this different medium, pen poised, something would happen. But nothing ever did. I often threw these notebooks into the fire. The biros too. Watch as the flame turned blue, engulfing the paper or plastic, heat energy flaring for a moment before vanishing. Something becoming nothing.

If I didn't get out for at least twenty minutes of fresh air daily, alcohol or something stronger would overwhelm me. At midday, I put on my thin purple fleece, blew my nose and locked the flat.

The sky was headstone grey as I wandered aimlessly towards town, passed the clogged shopping centre, onto Woodquay. The wind stung my face. Cigarettes died slowly in the sandy pot outside the bookies. I caught the waft of the meaty burger bar. Beauticians and hair salons advertised chemical products for natural looks. Stale beer lingered in the gutters along the footpath. People bustled about and a hop-on hop-off red bus turned the corner while I waited to cross over to Shop Street. I felt sorry for the tourists and the guide in their winter coats. How they had to rustle up enthusiasm for the city.

It started to rain, of course. A light mist at first but then a powerful torrent. I was hit in the head. Stopping momentarily at the Wilde-Vilde statue to brace myself, I thought it must be hailstones by the weight and intensity of the downpour but after repeated slaps by the hard drops, I wiped my forehead and looked at my hand to check for blood. Stunned, I peered closer.

```
              N
  V           U                       L
  E           A           A           I
  L           N           L           O
  V           C           L           N
  E           E           O           E
  T                       W           S
                                      S
```

I gasped and looked up. They were falling from the sky.

```
                          B
              H           L           P
  P           A           U           E
  O           L           E           L
  R           L           G           T           C
  T           O           R                       H
  A           W           E                       I
  L           E           E                       M
              D           N                       E
```

Thousands-upon-millions of them.

Rainwords.

People scampered all around me to get out of the storm but I was still, open-mouthed.

```
                                    D
                                    E
        H                           S
        A               T           P
        R               R           O
        L               E           T
        E               A
        Q               C
        U               L
        I               E
        N
```

I bent down and gently turned my palm to reveal a droplet. *CLARITY*, it said.

My eyes couldn't take them all in as they darted to the ground.

```
                            W
        L                   O               T
        U                   R               R
        N                   M               U
        A                   H               S
        R           W       O               T
                    A       L
                    S       E
                    H
```

Glancing around, I was barely able to breathe and put my hands up to the passers-by but they all just passed by.

```
                                        F
      H                                 R
      O                                 A
      R           H                     N
      S           I                     K
      E           J           Y         I
      S           A           O         N
                  C           U         C
                  K           T         E
                              H         N
                                        S
                                        E
```

I cupped a handful of the rain and protected it with my other hand as I rushed back to my apartment. The sky was clearing when I unlocked the door and shouldered it open. I left it open behind me, went up to my room and laid the rain gently on my desk.

It turned into a puddle.

'What?' I said, inspecting it, poking it. 'No. Please.'

But it was just wet.

Sighing, I mopped it with a faded towel that had an illustration of Marbella's beaches and palm trees and said, 'Wish You Were Here.' A wail got caught and muffled in my throat, an underwater scream. I sat on the floor and held my knees to my chest.

*

My chin quivered while I stared at threads of a spiderweb fluttering on the ceiling's coving. The shush of a light shower roused me from the ground. Rain drizzled sideways at the windowpane before trickling down it.

```
                          P
              B           I
  V           E           N           F
  I           C           K           L
  E           O                       A
  W           M                       S
              I                       H
              N
              G
```

My chest filled with elated air.

The stairs groaned as I raced down to the kitchen and when I pulled open the broom cupboard, the door nearly came off its hinges. I snatched the mopbucket, the basin. In the sitting room, I threw all the coal in the fire and brought the coalbucket too, sprinting out the back of the building to where the coin-operated washer and dryer were, sheltered under a tin roof. I put my word catching vessels on top of the roof.

'Wait,' I shouted. Too many words were being lost.

I ransacked all the cups and bowls we had in the flat, cradling them like a newborn in my arms, accidentally smashing one or two. Then I emptied the pedal bins onto the floor, took the lids off the saucepan, the blender, the kettle and left them outside.

It wasn't enough, I went back to the kitchen and grabbed four branded pint glasses I had stolen from the nightclub. Shot glasses too. With my hands, I scooped out jam and pesto from their jars, and spilled two of my secret stash bottles of red, but left a third spare bottle unopened in my wardrobe. I put rocks in reusable shopping bags to anchor them against the wind and even thought about leaving my boots and leather handbag out, but decided against it, not sure if they were waterproof on the inside and knowing I'd need them if I was to be invited to literary events again.

Utterly exhausted, I went for a nap and dreamt of walking barefoot on thick blankets of grass, lush and green. When I awoke, I was damp all over and my adenoids were swollen. It was still glum outside. I cheered.

*

Time had fallen away but it must have been late evening because I heard my housemate plod up the stairs. My fingers were whirring across the keyboard.

She called me as she walked across the landing. 'Can we talk?'

I kept typing.

'Do we have a leak?' she said, stepping into my room and then she noisily exhaled. In a softer voice, she added, 'Look, I'm worried. Do you think I should give your mother a call?'

Reluctantly, I lifted my eyes from the screen and turned to her. She was in her waitress uniform, a white blouse and black knee-length skirt.

'What's going on this time?' she asked. Her face was weary red.

'Poems, stories, worlds, can't you see?' I said, smiling widely. Trembling all over.

'No?'

I picked up a bowl and slid my palm underneath the water to cup some of it out. Drips of words fell onto the ground. 'Look closer.'

Salthill

Black Rock Diving Tower.

The Irish name for Salthill is *Bóthar na Trá*, which literally means The Road Along the Sea. Two hundred years ago it was a small village occupied mostly by fishermen. There was a cluster of cottages at Blackrock and another at what is known today as Rockbarton. The road west was bounded on one side by a high Landlord's wall.

Although the famine badly affected the area, things began to change for the better in the latter half of the nineteenth century. The Eglinton Hotel was built and brought a new level of scale and style, the tramway made the area accessible for tourists and visitors alike, and the promenade was built. Salthill rapidly became the jewel in the crown.

The twentieth century saw the transformation of the area from a small village to a resort to a large suburb. A huge amount of development took place and the population greatly increased. Many of the changes were geared towards amenities for the public—ballrooms, hotels, Pearse Stadium, Leisureland, the extension of the promenade and the building of the diving tower at Blackrock.

Today Salthill is sandwiched between the new suburb of Knock-nacarra and the city, but still retains an identity of its own. In terms of location it is hard to beat Salthill, facing the Bay and the Burren Hills, with the Aran Islands off to the right, Galway City to the left.

Una Mannion

IN BETWEEN DAYS

The night the nuclear reactor in Chernobyl went into meltdown it was raining in Galway. And while nuclear ash floated from the sky like snow over 1,000 miles away, Anna stood outside the Oasis in Salthill and lifted her face to rain. Kohl-faced students spilled out around her, jostling, the smell of sweat and damp-soaked wool suffocating and close. She'd drank too much, didn't know anyone, didn't have the fare back to Tirellan. She couldn't see Eithne, who'd been huddled with a microbiology postgrad all night. 'West End Girls' thumped from the walls of the Warwick next door. She shouldered through the crowd towards the black expanse across the road and heard it, the crash of waves, the suck of stones, the taste of wrack, salt-thickened hair. She breathed in, decided to walk. It would settle her.

The town was soundless, the hospital dark, save the random window in a lit hallway. She passed the college and the cathedral and walked through Woodquay. A taxi splashed by in the opposite direction. Ahead were the road works, high fences angled haphazardly and deep ditches either side of the road. During the day the noise was relentless jack-hammering and the crush of diggers on rock. At night the machines sat empty, mechanical arms reaching in mid-gesture. Driverless vehicles. Anna shivered. Dunnes' car park was empty, just a solitary trolley spinning.

Almost there, she thought. She could see Tirellan ahead, the slight gradient, the sprawl of houses. Then something moved ahead of her on the road. Maybe fifty yards in front, a dark shape at the edge of the ditch where the fencing and the streetlights stopped. It moved again. She wiped her face as if to clear a blurred windscreen. A man. He'd disappeared down into the ditch. She'd keep going, step into the road when she passed. Then she heard him.

'It's okay. Come on.' Like he was talking to a child, and she slowed.

'Come on, girl.'

Her heart thudded but already she was moving towards the ditch. She looked down. A man was crouched below at the edge of the dark gully, reaching towards something. And then she heard what he must have. A cry. Over and over again. In the middle of the sludge water, a kitten was stranded on a sunken trolley. Anna watched them. The kitten would move towards him, test the water with a paw, then jerk back. She looked around. There was a piece of metal, a broken barrier about halfway down the hill. She sidestepped through the muck to reach it, could feel the squelch of mud water in her shoes. The man was still talking to the cat.

'It needs a bridge,' Anna called, standing above him, holding the length of steel. The man fell forward on to his hands.

'Jesus! Fuck's sake. Where'd you come from?' She recognised him. Tall and pale. Quiet. He worked in the Quays. She'd seen him in the Crane playing in a session. She'd never spoken to him except when he told students in the pub it was time to go home.

'From the road.'

He looked at the cat. 'She's stuck.'

She pushed the metal towards him. 'Try making a bridge.'

He took the metal and edged it towards the cat, talking to it. 'Sometimes I feel stuck, too,' he said. 'It's okay.'

Anna couldn't think of what to say except, 'Here, kitty.'

When they had the rail wedged against the trolley, the kitten walked down the makeshift gangway, still crying. She made it half way, then retreated. Came closer, then backed away. He kept coaxing, calling the cat a *she*. Ginger-white. Anna tried to remember something from genetics class about why ginger cats were more likely to be male. It was muddled. The kitten approached and this time he reached out and scooped her up, tucking her under his coat.

'God, she's shaking. Feel.' He stood and leaned towards Anna and she put her hand under his coat and felt the tremble. He looked at her, waiting for a response. Touching the shaking cat against his chest felt intimate, and she pulled her hand away.

'We have to get her warm. Can we go to yours?'

'Okay. I'm in Tirellan.' She didn't ask why he couldn't take the cat to his.

The house was dark. She turned the key in the door and stepped into the hallway. No one was home. Eithne must have gone back to the microbiologist's and the lads always went home for weekends.

'Can we get her warm?'

The house was freezing even though it was the end of April. Upstairs she grabbed the two-bar heater and a towel and went down to the sitting room. He wrapped the kitten and they all huddled in close to the heat. In the light they could see she'd been attacked. There were cuts and scratches and a slice through the tip of her ear.

'Is there something to clean her cuts?'

'Like medicine?'

'Yeah, or Dettol?'

'No.' Then she remembered her mum soaking cuts in warm salt-water. 'I've salt.' She boiled the kettle and stirred salt into a bowl of hot water and they waited for it to cool.

His name was Liam. From Galway. He was leaving in a few days, going to a squat in Camberwell. Most of his mates had gone already. He didn't recognise her and Anna didn't say she'd seen him before. She'd only been out a handful of times, and most of those since Eithne had moved into the house. She told him how she'd left Leitrim with her mother before the Inter Cert. They'd gone to the Bronx and ended up in Rochester after a few years of moving. She'd come back to Ireland for college two years ago but wasn't sure it was working, how she'd thought here was home but then found it wasn't. Once in first year she'd gone up to Leitrim to see her uncle and scatter of little cousins. The young ones performed Irish dances for her in the kitchen and looked at her like she was from another planet.

'My uncle kept asking how was I finding things in Ireland and did I still understand the accent.' She'd seen how they saw her. But the States didn't feel like home either.

He cleaned the cat's wounds with the salt-water. She watched.

'We should feed her,' Liam said.

One of the lads had a mother who cooked him a full ham every week which he carried up on the bus from Clare. Liam peeled off a strip and held it above the cat. She sniffed, then dropped her head. He held it closer to her nose. She licked it twice, sat up, opened her mouth and chewed it. Then she ate three more pieces, curled up in a ball and fell asleep. He looked around the room. Anna's housemates had put up posters. *Rum Sodomy and The Lash* was sliding down the same damp wall where a votive was hung. The landlord had asked them not to move it.

'It's a sacred heart lightbulb that stays on forever,' she said.

'I live with my aunt,' he said.

'Oh.'

'She's religious. I know what votives are.'

Anna wanted to ask why didn't he live at home in his own house, but didn't. They sat staring at the bars and the sleeping cat. Liam stood and switched off the overhead light. The room glowed from the plug-in heater and the sacred heart bulb. The kitten was close to the heat and he felt her fur to see was she getting singed, then leaned back against the couch, took out a packet of purple Silk Cuts and offered Anna one. He struck the match, his hand cupping the flame that had cupped the kitten. He had a silver hoop earring and a shadow of stubble along his jaw. She wanted to touch him. She bent towards him, pulled on the cigarette to light it and sat back, blowing the smoke away from the cat.

'Do you know this is the second time in the last year I've met someone over an injured animal?' she said. After her first year in Galway she'd gone back to Rochester for the summer. One morning, really early before the sun got too hot, she'd gone to the high school running track to jog. Four laps equalled a mile and she was trying to run eight laps even though she had never done anything athletic. She was sweaty and gasping when she started the fifth lap. Ahead of her another jogger, a man, was examining something on the ground just off the track. She'd stopped. A bird struggled and flapped in a circle with a broken wing. Whatever had happened, the wing looked almost disconnected from the body. She thought maybe it was a cardinal; its vibrant red feathers fluttered an arrhythmic beat on the ground.

'We have to kill it,' he'd said. 'For mercy.' There was a pile of rocks at the base of a tree and he went over and picked up the biggest one. He held the rock over the bird, looked away, but couldn't bring himself to do it. She watched him, then walked over to the bin and took out an empty Burger King Whopper box, unfolded it and covered the red bird. She took the rock from him and dropped it on the moving Whopper box. Twice.

'Jesus. That's brutal,' said Liam.

'He asked me for my number after I'd scooped the bird into the trash.'

'Pervert. You can't trust men that jog.'

She didn't tell Liam that she'd given it to him and that the man, who was clearly in his late thirties, rang her afterward and she went out with him, because so far that summer she'd sat around watching *One Life to Live* and *The Young and the Restless* and needed to do something, and so she'd drank too much and had sex in the front seat of his blue Corolla down the street from her mother's duplex. That it had briefly charged her to be unabashed about her body with someone she barely knew or liked, who was probably her mother's age and told her he worked for the electric company. She'd never done anything like that before. She hadn't turned twenty yet, had barely had sex. She'd fumbled around with a medical student from Cork the year before but it was quick and apologetic. When she thought of either of them, the shamed boy or the middle-aged jogger, she felt revulsion.

'Why didn't you bury the bird?' Liam asked after a while.

She didn't answer. It had never occurred to her.

At their feet, the rise and fall of the kitten's breath had slowed, her orange fur pink in the glow of the two-bar heater, her small shape curled like an embryo, as if they were incubating something.

'I better head,' he said after a while. He stood and moved to the door.

'But what about your cat?'

'I can't take her. I explained. My aunt. And I'm leaving for London and all.'

'But neither can I.'

'Please. Just a few days? I'll sort something.'

Anna filled two hot water bottles, put them in bathtub and covered them with towels. She lay newspaper down by the drain and hoped that if the cat had to go in the night it would have the sense to go there. It was almost four. Eithne wouldn't be coming home. She put the cat on the water bottles. It barely stirred.

It was Tuesday before the news started reporting the meltdown. Detectors had gone off in Sweden. Finland was recording ten times the normal radiation levels. The Soviet Union had been forced to admit there'd been an accident after saying nothing for days and denying it. Anna had just finished her pharmacology exam and stepping into the afternoon light of the Quad met Eithne running toward her. Something was up. The cat must have been crying.

'Did you hear?' Eithne asked.

'No.'

'There's been a nuclear accident.'

'Sellafield?' She'd just signed a petition.

'Somewhere in the Soviet Union. A nuclear power station,' Eithne said. Radiation was drifting across Europe in plumes of radioactive particles.

'Come on. Everyone's going to watch the news in the College Bar.'

She counted back days. The night she'd met Liam. She hadn't seen him since. Both she and the cat had slept almost all of Saturday. Sunday she'd left it in the bathtub to go to town. Before she left, she'd refilled the hot water bottles. She stuck a note on the bathroom door in case some of the housemates returned. *There's an animal in the bathtub. I put it there. It will be gone in a few days. Promise.* She'd walked back at dusk when there was still a thread of light in the sky to the west. Coming up the path she saw things stacked against the door: a rectangular plastic box, a bag of kitty litter, ten cans of cat food and a brown paper bag.

No one had come home yet. She opened the paper bag. Inside was a brown bottle with a dropper cap. Iodine. And a note. *Went to the chemists. Can you put iodine on her cuts? Yours in gratitude, Liam.*

Ten cans was more than a few days. Her flight was booked back to Rochester the last week of May, less than a month. She felt shaky as she walked up the stairs to check on the cat in the bathtub. *Yours in gratitude.* Was he mocking her? The newspaper over the drain was wet. The cat looked alert and put its front paws on the side of the tub when Anna leaned over. She picked her up and brought her into the bedroom. She'd try to keep it a few days and say nothing to the others. The kitty litter box would go in the corner of the room by the window and the food on the other. Next to her bed she arranged the hot water bottles on the floor so she could check on the cat in the night.

Before bed, Anna held the cat in her lap and dripped the iodine across her cuts. The cat lay there, letting her. Anna parted the fur to examine a cut, turned her over, and talked to her, said what a good cat she was. The cat cried just once when the liquid hit the slash in her ear. Iodine leaked across the skin and fur, turning the ginger bits a deep amber and the white fur and skin a sulphuric yellow.

'Sorry, girl. You look dreadful. Like a little punk rocker.'

Late that night she woke when the front door clicked shut. She heard footfall on the stairs. Giggling. Eithne was home. She could hear the microbiologist's English accent. She leaned to look at the cat and realised it was lying against her ribcage. With the small shape breathing beside her, she fell back to sleep.

The past two mornings she'd left the house, first emptying cat food on a saucer and locking her bedroom door.

'Don't cry cat,' she whispered as she left.

Anna and Eithne sat with others in the College Bar each evening for the next three days. The Soviet Union said just two people had been killed. Western journalists claimed more than 2,000 were dead and that the reactor was still burning out of control and spewing radiation into the skies. Clouds of radioactive iodine were drifting across Europe. The Irish Meteorological Service said there was no likelihood of any airflow from the Soviet Union reaching Ireland. But by Thursday the winds had shifted. A radioactive plume was headed from the Ukraine towards Ireland. It would arrive overnight. Some of the science postgrads were saying that rain would wash radioactive particles out of the atmosphere and bring them to earth.

'Well Galway's fucked, then, because it always rains,' said Eithne.

'Poland's giving out iodine capsules.'

'Why?' asked Eithne.

'It gets absorbed by your thyroid. And if your thyroid is already saturated, it can't absorb the radioactive iodine.'

'Ireland doesn't sell the capsules over the counter,' said the microbiologist.

'Get the liquid,' said one the medicine students, 'and brush it on your skin.'

'We should get iodine.' Eithne nudged Anna. She was about to say she already had some for the cat.

They kept drinking in the College Bar, went to Mick Taylor's because it was May Day and Taylor's was a Worker's Party pub. Everyone was talking about Chernobyl, the clouds on their way. How it would rain on them. She was swept up in the flow of conversation and students. Because of the cat and Liam and the threat of a radioactive atmosphere, she felt weirdly alive, part of something. Then they were headed to the Warwick. Thursday night, student night. She'd had three or four pints already and was tipsy.

Outside the Warwick they queued with the pile of the postgrads they'd met in the College Bar, friends of the microbiologist. And he was there, Liam, standing with a group further ahead by the door. She recognised some of them, trad musicians who played in the Crane. He saw her, said something to them, and came down.

'Well. All good?'

Anna stepped out of line and stood with him. She could feel Eithne watching.

'Yeah. I guess. Your cat's face-bombing me every morning.'

'You got the stuff I left?'

'Yes. But I'm hiding her in my room. Kitty litter and all.' She'd been leaving the top window open and a towel at the door in case the others could smell the cat food. 'I'm going back to Rochester this summer. She can't stay.'

'I'm trying to figure something out. She's healthy and all?'

'Very. Though I'm totally unqualified to say that because I've never had a cat.'

He glanced back up the queue. His friends were at the door. 'I'll talk to you inside.'

Eithne was looking at her eyebrows raised. 'How do you know Liam Connolly?'

'I don't. I didn't even know his last name was Connolly.'

'But he just pulled you out of line and had a secret conversation with you.'

'We met last Friday night. I barely know him.'

It was dark inside the club. They danced with the postgrads. She'd seen Liam with his group. They weren't dancing. A geologist from London danced in front of her, saying wasn't it the best night ever. It felt like it. Later, she turned and saw Liam standing against the wall watching her and he didn't look away when she looked back at him. She tried to not be ridiculous even though the geologist was jumping up and down in front of her shouting the lyrics. Then The Cure came on and everyone got up to shuffle around the dancefloor. She told the geologist she was getting a drink. She walked up to Liam. *Go on, go on* echoed around the room.

'Let's get out of here,' he said.

She turned and went out the door with him. They walked up the road along the seafront in the dark. The song kept echoing in her head long after it ended, *it froze me deep inside*. This night would end, he was leaving and she already felt the loss of something that had never happened. They had a pint in an empty hotel bar on the Threadneedle Road. The barwoman with thick glasses wiped the counter with a cigarette held loose between her lips while an English station on the TV gave an update on the nuclear plant. Liam sat facing her on a bar stool, his knee between hers.

'Shouldn't you have said goodbye to your friends?' she asked.

'It's better this way. They'd a send-off for me tonight and dragged me down to Salthill.'

'You're leaving that soon?'

'Day after tomorrow.' He'd be gone in a day. Living in a squat in London.

'That makes me sad,' she said. She didn't know why she said it.

'We should name her,' he said.

'Who?'

'Our cat. She needs a name.'

'If we name her that means we're getting attached. So we shouldn't.'

They finished their drinks and came back towards the Warwick as it was emptying. It had started to rain. She could see Eithne and the others standing at the seafront.

'It's the radioactive rain,' someone shouted. And they all stood there together, greeting it with upturned faces. More and more joined them, like a solemn welcome committee for the dark plume reaching their shores.

'Headcases,' said Liam. 'Let's go see our cat.'

They walked through the town. Across from the hospital he knocked on a door near Supermacs and someone passed out cans. The rain kept falling. She thought if she had the choice to be somewhere else or here in the poison rain with him, she would always choose this.

Back at the house, Liam sat on her bed, his back against the wall, and threw the yarn balls she'd made for the kitten. He passed her a can.

'She seems happy here.'

'She's trapped in a box room. She's not happy.'

They talked. Neither of them knew their fathers. Anna's mother was a nurse. Since they'd gone to America, they'd moved four times until her mother got the Rochester job. It was just the two of them. Her senior year she'd gone to a high school with over a thousand students and met no one. When she came back to Ireland she realised that she didn't know anyone here either.

'Why would you come back? The whole country's leaving.'

'Where else could I go?'

'Like a thousand colleges in the sun in a country where there are job prospects,' he said. She didn't think of Rochester or anywhere in America as places in the sun.

'Anyway, it's not like it's really worked out here.'

'It looks like you have friends. The people you were with tonight.'

'The postgrads? They're Eithne's friends. I only met them in the College Bar, watching the news with Chernobyl and everything.' Anna remembered what they'd said about the iodine and told him how it's like protection. 'We have the cat's iodine. Let's use it on us. I'll do you first.'

She told him to lie down and knelt beside him holding the brown bottle. She waited for a moment, then moved his hair from his neck, still damp from the rain.

'The state of our cat after you went at it with that bottle, like Cyndi Lauper on an extreme hair day.' He turned his head away. 'Somewhere less visible, please.'

She pulled up his sleeve and looked at his arm. His skin was pale with dark hairs. She turned it so she could see the vein in the hollow on the inside of his arm. The median cubital vein. She knew from anatomy class. She squeezed the dropper, letting six drops fall, pressing them in with her finger.

'Now I've marked you; you're protected.'

'Your turn,' he said, pushing her back on the bed.

She closed her eyes. Waited. He lifted the leg of her jeans and she felt his thumb on the inside of her ankle. Then the drops. Being touched at all made her throat tighten. He lay down beside her, holding the kitten on his chest.

'We should call her Cyndi Lauper,' he said. With the shock of iodine orange and the scrunched face from the cuts, Anna could see a resemblance.

She told him too much, how at Christmas she'd gone back to Rochester. Her mother worked night shifts and Anna felt alone. She drank vodka and thought about where she could go. The roads were grey slush and banked with dirty snow. She felt frozen and dead. And she did something disgusting and desperate. She rang the jogger who picked her up and they went to a bar.

'I'm not even the legal age to drink there and he wanted me to go into the bathroom with him.' He was worse than she'd remembered. Liam was quiet and Anna thought now he knows the worst about her.

'When we talked about you developing social skills, Anna, that's not what we had in mind.'

It made her laugh. He told her that when his mother was sick, he never went to see her in hospital. His aunt said maybe he should. But he didn't and he could never fix it.

'You didn't want to see her sick?'

'It was a mental hospital.'

They talked until they fell asleep. He lay behind her, his knees tucked into hers, his arms wrapped around her. Their cat lay on the bed with them. She had a vague sense of him leaving. Rubbing the cat, her cheek. And then he was gone.

Days passed. There was heavy rain and talk of contaminated milk and lamb. High ground was the worst. She heard on the radio that the poison from Chernobyl could last a thousand years. In the College Bar, Eithne's microbiologist said it would be even longer than that. The college was emptying. The lads had left for home. Eithne was packing her stuff for the bus to Ballina. She'd been out the night before at the Warwick and heard Liam Connolly had emigrated.

'He's left the country. Are you sure you didn't sleep with him?'

'Fuck off.'

'Well, he's gone and left you holding the cat.' Eithne cracked-up at her own joke. Cyndi Lauper was now roaming the house, finding pools of sun on the sitting room floor and garden, jumping on the windowsill to be let in, pawing her door. Anna had brought her to the vet. She was too young to get fixed yet, and she was a she.

Anna puttered around the empty rooms. She was supposed to be getting ready to go back to New York. She went around town, walked to Salthill. One day when the sun was out she borrowed the microbiologist's bike and cycled to Spiddal. The day before her flight she went to the phone box at the bottom of the estate to ring her mother and say that she'd found a job in a hotel on Eyre Square. Chambermaid stuff. She was staying. She rang the landlord. The house had been empty last summer, could she stay? He agreed same rent.

'I have a cat.'

'They're good for the rodents,' he said.

One evening in June she came home from the hotel to find a brown package dropped through the letterbox, postmarked London. Inside was a mixed tape. Cut out newspaper letters made a cover. *Listen to this when you are falling asleep.* Inside a smaller envelope was a fifty-pound note and a slip of paper. *Cat maintenance. Can I see you both at Christmas?*

Knocknacarra

Knocknacarra — *Cnoc na Cara* in Irish, meaning The Hill of the Stone Crossing — was once a rural area, just west of Galway, mostly made up of small farms. Many of the natives were Irish speakers, such as Dónall Mac Amhlaigh, a distinguished author and journalist, and golfing legends Christy O'Connor and his nephew Christy Junior.

It seems just a short time ago that Knocknacarra was all green fields, then suddenly these were being swallowed up by housing estate-after-housing estate, as it continued to grow into a huge sprawling suburb, complete with a church, a pub and a shopping centre. The only concession to the area's heritage is the retention of local poetic Irish-language place names, which are now used to identify the different estates.

Hugo Kelly

STATISTICS ARE AGAINST US

My father is talking about abortion again.

'I just can't believe Fine Gael is responsible for introducing it into Ireland,' he says.

We are in my car and I am driving. Ann, my ex-wife, is sitting in the back seat. Even though we've been separated for over four years she keeps in touch with my father.

'The party of Collins and Cosgrove has brought in abortion,' he says, shaking his head. 'It will be euthanasia next.'

I look at Ann in the rearview mirror. She smiles but there is distance in her eyes. Our silent communication is dying. The thought depresses me.

My father leans back, lapses into silence. I imagine gears and cogs grinding beneath the surface, producing a low disappointed hum that I have become accustomed to. Five years ago my mother died and he has not been the same since. And now Fine Gael have let him down.

We are on the Western Distributor. It's early summer. The rinsed-out green of winter has finally given way to something more fertile, hopeful even. My father has agreed to leave the house for the first time in weeks. When he heard Ann was coming, he was willing to be more adventurous. So today has turned into a day out.

I catch another glimpse of Ann in the mirror. Her hair is now a sandy colour, lighter than it was. I'm pretty sure that she's been getting her teeth whitened too. But I don't feel comfortable saying these personal things to her anymore. This makes me sad as well. My father hasn't really accepted that we are no longer together. I keep having to tell him our relationship is over, but I have some sympathy with his confusion. On paper, a bank manager would have liked our chances. But it didn't work out for us. We were independent people; too much education, not enough life. Our relationship became a form of compatibility. But in the end, it wasn't enough.

My father now points to the approaching roundabout.

'Take the left here.'

'I know,' I say.

'And the second left,' he instructs. 'That's Sliabh Ard.'

'*I know.*'

Our first trip is part detective work. Because of a similarity in address, we think that an important parcel meant for my father may have been delivered to a house here by mistake. My father, you see, collects books about Michael Collins, his personal hero. He has a glass-fronted bookcase that is thick with titles. But there is one book that he is missing *My Time with Michael Collin* by Batt O'Connor TD. It took a while, but I located a copy online in England. The book never arrived. There then followed some unsuccessful engagement with the postal sorting office.

'You know Michael Collins worked in the post office in England,' my father shouted down the telephone line, 'and he wouldn't have been bloody impressed with you lot.'

I pray that we locate the book here.

The estate feels typical, neither new nor old. Some ash trees have grown spindly and unloved. The red brick, darkened by recent rain, feels heavy. We find the house. A large palm tree obscures the front window and I can see a folded copy of the *Advertiser* leaning against the dark glass beneath the postbox. I am not surprised when no one answers the door.

My father presses his face against the glass.

'I can see loads of post on the floor. I bet it's there.'

Before we get back in the car Ann extracts a piece of paper and biro from her bag. She writes a quick note and leaves it tucked in the postbox.

'I have left some details,' she says. 'You never know.'

My father is despondent but Ann insists that we will track down another copy if needs be. Yet again I am glad that she is here.

For a few years we tried for children. When they didn't arrive, I thought it was all for the best and headed off on sabbatical to the States for six months. Ann, who is a teacher, joined me for the long holidays. We were in our late thirties with money, living in the green belt outside Boston. It should have been wonderful. Instead, it was there that it fell apart. Away from home and our routines, the compatibility dissolved, and the grievances came out. We came back separated.

It's important to keep my father busy so now we head the short distance to Knocknacarra Shopping Centre. My father needs some clothes but refuses flatly to go into the city centre. Ann suggested trying Dunnes.

The car park is busy with Sunday shoppers and I have trouble finding a space. I end up some distance away in the corner near B&Q. My father, I can tell, is not impressed as we trudge diagonally to the entrance for Dunnes.

'Rain is forecast,' he says. 'I hope we're not caught later.'

Inside the store we locate the men's clothing rails and my father tries on a moss-green fleece. Self-consciously he stands in front of us, next to a full-length mirror. I note that today he is wearing his natty brown corduroy trousers that Ann bought for him at Christmas. I am glad to see that he has made an effort.

'That looks very cosy,' I say. 'It will keep you warm for winter.'

He ignores me and turns to Ann.

'Hmmm,' she says, unconvinced. 'It's kind of like what you have already.'

She disappears into the rails for a minute, and then comes back with a couple of different types of puffer jackets. My father, as I do, views them sceptically. But he takes the fleece off and tries on the navy one. I have never seen him wear anything so remotely cool before and I am not sure what to say.

'It fits you well,' I murmur.

'I think it's great on you,' Ann says. 'It makes you look at least five years younger.'

'Ah,' he smiles and looks down at himself, proudly.

We buy the jacket and then some vests, socks and a new pair of pyjamas.

We pay and make our way to the coffee shop. This is above a pharmacy and shares the floor with a hairdresser's. It is my father's favourite coffee shop in all of Galway. He always takes a peek at the busy line of sinks and mirrors behind the partition, studying the various hair products with ethnographic interest. He then sits, facing out watching as the women come and go. I realise that he likes it because it is a repository of all that is gone from his life. He misses women and everything that entails. This is not an issue that I feel capable of dealing with.

My father wants a white coffee but the young woman serving us thinks he means a latté. My father responds crankily that he wants a white coffee. The young girl looks confused and I feel embarrassed.

Ann explains to him that a latté is similar but just uses better coffee. Mollified, my father agrees to try one. We sit down but after a few minutes my father complains of a draught so we move again. When we finally get our coffee and scones I find that my appetite is gone.

My father quizzes Ann about her job as principal in the school. She talks easily about the pupils, about the pressures of being young these days. She asks him how he is doing. As always, he is open with her.

'The nerves aren't great some days,' he says. 'I feel a bit anxious. I have trouble sleeping.'

'We all feel anxious,' she says and rubs the back of his hand with her fingers as he falls silent and stares into his coffee cup. 'But if you just get out of the house it will lift your spirits. Will you make an effort this summer?'

My father nods, wanting to appear reasonable.

Ann asks me about the university.

'How is the new MA you were working on?'

This is a new postgraduate course in green economics that I helped develop. But the course was cancelled due to only five applications. Overall, I think the students are more stupid and my colleagues are more angry. But I don't say this because I don't want to appear negative. I tell her that the course is on hold for a while but hopefully next year it will get off the ground. We just need better marketing.

'A business is only as good as its sales-people,' my father interjects. 'Business is selling.'

Ann smiles. In the dim café light I think that she has never looked lovelier. The laughter lines at the side of her eyes are so fine they appear graceful, like elegant veneers. On her last visit she told me that she is seeing someone.

This news has taken time to percolate through all my layers. She asked me had I met anyone. I shrugged my shoulders and she didn't pursue the question. I wonder how my father will take the news if her new relationship develops further. Invariably she will lose contact with him. That will be hard. The new man is called James. I try to not think of him.

We drink our coffee and then set off for the final leg of our journey to Aldi, my father's favourite supermarket. This involves driving out of the first car park and then making our way the hundred yards to the new car park. In terms of green behaviour, this is not good on many levels, but I don't want to argue with my father.

There we take a large trolley and walk up the aisles. My father picks an occasional item and leaves it flat on the bottom of the trolley. By the time we have wandered up and down three aisles, there is a packet of almonds, a French brioche loaf—which my father has somehow discovered a liking for—and a small tin of sardines. I feel like I am being tested. He wanders over to the large steel baskets arranged in the centre of the floor where the special offers are kept. Toolsets, cycling tops, garden shears. All the much-loved suburban bric-a-brac.

'What about this?' he says, holding up a large grey boxed item that says *Smoothie-Maker* in bright red letters.

'Do you even know what a smoothie is?' I say, regretting my crankiness, but still unable to avoid it.

'I could use it to make fresh orange juice for myself. The doctor says I need more roughage for my sluggish bowels.'

'You would never use it,' I say.

'I would use it,' he says. 'And it's only twenty Euros.'

Ann walks up beside him and examines the side of the box.

'This does look pretty good,' she murmurs. 'But you know what? Cleaning would be a real problem. A lot of trouble taking it apart and all that. Sometimes you have to leave it to soak overnight.'

'Oh,' my father says, 'cleaning and soaking. I didn't think of that.'

'You know you could buy some of the freshly-squeezed orange juice they have here instead.'

'That's a better idea,' my father says and replaces the smoothie-maker.

They head off in search of the fresh orange juice, but I feel too tired to follow. Instead, I hide at the side of the aisle. For a few minutes I think about writing an article based on our day. It could use this trip as an example of what is wrong with modern living. The shopping centre, a three-sided quadrangle, wrapped protectively around a giant car park, facing inwards, away from the hundreds of houses in its hinterland. It wouldn't have to be academic. It could talk honestly about our day-to-day existence and the choices we make. I am lost in thought until I see that Ann has stopped and is talking to a man with a trolley. A young girl stands beside him. It takes me a few seconds, but I somehow know that this is James. To my dismay he is fit-looking, coolly dressed, in a t-shirt and jeans that make him look youthful and at ease with the world.

They talk slowly. I sense the intimacy in Ann's movement. I note as he reaches out and touches her elbow, absorbing her into his drama. A pain gathers in my stomach. I should follow her and meet this James. Instead I linger, hoping that I can escape. My father, surprised at finding himself alone, retraces his steps and stands next to Ann. Too late I see the confusion in his face. I am almost with him when I hear his voice raised.

'Isn't it terrible that Fine Gael is after introducing abortion into Ireland?' he says. 'The party of Collins and Cosgrove.'

I survive the awkwardness as introductions are made. Shaking hands with James and smiling amiably at Rebecca, his daughter. I lead my father to the checkout and give Ann and James a few private seconds of conversation.

There is little talk on the way home and I can tell that Ann is distracted.

'Have you a minute? I need to talk to you,' she says, as we get out of the car.

My father glances at us and then goes inside, carrying his bag of clothes. He closes the front door but does not shut it.

'What's up?' I ask.

'I have some news,' she says.

'This sounds ominous,' I say.

'It's... something.'

'Yourself and James... moving on... shacking up?'

I try and sound light-hearted, but my words curl and fade in my mouth like dead, dry leaves.

'I'm pregnant,' she says. 'James and I are going to have a baby.'

There are no words for my confusion. I replay the sentence but the meaning does not change.

'You are going to have a child?' I say stupidly.

'It's frightening. I can't believe it myself.'

I see her eyes have filled with tears. I know how raw she feels delivering this news to me. I have to reciprocate.

'I am happy for you,' I say. 'You will be a wonderful mother. It's amazing.'

'I am so nervous,' she says. 'I never thought it could happen. Statistics were against us. It kind of feels like a miracle.'

We both tremble as we hug. I smell her hair, thinking this will be the last time. As we part I am aware that the phone is ringing in the hallway. My father answers it. His voice rises with excitement and I struggle to ignore it.

I walk with Ann to her car. She looks at me expecting me to say more but the words are trapped at the back of my throat. I sense a gnawing pain, a final acknowledgement that I have truly lost her. I am aware that my hand is shaking as I open the car door for her.

My father appears at the hall door. He is confused that Ann is leaving.

'Are you not coming in for a while?' he asks.

'I have to go,' Ann says. 'But I will visit soon. Don't worry.'

'It was great to see you,' he says.

She flashes me a smile and then gets into her car.

I watch her drive away until the car slopes around the corner and disappears.

As I turn, my father practically jogs towards me. I see that he is wearing his new puffer jacket.

'That was the man from Sliabh Ard on the phone. He's just back from holidays. He thinks he has the Collins' book for me. We should go back now while he is there. What a piece of luck!'

I stare at him, digesting this latest news. My heart is beating in an odd rhythm and I feel weak. My vision tightens and the colours fade as though I can only see in black and white.

My father is already getting into my car. There is nothing to be done but to drive back to the estate to get the book.

'It was Ann's idea you know to leave the note. She's a great woman,' my father says.

'Yes,' I agree, turning on the ignition.

Back on the Western Distributor, the grey sky finally opens and rain begins to fall in thick drops. I drive on slowly. There is an odd aching in my body. The rain increases in strength. Soon it is hard to see.

'Turn on the windscreen wipers,' my father says. 'What's wrong with you?'

But I don't turn them on.

My hands seem to be locked on the wheel and any further movement is impossible. The road is mercifully quiet and I manage to pull off into an estate, letting the car slide to a halt. My hands, my useless hands, still grip the wheel. The knuckles are white, angry-looking with stretched skin. But I am not angry. I am forty-five years old and I am dying of a broken heart. For a moment I think I am going to be sick.

My father shifts uncomfortably beside me. He clears his throat. The silence is bottomless.

'I was thinking,' my father says, 'maybe you would be interested in taking my Michael Collins' books when I'm gone. They will need a good home. Especially if there is a complete collection.'

I don't say anything. My grip seems to increase on the steering wheel. I can feel the pulse of the car as wind rises.

'Is this about Ann?' he asks.

I nod, words refusing to form in my throat.

'Something to do with that fellow she was talking to in Aldi?'

I close my eyes, which my father takes as agreement.

He strains to say something.

Suddenly he reaches over and pats the back of my left hand that still grips the steering wheel.

'Good lad,' he says, reassuringly.

I nod and take deep breaths. Finally, I can unclench my hands and simply sit.

My father leans forward and studies the mercurial sky. He does it in a doubting, sceptical manner that I imagine thousands of Irish people have similarly done down the ages.

'It's going to pass,' he says. 'This rain,'

As though preparing for this eventuality, he half unzips his puffer jacket.

'No rush,' he says.

I put the car into gear, flick on the indicator and slowly drive on into the spitting rain.

Roscam

The round tower in Roscam.

Roscam, derived from *Ros Cam*, meaning Crooked Peninsula, is a small townland a few miles east of Galway that is divided by the old Oranmore Road and juts out into the inner part of Galway Bay. It was the ancient territory of Clanfergail, of which the O'Hallorans were dynasts.

Roscam is an important medieval ecclesiastical site. Its 'moor' grave-yard has a four-foot high stone, referred to as the 'Holed Stone', which supposedly has powers associated with fertility rites; hands were joined through the opening, symbolising the emergence of life. It also has a Ligaun Stone of prehistoric significance dating back to approximately 2,000 B.C.; a 5th century monastery ruin, which legend connects to St Patrick and which was later attacked by Vikings; an 11th century round tower said to be the smallest in the country; and the ruins of a 15th century church.

In the 19th century, there was a duelling field in the area, easily accessible by land and by boat. During the War of Independence, an Oranmore man named Darcy was shot in a field here by the Black and Tans. Today this once quiet area is gradually being developed with new housing, as well as a public park with walkways, playgrounds, pitches and basketball courts.

Danny Denton

MOTORBIKE ACCIDENT, ROSCAM

The electricity pole's about six metres from where Whitey's body comes to a rolling stop. That's about sixteen metres, they'll determine a few hours later, with measuring tapes and wheels and unhurried steps, from where Trev's body has landed. Or, *has been flung.*

So the difference between driving the bike, guiding the handlebars, and riding pillion mere inches away, still within the embrace of a passenger and a driver, is therefore ten metres in two directions. Inches become metres, in a moment. Whitey and Trev grew up three doors from each other on the terrace, a distance of about twelve metres; Whitey is younger by seven weeks.

*

What's dominant is not pain, or panic, but an awareness of pain in images. There's pain in the electricity pole crackling above him, casting light across a dense sky. Unmoved, despite the speed at which they struck it. *STRUCK* as a word that he'll use in later years, at first subconsciously, then, after some minor revelation, consciously. It will feel right because of the way its pronunciation seems to tear apart at the beginning (*S T R*) and yet collide again at the end (*CK*).

And there's pain in the bank of spindly leafless poplars that shiver on the horizon of his vision, and pain in the crayon line of silver cloud running three-quarters of the way across the dark sky, across what might be Galway Bay, if he — Whitey — happened to know the direction he's facing.

And the awareness of pain results from wrongness. Everything in the world is wrong now, because the world just happened to come apart for a minute there (like the word *struck*), and, when it collided back together again, it was all crooked, all pain. Or an awareness of pain in images.

*

The language he'll use when, months later, he finally starts talking about it, will make it seem like he was in a sequence of battles with the world — like a rivalry — and his narrative will be that he lost this particular battle, this particular battle of course being a major one in the course of the war. His physio, Darren, will initially like Whitey, as they go through rudimentary post-paralysis routines, but eventually the *I got caught* language, and statements like, *You make one mistake, Dar, and the world fucks you…* will get to Darren, because — as he'll later, often, explain to his housemate, Kitty, in the evenings — in that physio suite, lined as it is with mirrors, this guy, who insists on being called 'Whitey' by the way, and not simply 'Graham', this guy just can't see himself.

'In a roomful of mirrors he's blind to himself,' Darren will say, more than once, himself needing these de-briefing sessions with a Supportive Other. 'He's there, and he's surrounded by himself, unable to avoid his banjaxed legs, the scar on his jaw, the re-built shoulder, and he *simply* can't fucking see that it's his own fault. The world didn't fuck him. *He* fucked up. Majorly. There's no one to blame but himself.'

'That's so fucking patriarchy,' Kitty will (repeatedly) say. 'To blame the world for your own bullshit choices.'

But would it be so wrong, under the amber glare of this streetlight—the streetlight tall and steadfast, cyclopic, utterly unwavering, glaring down on all it beholds in the street: the bike, half-shattered on its side, the right fork buckled completely, pieces of frame and windshield strewn across the Old Dublin Road; Trev's body, unmoving, twisted and wrung like a dish towel; Whitey's body, unmoving, half-unfurled on the flat of its back, submitting to the cracklewhispering streetlight, to the long row of leafless poplars that shiver in the night-turning-morning, running out beyond the streetlight's scope, waiting nervously for a response to this collision, for what will happen next—would it be so wrong to say that maybe the world *has* always been wrong, since the day Whitey was born? Or that Whitey's world was wrong, and what's happened is that he's finally come face to face with it?

Maybe, maybe.

*

Later, there will be a courthouse, and there'll be some time spent shivering in a wheelchair on the courthouse steps, waiting on a verdict, the words *suspended sentence* reverberating in the mind. But actually, looking out from those courthouse steps onto the cold columns of the Town Hall Theatre, he'll be thinking of before, long before, when he was 'Graham', during an under-15s Gaelic football game, when he went up to catch a kickout, the ball falling from the sky into his reaching arms.

Time can slow in moments like that.

But as he reached to receive it, somehow — some calibration of the jump or the catch being slightly off — the ball bounced off the tops of the fingers on his right hand and suddenly there was stunning, crackling pain in the baby finger of the right hand. As he landed he cried out. The baby finger in its Mikasa glove seemed to be flopping out sideways, at almost a right angle to his other fingers. It was utterly wrong-looking. Of course the game had gone on past him, the ball gone away up the field and everyone — the two coaches, his mam on the sideline, the other parents and spectators and subs — was looking after the ball, and no one was looking for him as he crouched and squeezed away tears and cradled one of his hands in the other. Everything moved on so quickly. No one saw him, or felt that fluttering of panic like a bird caught and flapping in his skinny chest, or saw when in that panic he grabbed the baby finger and wrenched it straight again. No one heard the series of audible clicks.

He would later tell it a few different ways — the story of the dislocated finger would evolve, like all stories — but he always included the fear that the top part of the finger had severed in the glove, and he always tried (consciously or sub-consciously) to use language that made people wince, words like:

jagged

                                               wrenched

                  torn

             cracked

But he had fixed it, he would say, without the help of doctors or physios. He had fucking sorted that finger out himself. The same digit with which, when it had still been swollen, he'd gotten laughs in Biology class by feigning to finger Nora Finlay as she wrote on the board with her back to them. But having remembered that, there on the steps of the courthouse, while, in a room inside, a number of well-dressed citizens deliberated upon his fate, he'd then question whether the lads had laughed because it was funny, or out of sympathy for him, or awkwardness, or, worst of all, fear.

Later than that, there was the time it swole up again, *massively*, when he bashed Al Finnegan with the umbrella right outside the school gate. The gay fucker had worn black nail varnish that day, and Whitey felt again, on the courthouse steps, looking out on a queue of traffic from the university side, the pain shooting through his baby finger as he leathered away at Finnegan's head and back, the umbrella coming more apart with each blow struck.

And later again, here's the dark heavy mass of the sky, and a paramedic's head coming into it, saying, 'Hello?' as if he's on a phone call with a bad reception. 'Can you hear me?'

And later again will come the continual surprise of brokenness, in the mornings, upon waking in the bed with the telly still on — or, sometimes, on the couch in front of the telly — unable to move his legs, feeling excruciating pain in his bony, muscle-shorn ass.

And even later his father's voice from behind him in the chair, as he is pushed for a change, along the Prom perhaps, saying, 'Your mother's grand, Gray. It's hard to say because it doesn't make sense, but, actually she's happier now. She doesn't have to worry about you getting into trouble anymore. The way you — the way things are now. The trouble is over.'

And he will say to his father: 'That's fucked up, Da. That's *massively* fucked up.'

He'll say that because he can say what he likes now. Because he *is* massively fucked up.

*

See him now, a boy of eight in the sitting room, sitting right up in front of the telly, inches away from it it because no one else is up yet, and the flickering of repeated roadrunner cartoons (and later James Bond Junior, and the Animaniacs, and all the rest) bathes his eyes in colour and light. The dog is in the window, barking at a car in the estate outside, and he's telling the dog to shut up, and he thinks that because he's got his sheriff's badge on (the badge that will never get lost, that will end up in a box kept for decades under a bed), the dog should do what he says. Because he's got his sheriff's badge on, the sitting room is *his dew restic-shun*, but for some reason the dog just doesn't understand that.

And, not long after, a struggle on the beach near Barna, when his brother will eventually get him down and start stuffing sand into his mouth, saying, 'Eat up your breakfast now, Gray!' while the panic bird tries to escape his chest and his father looks on with folded arms and a boys-will-be-boys grin, eventually saying, 'Cut it out you two, it's gonna rain soon,' and walking on, away.

*

So maybe the world *has* always been wrong, and has in fact caught him this time. He'll eventually get used to phrases like, *I've made mistakes...* during intimate conversations, and in rehab, and at family occasions (his wedding, for example, when they'll strap his legs to his father on one side and his brother on the other side so that he can walk up the aisle to meet Sadie, who'll fall in love with him for his habit of wearing a toy sheriff's badge while he watches TV, calling the channels his *jurisdiction*; Sadie, who it'll take nearly two decades to drive out of his life)...

'I've made mistakes...' he'll admit at the coffee mornings the rehab centre will occasionally ask him to turn up to, where he'll see Darren again and they'll make such awkward small talk, but when he says that he's made mistakes he won't be thinking of the decision to drink and drive, or of Trev at his back, helmetless, yelling into the wind of their speed on the road, and then chaos; he'll not be thinking of jangling the keys of the bike at the table in O' Connor's, saying to Trev in front of them all, 'I'll show you a fucking road you haven't driven on before,' or grinning in the car park, egging Trev on with the grin—that gaunt square jaw of his that'll forever be marked with a jagged line, that he'll actually grow to love because it gives him some kind of authority (the scar itself a story, a character)... Actually, at such coffee mornings, and occasional AA meetings, when he recites the details of what happened that night—the darts, the pints, the lads, the craic—reciting them like prayers he knows the words to but never thinks about the meaning of, he'll be thinking of the sirens, as the awareness of pain dawned on him... As he tells the story in a way that makes it seem inevitable—as if he'd been chased by some demon through life to this very mistake—and as he's explaining that telling the story helps him deal with the horror, to the point that once he started talking about it, months after the accident, he found that he couldn't stop talking about it, as if he was trying to exorcise the trauma by talking it out over and over and over again, he'll be thinking of the electricity pole glaring down on him in the grit and glass and sharp plastic of the road, and he'll be thinking to himself, while meaningless recited words pour out, *You fucking caught me, cunt. You prick of a world. I made one slip up and you fucking caught me.*

Cunt. That word running over and over in his mind, a tsunami of pure hatred in a word, until he's not sure whether he's calling the world a cunt or calling himself a cunt.

*

And that's the very point—the very moment he's thinking back to, there on the road, lying twisted and broken, in body and time and space and perception—that Trev begins to disappear into the world. Trev: lying dead ten metres away, completely broken, forever. Not only the legs and the back and the neck and the brain, and the lungs and finally the heart, but the memory of him is broken too. Every time he's not mentioned in Whitey's story—those little imagistic details—or the anonymising rumours of *Yer man there killed a fella*, Trev disappears further into a void of forgetting, becoming a speck, a pause where a mention might have been made. Because when people's lives go on their stories go on too, and other things and other people get forgotten, until only his mother and father say his name, once in a while, privately, perhaps when they stop to glance at his photograph in the frame by the bed, or on his birthday, out in the house by the Swamp in Salthill, until they die too—one of a stroke, the other of cancer, less than three years apart—and Trev is gone then entirely.

And so when Whitey recites, *I've made mistakes* for decades afterwards, until the end of his life, at 78, in the Renmore hospice, Trev is not named among those words. It's as if Whitey were alone on the bike. Trev is present only as an unspoken hint, a faded, hidden stain on a broken person's memory. Trev dies on the road, at about 2.30am that Sunday morning, of his injuries, utterly unaware of any pain.

GALWAY COUNTY

Diamond Hill in Connemara National Park.

Ballinasloe

The name Ballinasloe is derived from *Béal Átha na Slua*, The Mouth of the Ford of the Crowds. It was situated at a crossing point of the River Suck, a gateway to the west, which would suggest it was always a meeting place. The town is fairly modern in origin with the local agricultural fair for a long time the largest cattle mart in the British Isles. This annual October event gradually evolved into a fair exclusively for the buying and selling of horses, the biggest horse fair in the country.

A number of industries opened up towards the end of the last century, but they have ceased trading now, and along with the closure of St Bridget's Hospital, it has caused a serious economic downturn in the town.

Some of the writers associated with Ballinasloe are Rita Kelly; Eoghan Ó Tuairisc; Desmond Hogan; Fr Patrick Egan, the historian; and children's writer, Sandra Warde Kilduff. Classical guitarist John Feely and artist Eileen Quinn also come from Ballinsloe.

Close by is the site of the Battle of Aughrim, as well as the River Suck Callows Special Protection area.

Nuala O'Connor

FUTURETENSE®

'It's actually good that you're a foreign national,' Donncha said. He leaned back in his chair, hands behind his head, elbows splayed like wings. Cock-of-the-walk.

Maria smiled down at him; the smile hurt her cheekbones. 'For what reason?' she asked.

'The clients like it when the descriptions sound a bit broken-Englishy. It's sexy, you know?'

'But I'm Irish. I'm from Galway.'

Donncha snorted. 'Yeah, OK.' He shuffled papers on his desk and Maria dipped from foot to foot, weary of standing. 'Listen, when you're writing, think effervescent.' Donncha waggled his thick fingers. 'Think staccato.' His skin was the same mottled, churlish pink as a cow's udder; Maria wondered if it smelt of milk and dung. He swung in his chair and pulled himself to stand, his belly pouching forward, slack. 'Welcome aboard, yeah?'

Maria hoped he wouldn't try to shake her hand; his bovine fingers would be too much, too much altogether. She nodded at Donncha, lifted the basket of perfumes from his desk and carried it out of his office to her own. She sat and picked out a grenade-shaped bottle; she imagined throwing it at Donncha's temple and the nice thwack it would make as it hit flesh. Maria conjured the rainbow of bruises he would be left with, the welts and, eventually, the scabs. She twisted off the lid and sniffed deeply.

Terroriste®—*Scent-bomb your territories with this explosive cocktail of masculine cyprus and wood, lashed to feminine frangipani. Terroriste*®—*for the woman who wants to be a man. Terroriste*®—*Forceful. Fragrant. Full on.*

The office was in a warehouse in an industrial estate on the Naas Road. Maria had taken her flat in Fairview so as to be near the city centre; she wanted the throb of it close by. Now, every weekday, she went through the city on one bus and out past it on another, to a suburb on the far side. She left Dublin Bay at her back to enter the long, grey corridor of the town. Maria wondered about all the lives that went on in the apartments on the quays and the houses in Inchicore and Bluebell: the sex, the sorrow, the shame that filled those rooms, under lights and in darkness, seven days a week. But some of the people must be happy, she thought; they were bound to be, weren't they?

The buses she took chugged and stopped, stopped and chugged and, by the time she got off her last one for the day, it was late evening. The diesel smell of the buses reminded her of her father's New Holland, stinking up the boreen and the yard with its black fumes. Her mother called it 'that fucking yoke'; *her* family had always had Masseys, like *normal* people.

Maria would have to go west soon and show her face; she would have to endure her mother, complaining about her father and weeping into her apron over a dead calf or a vanished hen. The same woman who never dropped a tear at her own son's funeral.

HerStory® — *Tonka bean and orange blossom vivify this homage to the female spirit. Childlike and luminous, HerStory's*® *vibrant top notes slide sensually above an earthy heart and silky accord. Tough and seductive, HerStory*® *is the new woman's fragrant manifesto. Wear it. Own it. Live it. HerStory*®!

Dublin city unfurled before Maria at the weekends. Her mother had proclaimed it a foul place but Maria enjoyed the mix of oil and hops and exhaust-stink; she liked the moss-and-mud smell off the Liffey that was like no river in Galway. The buildings were various: a pagoda of glass floated above the Liffey; there were the columns of government, and soft red brick everywhere. Dublin's crowds energised Maria. She liked their push-me-pull, the endless spate of bodies and faces, everyone hurrying towards something and, later in the day, hurrying away from it.

'Dublin is awful depressing, Maria,' her mother said. 'And you can never tell what's what or who's who; the place is wedged with gutties. Keep yourself to yourself.'

Maria liked the southside of town as much as the northside. She spent Saturday afternoons strolling up and down Grafton Street to watch the whole clatter of life it held. She loved the flower-women with their rough faces. And the man who made a sand Labrador and stood over it all day, finessing its coat, as if the dog were real. Maria appreciated the buskers — the shy and the brazen — who tootled for the tourists on tin whistles and crooned in County America accents. She wondered if John had enjoyed the town when he lived in Dublin, or if London called to him from early on. Her brother had always wanted the next thing and the next; nothing in the now ever satisfied him.

John had worn a benign aftershave, remarkable only for its subtlety; Maria chose it for him though she was only a girl at the time.

'You can't wear Daddy's aftershave forever,' she said, standing behind John on the cold lino of the bathroom, watching him douse himself from the sailing ship adorned white flask, that reminded Maria of a baby's bottle.

'And what would you suggest, missy?'

'We'd have to go to Ballinasloe so I could show you.'

John drove her to the town in their mother's Fiesta, and he let eleven-year-old Maria sniff her way through every men's fragrance in every chemist's shop in Ballinasloe, until she found the right one. The scent she chose was called Futuretense and it came in a squat silver flacon. John had never heard of it but, when he sprayed it on, he told Maria it was the perfect one for him. He smelt his wrist and said, 'As comforting and elemental as a new lover.'

Maria grinned. She loved the way John spoke, like someone making up a poem on the spot. She was happy to be seen walking Society Street and Dunlo Street with him, proud to be his sister. John paid for the aftershave and they celebrated with tea and fairy cakes in the Bread Basket, and a breakneck spin back to Ahascragh in the Fiesta. John overtook every other car on the road and roared, 'Bogmen! Bogmen!' out the window as they sped by.

On one of Maria's wandering Saturdays, a man wearing Futuretense wafted past her and she swooned under its warm, woody scent; it brought her brother to her like a swift slap. She followed the man for a while, soaking up his trail of cyprus-tobacco-ginger, but she let him go once he crossed over into Stephen's Green. The moon was a yellow lantern rearing up behind the trees that rimmed the park; it was time for Maria to get back to Fairview and make her tea.

Luna Bella®—Unmask the urban emotion of Luna Bella®, an unprecedented mix of patchouli, leather and moon iris. Let your soul hover above its sophisticated intensity and be swept away on its urgent, ice-lily base. Everyone deserves the indulgence that is Luna Bella®.

'Cheer up; it might never happen,' the bus driver said.

Maria stood at the front of the bus, waiting to get off; the driver looked at her in the rear-view mirror. She wanted to say, 'It already *has* happened.' But that brought too clear a picture of John, hanging in his London flat, his skin darkening as the days passed. So she smiled instead, into the mirror, before turning to look at the driver. He grinned back, showing two rows of bright, even teeth; Maria was always drawn to nice teeth.

The bus pulled in at her stop and the driver opened the doors. Maria stepped forward to alight but the driver closed the doors quickly before she could leave the bus. Maria turned to him again and he winked. He had choppy, fair hair like a footballer's. The bus driver was taking her in, noticing her as much as she was him.

'Ah, I'll stop messing now,' he said, pressing the button to open the doors. 'Go on. Cheerio.'

Maria thanked him and swung off the bus into the Fairview dark, bringing a small piece of the driver home with her. She savoured him as she ate her tea of tinned salmon and batch loaf; she sipped him up with her coffee. Later, in bed, his golden hair lay beside her on the pillow, smelling of sunflowers and honey and cognac, and Maria rubbed herself into ecstasy on his scent.

Tower de Nuit®—Abandon yourself to the glamorous ride that is Tower

de Nuit®, *let it fill you with the lush, juicy undertones of star anise.*
Surrender to the joie de vivre of virile, glistening black orchid. Tower
de Nuit®: *Provocative. Risqué. Orgastic.*

Donncha stood over her desk; Maria had seen him lumber towards
her. She held her breath; she did not want to smell him. He had that
fat-person aura: a curdled, damp warmth that spoke of unwashed
folds.

'Maria!' He blurted her name as if it embarrassed him to say it.
'Listen, I'm just thinking and, don't get me wrong, but you might want
to tone it down a bit.' He wouldn't look at her, keeping his eyes instead
on the print-out of Maria's work in his hand. She could see that he
had yellowed-in parts of it with a highlighter. 'We're in the business
of words, yeah? But "orgastic" — is that a real word? What does it even
mean? It sounds, you know, rude maybe. What do you think?'

Maria placed the bottle of Tower de Nuit on the palm of her
hand. 'What does this look like to you, Donncha?'

'I don't know. The round tower at Glendalough?' He squinted.
'A lighthouse? The Spire, maybe?'

Maria curled the fingers of her other hand around the perfume
bottle. 'And now?'

'Well, I can't really see it when you have your fist around it like
that.' He sputtered a laugh.

Maria moved her closed hand up and down the shaft of the
bottle. 'Now, Donncha? What does it remind you of when I do that?
Slowly, like this, then a little faster. Oh!' Maria stilled her hand.

Donncha backed away, his face shining red as a Sacred Heart
lamp. 'Ah, yeah, I see what you're saying. You're doing grand. Work
away, work away.'

Maria watched him stumble over to the water cooler; she listened
to the glug of its innards as Donncha helped himself to one cup of
water after another. She took out a perfume bottle from her basket

and popped off its lid.

Ishka® — *An aquatic interpretation of pure Irish water, Ishka*® *flows from a top note of crisp green tea through to a base of shamrock dew. Natural and earthy, the watery accords of this fragrance's core tell of the man with an endless need for adventure. Ishka*® — *slakes every unquenchable thirst.*

The bus driver's name was Eddie Laharte. Maria knew this because he had a totting-up sheet on a clipboard that sat behind the steering wheel and, with her good eyes, she could read it. 'Maria has great eyes; brilliant eyesight', was her mother's only boast about her as a child and, even then, it was as if she took credit for the fact.

John, of course, was beyond compare; there weren't enough superlatives for him. John of the top marks at school. John of the gobsmacking good looks — 'I don't know where he gets it from! But it's more than likely my side; the Uncle Jack was a fierce handsome man.' John of the thoughtfulness — 'He brings me breakfast in bed every Saturday; I kid you not, missus. He's a great lad altogether.' John of the lovely Ballinasloe girlfriend — 'She was Queen of the Fair last year!' John of the Dublin boyfriend. The Ahascragh girlfriend. Another Dublin boyfriend. Their mother couldn't keep up and, by the last boyfriend, she had lost any desire to try.

Eddie Laharte sang snatches of songs to Maria as he drove the bus, looking up at her from under his thatch of hair. He called her Roxanne and told her she didn't have to put on the red light or sell her body to the night. Maria liked his name. Eddie Laharte. In her mind she called him Steady Heart.

'So, Roxanne, what's your real name?' Eddie said and, when she told him it was Maria, he wondered how to solve a problem like her.

'You could take me out,' Maria said, appalled that the words of fantasy had fallen from her tongue.

'Grand so,' Eddie said, 'I will.'

And he ignored the complaints of the other passengers while he stopped the bus on the North Strand and took his time swapping mobile phone numbers with Maria.

Cherrybomb* — Bold but with a soupçon of lux, Cherrybomb* is a candied, berry surprise. The top, heart and base notes of the fragrance sing to the innocence of the young while anticipating the mature yet vibrant accents of cerise and vanille. Cherrybomb* — the rubescent scent of youth, just waiting to be plucked.

Maria was summoned west. Her mother met her off the train in Ballinasloe.

'He's taken to the bed,' she said, as she swung the car out into the road and turned left towards Ahascragh.

'Daddy?'

'Of course Daddy. Who else is there? He's asking for you morning, noon and night.'

Maria looked at the houses they passed; some neat and cared for, others with crumbling stone walls and broken windows. The next house along, she knew, had a Virgin shrine at the bottom of its garden; Mary standing with pleading arms and a let-down look. Blessed Mother of Ballinasloe. Virgin of Ahascragh. Mother of Sorrows. Our Lady of Suicides. Sancta Maria. Pray for us.

'I have bad news,' her mother said.

Maria looked at her. 'Oh God. Is he very sick?'

'Is who sick?'

'Daddy.'

Her mother jammed her foot to the brake and Maria jolted forward. 'Not him! The dog! The dog died. Boy—John's old pal.'

Her mother started to whimper and Maria told her to pull over; she parked beside the house with the shrine. The Madonna's halo of bulbs sparkled in the dusk, a sapphire torc; Maria was enchanted by the blue glow and only gradually became aware of the sustained sobbing beside her. She switched on the map light and saw that her mother's face was flooded with snot and tears.

'Here you go.' Maria handed her a tissue from her bag; it was a dusty lump that held a portion of the gallons of tears she had leaked over the loss of John.

'You'll have to bury Boy,' her mother said. 'With himself in the bed, I can't manage the digging of the grave, the lifting, all that. Poor Boy, he was a terror but I loved him. Who will I have left?' Her mother pushed out another few tears and dabbed at her eyes.

'I'll drive,' Maria said.

They picked their way over cow pats to get to the place by the horse chestnuts where the pets were buried over the years; there were crosses for gerbils, dogs, cats, goldfish and Maria's beloved pet duck, Bernie. Maria wore a pair of wellies that may have been hers or may have been John's, she wasn't sure; they felt dank on her feet.

'Do you remember, Mam, you used to heat up the insides of Daddy's wellies with the hairdryer before he went out in the mornings?'

'What? Not at all. I did no such thing.'

Maria looked back up at the house, standing like a headstone on the hill; geese squabbled around the pond in the low field. How had Maria never noticed before that the pond was heart-shaped? A deep, steady heart. She wondered if Eddie would send her a text while she was at home and, if he did, what it would say.

When they reached the spot her mother had chosen to bury Boy, Maria began to dig. The peaty, wormy clay threw up the smell of childhood to her nose. She and John had spent hours in these fields, digging to Australia and making Sindy doll graveyards. Maria began to enjoy the cleave of the shovel through the quaggy earth, the primordial feel of it. She moved the clods quickly and felt as if John was beside her, helping to open the ground, sure now that he wanted a Galway burial and not the ash-scatter on the Thames of his note.

Her mother sat on the grass, holding the swaddled Boy to her chest. She dipped her face close to the bundle of him and sighed. Maria worried that she might kiss the old sheet that covered the dog. Or worse, unwrap him and put her lips to his coat. She kept digging. Boy was a squat terrier and it did not take long to fashion a big enough hole, or fill it in above him. They stood over the grave. Her mother's eyes were closed and Maria hoped she was not going to recite the Rosary or anything like that.

'He was the needle in my compass,' her mother said.

The trees rustled and Maria watched a chestnut drop to the earth and split.

'He was a lovely little dog, all right.'

Her mother's eyes sprung open. 'What are you saying? Not Boy! John! John! Sure I'm lost without him. Lost. And your father is useless to me. The whole thing has fallen asunder.'

K9*—Make a statement with quirky K9*! The Irish Setter-shaped flasque will be a favourite talking point. Loyal and fresh, with a blend of emerald grass and bright satsuma, K9* is a strong balance of the classic and the modern. K9*—rugged, faithful, true.

The bus was wedged with people as it always was in the evenings. Eddie was not the driver and Maria worried that by going west she had upset some equilibrium, knocked things skew-ways. She left Eddie driving the bus on Friday—he was there, safely there where he should be — but now he was no longer behind the wheel. There was a man with onyx skin in his seat.

'Where is Eddie Laharte?' Maria asked the driver, put out that this man was at *her* man's wheel. He shrugged and shook his head.

Maria sat. The young fella sitting in front of her had lipstick on his cheek, a perfect pink pout; the girl beside him eyed it manically. A teenager across the aisle had blood dripping from no discernible wound on her ear and it tattooed her collar. Maria wanted to tell her; she would like to tamp the blood for the girl but could find no way to say it, so she said nothing. The elderly man who sat beside Maria talked about Blackhall Place and Fitzwilliam Square and the women who roamed those places.

'It's all gone on the internet now,' he said, 'all *that*.' He licked his lips and caught her eye. 'Isn't that right?'

'Maybe,' Maria said, looking out of the bus to see an aeroplane leave its scribble across the sky.

She thought of her father, how small and vulnerable he had looked in her parents' bed, with his hair tossed into a silver peak. The room smelt, as it always did, of mildew and soup.

'Hello, Daddy,' she had said, an offering from the doorway of the bedroom.

'Maria! Thanks be to God. Get in and close that door. I haven't got long; your mother is killing us off one at a time: first John, then Boy. She's after me now. I needed to warn you.'

'John hung himself, Daddy. And Boy ran under the wheels of the New Holland, didn't he?'

'Is that what she's telling people? The fucking witch. She strangled the pair of them with her hands. I saw her.' Her father gripped Maria's arm. 'Listen, 'til I tell you. Stay away from this house. Stay away from Ahascragh. Settle yourself well in Dublin and don't be coming back here at all.' He glanced at the closed bedroom door and lowered his voice. 'She's threatening to put me into Brigid's in Ballinasloe. *She's* the madwoman and she wants to shove me into that place full of

gombeens and nutjobs. If she doesn't squeeze the life out of me first.'
He whispered: 'Stay away or you'll be next.'

Le Fou — *Experimental rose, combined with edgy accents of sambac jasmine, lift the wearer of this scent into new realms. The skin tingles under the powdery warmth of Le Fou's* *exceptional heat, and pink peppercorn adds a sparkling facet. Le Fou* — *Kooky. Exciting. Fantastical.*

Eddie brought Maria for a picnic in the Phoenix Park. They sat on a bench and he took cheddar sandwiches from a Tesco cool bag. They both decorated the cheese with Tayto and crunched through the sandwiches under the eye of the Wellington Monument that rose up from the grass like God.

Eddie handed her a Double Decker. 'Bus chocolate,' he said, and they both laughed.

When they finished eating, Eddie stood and suggested a walk. He put his arm around Maria's shoulder and they strolled deep into the park, into the wooded, quiet part. The smells were welcome to Maria: the pinch-cool air of autumn, muck, grass and Eddie's warm, masculine fug — a mix of sweat and cheap deodorant. He took a small rug from his Tesco bag and they sat on it, their ears full with the friendly sounds of the park: the burr of distant cars, leaf-loss from the trees and murmurs from the living earth.

Eddie tilted Maria's chin and she watched his golden fringe fall over his eyes as he closed them and leaned in to kiss her. He tasted not of crisps or chocolate but of something sweet and rosy, something like hope. Maria let her tongue slip over and around Eddie's. Soon all there was in the world were their two mouths and their meet, tease, and delight in the soft heat of the other. When they broke away, Eddie smiled and Maria felt a lurch from groin to throat. He pushed her back gently so that she was lying down and he lay beside her.

Maria looked up at the sky. 'My brother topped himself in January,' she said.

'My little brother drove his car into a wall. We don't know if he did it on purpose or not.'

'The Dead Brothers Club.'

'I know a few more in that,' Eddie said.

'Me too.'

Eddie took her hand and they both closed their eyes. The park hummed around them, keeping up a hushed banter while they dozed. When Maria woke she saw a pair of fallow deer standing a few steps away, the stag's antlers poised like question marks, the doe's jaw working on grass.

'Eddie,' she whispered, nudging him.

He opened his eyes, hunkered into his standing and helped Maria to her feet. They picked up their things and backed away from the deer. The stag nodded his head as if in blessing and the doe kept up a rhythmic chewing and stared at them from succulent eyes.

Herne du Bois® — *A strong base of oriental musk coupled with oak-moss makes Herne du Bois*® *a deep yet soaring scent for the discerning man. Smoke fuses with green chypre in the base notes creating an earthy, masculine body. Herne du Bois*® — *taming the wild.*

Maria sat at her desk, feeling suddenly slick all over; sweat pushed between her breasts and slid inside her thighs. It was her body remembering — before her mind caught up — the sex she and Eddie had had that morning. He lay over her and held her gaze and his tongue lifted behind his teeth as he moved. He had sleep scars on his cheek, as if his skin had been folded and refolded. Maria recalled his low grunts when he rocked over her, and the final, giddy fall to her neck, and the way he kissed the skin there in small, picking kisses. She conjured the soft wet of his tongue; remembered the astounding tenderness of him.

'Erm, there's someone here to see you.' Donncha stood in front of Maria's desk; she hadn't heard him approach.

'Someone for me?' She rose and looked behind Donncha. Her mother stood there, alien and uncertain in the middle of the floor, her dark coat making a jackdaw of her. 'Mammy?'

Maria went and put her arms around her mother, breathing deep on her grease-and-sherry scent.

'I'm sorry, peteen; I had to get away from your father. He's raving. I hopped on the train.'

Donncha stepped forward. 'You can use the canteen to talk, yeah? Get yourselves a cup of tea.'

Maria nodded her thanks and steered her mother towards the door. She sat her in a chair and knelt beside her.

'He's saying John is better off dead.'

'Daddy doesn't mean that, Mam. He was mad about John.'

'How can he say it then?'

'I suppose he's hurting still and doesn't understand.'

'I'm afraid of my life of him. He half-choked me this morning and I ran from the place.' She put her hand to her neck.

'You can stay with me tonight, Mammy. We'll go to Ahascragh in the morning and see what's what.'

Donncha urged Maria to go home and she thanked him and bundled her mother to the bus stop.

'I don't know what to do with your father at all. As if I haven't enough to be dealing with.'

Maria leaned into her mother's side and tucked stray hairs behind her ear. 'It'll be all right, Mam, we'll get Daddy sorted. You'll be OK too. We have to stop looking behind us now and start looking ahead.'

Her mother nodded and patted her hand. 'You're a good girl, Maria, a great girl. You always were.'

They sat with arms linked on the bus into town, her mother stiff at first, as countrywomen always are in the face of Dublin's grime and hustle. But Maria could feel her mother's body slacken as the bus trundled on past the canal where swans performed their watery skirr.

When they stepped onto the Fairview bus, Eddie said, 'Hello, honey.' Maria smiled and indicated her mother, hooshing her into a seat near the front.

'They're a bit familiar these Dublin bus drivers,' her mother said.

Maria turned to face her. 'Actually, he's not just the driver. He's my boyfriend.'

'He is not!' Her mother leaned off her seat, into the aisle, to get a look at Eddie. 'What's he called so?'

'Eddie. Eddie Laharte.'

'Laharte? Is that some kind of came-over-with-Cromwell name?'

'I don't think so. His people are from Kilkenny.'

'Oh,' her mother said, nodding. 'Eddie Laharte.' She tested and re-tested the shape of the words on her tongue. 'Eddie Laharte.' Finding them pleasing, she settled back in her seat and grinned approvingly at Maria. They both fixed their eyes forward to the front of the bus, to where Eddie sat, whisking them onwards to Fairview and the future.

Futuretense® — *A light top gives way to deep, steady heart notes that seductively lead to a harmony of relaxing tobacco and warm ginger. This is a fragrance that thrusts its wearer forth into unknown realms. Futuretense*® — *promise in a bottle. Futuretense*® — *the only way forward.*

Barna

Silver Strand Beach.

Barna was a quiet coastal farming and fishing village west of Galway. Most of the land was originally poor and it was fertilised gradually using seaweed so that the soil eventually became quite rich and productive. Local farmers travelled into Galway regularly to sell their products at the various fairs and markets. Many of them were native Irish speakers, but as the population increased, so the influence of the language weakened, though it is still a strong feature of the area.

There was a lot of activity in the parish during the revolutionary decade between 1913 and 1923 as the Black and Tans burned many houses on the Pier Road. They also tortured and murdered Father Michael Griffin and buried his corpse in a bog at Cloch Scoilte.

Today Barna is an upmarket suburb of Galway, with a strong sense of community. It has an 18-hole moorland golf course and Barna Woods, a lovely location for walking, which has the last natural-growing oak trees in the west of Ireland.

Silver Strand Beach in Barna is named *Trá na gCeann* after a bloody battle that took place there a few hundred years ago.

Órla Foyle

IT CAN BE GOOD

F ist punch. Foot kick. Body bang.
'You fuckin' bastards. Call this a cop shop?'
Someone walks close to the opposite side of the door.
'Stay quiet in there!'
Fist punch to the approximate point that voice came through.
Mouth on my side of the door. 'Is that you, you Big Foot Bastard?'
Fist punch on his side of the door.
'Pipe down now.'
I pipe down and my breath sounds hard. Give him a few seconds of thinking he's got me done. Now. *Fucking bastard cops. Wankers hauling me in here.* I can see them shaking their heads, smiling, calling me a sorry bitch, some returned daughter of the isle now all misshaped and foreign with an accent.

I pissed on the side of the road in Turkmenistan in front of a bus of travellers, I yell now. *Do you think being arrested frightens me?* The bus driver whorled his tongue through his broken teeth when I got back on the bus. Other men said things. I didn't understand the language but my new husband dragged me down to my seat and said, 'Why couldn't you hold on to it?'

'I'm a nurse. I know what it does to the pelvic floor and bladder if you do that.'

An old woman drew her scarf from her mouth and spat at me.

We were on a kind of honeymoon through Central Asia and beyond. We hadn't any rings but Jerry said we could pick up cheap lapis lazuli in this market he had heard of in Herat, in Afghanistan. The bus bumped along the road to the border checks between here and there. Old men tugged at my dress. Young men clicked their tongues. Young women gave me their eyes, dark and watching. I smiled at them. Most of them looked like the girl from the *National Geographic* photo. Jerry said to come on, let's get the next bus. There were more chickens than goats on this new bus. We sat at the back. The hot dust rose up through the window. I was far away from home. I was twenty-two. I was married to a man with a beard and beautiful eyes.

Fist bang from the other side of the door, then the door unlocks and opens.

Big Foot Bastard stands there.

'Hello, Sergeant,' I say.

He is joined by Little Miss Nice, a small and round female guard.

'Stop yelling your useless stories at the top of your voice,' Big Foot Bastard says. 'We don't need to hear about your Turkmen... sten... trip.'

'Never been abroad, Sergeant?'

'I've just back from Lanzarote,' Little Miss Nice says. 'I'm all brown from there.'

Big Foot Bastard holds up his hand. 'You were arrested for being drunk and abusive in Knocknaccara...'

'I was pushed.'

'Witnesses say you mis-stepped.'

'Mis-stepped? Whoever says that word in real language? I was pushed by my sister's boyfriend, and wankers with their mobile phones filming me. You didn't arrest them did, you?'

The ground spins below my feet. I haul myself upright against the faint. I think of Jerry. Jerry dead and on the bed. The rhyme won't leave me now.

'You don't understand,' I say.

'If you stay quiet, I can bring you a cup of tea,' Little Miss Nice offers.

'I'm grieving,' I say.

Big Foot Bastard looks at me. 'Over what?'

I say nothing.

Big Foot Bastard says, 'You're going to have to sober up now, aren't you?'

'Go fuck yourself,' I say sweetly and I think of Jerry smiling at me. Go fuck yourself, we had sung to each other across hotel rooms and finally in our home in Eastwood, Sydney, Australia until he was dead in a bed.

Fist bang on the door. *I've been in better cop shops than this. I was in Darlinghurst with all the prozzies and junkies, and they were the cops. You know you always made sure to have someone with you, when you called the cops. The rapes they got up too, otherwise.*

Jerry said, 'You idiot, letting them near you.'

Our flat had been burgled so I called the cops. They came into our sitting room and picked up things. One of them picked up me.

Jerry cried next to me in the hospital. I was open-raw and bloody. I screamed go fuck yourself at him. Later he said he couldn't break my barriers, he couldn't climb my walls, and I was failing to see his own pain. I said what pain. He said, you know. I said the pain of some bastard's dick inside you? That pain? The pain of some wanker's fist against your throat so you don't scream? That pain?

Kick the door. Kick. Kick. Kick.

A kick from outside. 'Shut up in there!'

I think of Jerry's dead white face on the bed. His teeth are white too. His eyes and mouth are open as if he has just yawned.

'Jerry,' I say and he says nothing.

Sudden Adult Death Syndrome. It is as common and rare as cot deaths.

Big Foot Bastard tells Little Miss Nice to return to her station.

He stands in the doorway. 'You're quite the article,' he says. Then locks me in.

I punch the cell door. I kick and kick and kick.

I was pushed!

I hurt my face but stood up fast, fists curled. A crowd was around me.

'She's drunk. She's plastered. She fell,' my sister's boyfriend explained.

Someone put his mobile phone to my bloody face. So did a girl dressed like a student. I tore her mobile from her hands and threw it on the ground. She fell to her knees to look for it. She wailed when she realised it was cracked.

More mobile phones clicked and clacked.

'Fuckers,' I screamed. 'Wankers. Pricks with phones.'

'The language out of you,' an old woman shouted.

'Fuck you,' I told her.

Ambulance men came first. I shoved one of my fists into one of their faces. The cops arrived. A big one of them got out of the Garda car and told me to behave myself. I spat and buzzed with swear words. *Prick cop. Wanker. Fucking tyrant. Bastard shit on a stick. Is this how you treat your returned citizens? I fucking emigrated when bastards like that little prick did this country out of our money.*

Jerry dead. Jerry dead in our bed.

Cop on top of me. Cop inside me. Cop grinning from the fridge eating my home-made coffee mousse. He left some and I fed next door's dog with it. He threw it up later and I listened to it hurl and puke, wishing I could hurl and puke the bastard's scum out of me.

Jerry said, 'I think you need more counselling.'

I was brushing my teeth and told him to go fuck himself. I thought I sounded almost better.

I came into the room and he was lying quiet on the bed.

I lay back on my pillow and looked sideways at his eyes.

'What's on the ceiling?' I said.

I touched him and he didn't move. I slapped him and he didn't slap me back. I hit him and his skin just shuddered. I climbed on top of him and yelled into his open face. He didn't do a thing. I shoved my hand onto his heart and I tried to punch through. His body lifted a bit but nothing else.

I cried oh Jesus god oh Christ oh St Anthony oh all the saints oh Jesus Jesus. His beautiful teeth, his lovely beard and his dark open eyes. When we had made it to as far as the coast of Sri Lanka, we had our lapis lazuli wedding rings and we decided that gold didn't matter at all.

I called the ambulance. The cops came too. I recognised a couple of them. I went berserk and they hauled me in on suspicion of nefarious murder. I laughed mad into their faces. I kicked and kicked and kicked. I punched the cell door.

My sister took me to see the swans in Claddagh bay. She said the Spanish Arch Museum didn't know if it was an art gallery or a museum. We stared at the large Galway Hooker suspended from the museum's ceiling. We admired photographs of our ancestors in nineteenth-century Galway. We walked through Shop Street, Quay Street, Cross Street, Mainguard Street. We shopped in the Saturday market and bought vegetarian curry from hipsters. We attended book launches and plays in the Town Hall Theatre. We swam through women buying stuff in Penneys. We went travelling in her car and she patted her steering wheel in time to the song on the radio.

'I was raped once,' I said.

She took her eyes off the road for one second then put them back on to it again. She whispered, 'Oh, Jesus,' then she drove on beyond Knocknacarra and further to a beach I never saw before. She said it was Silver Strand and there was a line of silver between the sea and the sky. She lit two cigarettes and gave me one. She stared at the sky. A wood-pigeon called out from a few trees inland. *Caw caw caw caw— caw* and on until it stopped then started again. I followed its rhythm in my head while watching little flies alight on dry seaweed. My sister was crying.

I told her all my thoughts were snapped into pieces and they shifted places in my head. Now there, now here. Now Jerry, now the cop. Now Jerry dead, now me still alive.

I laid back on the warm dry sand. The waves came in and out close to my feet.

The counsellor had told me a long time ago that I would have to string my life back together again, like one of those old dolls with wire running through the gaps in their bodies. Jerry's mother thanked me for loving Jerry. Jerry's father said even though it was a short marriage for me, maybe I'd find another soon enough. My sister said, come home. My parents said we love you.

I worked in a library for a while, glad to whisper instead of talk. Then I moved into Revenue. Head down and into a computer. Yes, Sir. You owe us tax, sir. Yes, Madam. We live to cream off your hard work. Thank you for your abuse, Sir. I don't mind, Sir. We are coming for your money, Sir.

I found out from Facebook that my rapist cop was getting married. I befriended his wife-to-be and told her about her husband's penis in my vagina. I described it exactly. She said she wanted to FaceTime me. Her face was pretty. She had long hair. She said he said I was lying. She said he said that I was just this mad Irish bitch whose husband died in serious circumstances.

I almost laughed. 'You mean curious,' I said.

She ended FaceTime.

Then I met my sister's new boyfriend for the first time over a drink in Tigh Neachtain's.

'Oldest medieval pub in the world,' he said.

I drank vodka and began to cry.

'She's remembering her Jerry,' my sister said.

'Hasn't he been dead for almost a year?' her boyfriend said.

'You don't forget them that quick,' my sister said.

Her boyfriend nodded, not interested. He was moving in and I was upsetting the scene. I drank more vodka in the guest bedroom. I sang Go fuck yourself at the top of my voice. My sister's boyfriend stalked backwards and forwards in the kitchen downstairs in the morning. He said I'd have to move out. I threw a kitchen chair at his head. I missed.

He said he was calling the guards.

I stood at the front door. *Let them come. I'm ready for them.*

My sister's boyfriend followed me out. I hit him and he hit me back.

Fist punch. Kick. Shoulder shove.

Wanker, fucking bastard.

'Quit that language,' Big Foot Bastard shouts through the door.

'Jerry's dead,' I scream through the door.

I sit down then I laugh because it is a normal afternoon outside and I am inside a cop station. I laugh because Jerry died after a cop raped me. He died so quietly. I laugh because I told my sister that I am all snapped up into pieces. I laugh because this only ever happens in nightmare fairy tales. I keep on laughing because the tears are coming and I want them nowhere near me. I laugh so hard that I have to kick the door.

Kick. Punch and a shove. *Fuckers, you wanker cops. Let me out.*

The door opens and my fists go first, punching through the air. I see cops in their light blue and dark blue uniforms. They stare at me. My toes tense in my sandals. My heels slick in sandal sweat. My sister is standing there. She smiles at me. She is wearing a blue summer dress and looks sun-dirtied and alive.

'Oh God,' I say.

'Let's go home,' she says.

She holds out her hand to me but Big Foot Bastard warns, 'We won't be so lenient next time.'

Little Miss Nice asks me to sign a piece of paper then gives me back my bag.

'Thank you,' I say.

'It's a pity you won't thank me,' Big Foot Bastard says.

My sister and I walk towards the entrance. The sun is hot coming in through the doorway and onto the floor. My sister squeezes my hand. A man comes up towards us and for a second he looks like Jerry. But he's not. I turn and shout into the cops.

'Motherfuckers!'

The man falls back and my sister laughs. We half run to her car and she screeches it out of the car-park. We don't talk for ages but we smile and smoke cigarettes. I look out of the passenger window at everyone swimming in Salthill. They look happy. How many are dying, I think, then I think of Jerry all dead and the cops asking what did I smother him with.

I pull down the passenger mirror and look at my eyes.

'That was an afternoon and a half,' my sister says.

She turns on the radio, zooms down her window.

'Motherfuckers,' she calls out.

I smile. 'Motherfuckers,' I chime.

I close my eyes. The sun is hot. I can hear people laughing. I open my eyes. I can come back. I can make a new life. My sister's singing is in my head, off-key and lovely. She flicks her cigarette. She laughs and her freckles jump all over her face. She is alive. Her blonde hair spurts out from its top-knot. Sweat shines up the tiny creases in her throat.

She says her boyfriend is history. She says stop drinking and get some help.

She says life can be good.

She smiles and repeats. Life can be good. Smiles and repeats.

We stop at Silver Strand, leave the car and walk along the promenade towards the cliff. Tourists walk and talk. A man and his dogs run into the water.

'Look at that,' my sister says and points out a warning sign for dogs to be leashed while on the beach or pay the maximum fine of €1904.60.

'All of that for a dog plus sixty cents and nothing for that Aussie bastard cop,' my sister says.

'Come on,' I say and we wander down to the beach. I don't tell her that sometimes I imagine his sweating and his breath and I imagine punching my two hands into his face until there is only skin left, limp and skull-less, and now I imagine tossing it to the dogs playing by the sea. Here's dinner, dogs. Chew him up between you.

My sister and I hop and skip amongst the stones beneath the cliff then we sit and watch tourists and natives with more dogs walk up along its edge, not minding the official warning sign: Danger. Keep Clear of Cliff. Falling Stones. Someone in a white sunhat leans over and looks down.

'Get back, you idiot,' I shout up at them.

We laugh and wander back over the beach past elderly sunbathers and swimmers, past a little girl in a green swimsuit splashing wet sand onto her knees. We sit down close by and share a cigarette.

'You can see Clare from here,' my sister says. 'And the Aran Islands.'

'They look like a giant's blue-grey knuckles,' I say.

My sister blows out her smoke and crinkles her eyes in the sun. 'Hmmmm.'

'Thank you, Evie,' I say.

She grabs my hand hard then kisses it. 'Life can be good. Don't forget. It can be good.'

'It can be good,' I say.

A wood pigeon calls out *Caw-caw, caw-caw...caw...*

It-can be-good, the wood pigeon calls. *Caw-caw...*

It can be good.

June Caldwell

MALACHI DREAMS IN A CUPBOARD

Two gombeens in blue uniforms strolled up to our Malachi's newly acquired semi-D in Barna to throttle his noddle with news that he was a leprechaun. The doorbell went bingdroomdring. T'was just him inside, courting a Tuesday. Caoilainn herself was out working Reception at the spangly Glo-Tel in Salthill, made of seaweed pillow cladding. 'Sorry to bother' or some flange like that. 'Are you Malachi Ó hÉalaighthe?' Him thinking it might be dems from the council over-concerning about sewers carrying unsolicited gunge towards fish farms owned by that tool of a quadrangular-headed politician whose nephew is a serial killer. 'That's right,' he says. 'If it's local election drivel lads, I'm not easily swayed.' Beneath the enflamed hair on his s'tickly chest, that fattened pounder going at it like a bodhrán on a sawdust floor at last orders: lub-dub-lub-dub-lub-dub-lub-dub. Him about to be exposed, whether he wanted or whickered.

He was only married a drizzly twenty-two weeks and according to all it was going mighty. The only nit in the grit was the unemployed bit. Piddling hours away picking at musical instruments he couldn't master or make sense of. On Caoilainn's days off he'd put away his trioblóidí, romping about the house doing the sexy cheese, not giving a hoot or a hickle. The sputters outta them and who'd dare scoff having been there themselves or about to be?

Once, on account of Malachi's increasing low moods, she let in two Mormons of an afternoon to wreck his cranium. Assumed it'd give him a bit of a chuckle and the two of them could wet themselves about it in the pub later. There'd been a bad barney that week with him buying the wrong colour [and size] Creuset. Rosemary Green with a Volcanic stripe in an 18 cm, instead of Cotton Grey in 26 cm, for her low-carb casseroles. Even I could see she was a bit croíbhriste about the state he'd got himself into. Everything was a fuddle and a jiggle. The smallest of tasks making him feel fierce tired, inadequate. She sweated about him a lot, but also learnt how to suppress her disappointment. Taking thoughts of him to the toilet, and again deep into her dreams where she'd attempt to recalibrate his sham ways of thinking.

In my day our kind didn't marry or get with womenfolk much at all. Well, I'm about to contradict myself here, thinking about it now on the hoppity hop. Us lot being male and solitary by nature, sure. But there were no female counterparts to be chasing after and moping over. Those that lived on the fringes of common sense, the not-all-theres, as the saying goes, they'd take us on alright. Had an appetite for it. In secret, small bouts. Intense ravishes in fields and ditches. Bouncing about in the lichens, liverworts and algae. In truth it took a lot of darting up legs to get used to these strange new geographies. Different basins and bales, smells and such like. The slower types were a bit more open-minded. But I suppose, like everything, it had its run until word got around and the clergy got involved. Those kinds of interactions were the death knell for a farmer's daughter, as you can imagine. The Christian-centric lifecycle an' all, I tell ye. Jaysis. There be no messing with that. Some ended up behind high walls with no chance of free air. That exact type of saga, I says, an identical narrative, is what the bible is sold on. But who'd pay heed to the oldest leprechaun in Ireland, Tomás Ó hÉalaighthe? They'd rather stick with duplicities, dem lot, and micro-manage. People along these stretches were always better able to maintain genetic diversity in beef stocks than in themselves. Ah sure, if I'm viciously honest, t'was a dirty business. No-one sets out to try and wipe out their feckin' tribe, you know? Pleasantly lustful one minute, howling at the Maumturk. The next it's hiding lumpy heads of newborns, those fluctuating facial symmetries, crooked legs. Sometimes the little squealers were smashed up with shovels by uncles or brothers. Buried in the sands up at Mannin Bay. Over time it made people a lot smaller, but smarter on the hoof. That fitted right with us. Then it had to be stopped altogether. It'd hook ye in looking over its own shoulder trying to start itself up again. Ah sure, before it was bad it was good and after it felt good it turned bad. Back down the line we lived in harmony, tis what I'm saying. For small pockets of time in anyways. Then we were cast out again, when mutations got a bit more obvious. Our Malachi wouldn't be here at all if it wasn't for that buck teeth girl with dull eyes from Claddaghduff.

Nope, t'was nought political, the two lads at the door tells our Malachi. Him in no mood for this at all, de head on him. They were straight up, no joking about. From the West of Ireland Family Association (WIFA). A coordinating body for a network of government-approved genealogical research development projects, based up there at NUIG, and unaffected by Brexit. Enjoying independence and non-interference from the hard sciences. Autonomy and the likes. They were able to make startling discoveries. He should sit and take a bit of a breath, they says. None of this was going to be comfy on the gulp down. Going back a rake of generations, unquestionably in the affirmative. Malachi belonged to the purist and most majestic class of ancients. Older than the Celtiberians, and not even vaguely connected to the R1b haplogroup.

By the time he was starting to take it in or give them any cre-
dence at all, they had their hooves in the doorjamb, and Malachi was
not minding his sap too well. Spinneying, so he was. Trying to figure
who'd be up to it. Lots of headway with Irish DNA, they were finding
out the full extent, beardy of the two explained. Had Malachi always
had that spinal curvature? Was he teensier than most going back to
the early years? Did he have woeful concentration? An affliction with
giddiness mixed with a short temper. Halitosis and headaches. An
ability to foresee and forecast? For the love of horseshoe crabs, the
fucks wouldn't shut up or put a thwack on it. He slammed the door
and told them they had twenty-two minutes, is all.

There was only one long-ago fíoras stopping him kicking dem
boyos in the nuts or flinging them onto the tarmac. A series of
blackouts and brain blips when he was a very young yoke. Months of
alarming visions and nightmares that left him hospitalised. What the
psychologists had whittled down to plain old neurosis. He imagined he
was living in fear of the mallachd. A situation that could mash you up if
you reeled a pointed foot wrong. Destined to spend his nights roaming
the landscape with nothing but yellow stainer or horse mushrooms
for company. His head pounding with the arrival of unlucky quarter-
moons; being chased goodo by barbaric badgers. Ones that lacked
the mental schooling to realise he might have social standing amidst
the crags and scarps and magic peoples of the tírdhreach. Didn't
he have to grab on to the substratum of a stinking sheep to escape
some forest animal's instincts to batter the fuck out of him. These
dreams or whatever they were, daymares, showed a different face. An
old hospice face stuck onto a liquid-cack frame of a toddler. In these
visions, he may have been seeing himself in the far past. Thought the
whole place was out to get him. Word getting around, posters yopped
up on hedgerows, with rewards for hunting him down. It seemed so
real. And for a while it was concluded he must be proper sick in the
head. These were no dreams though, and I had no way, being caught
in-between worlds, of letting him know what it meant. T'was normal

to be feeling these things. No shame in it. These days there's so many feckin' festivals and public upchucks of artistic frippery by way of an overdeveloped arts sector that any bollox could wiggleweave the cobbled streets of Galway going berserk, calling himself a fairy or a mad man. But inside these terrifying incubuses, which were analysed the piss out of and made factual by an authentic fear of having been adopted, he couldn't escape the inkling that he wasn't on a par with everyone else. Something seemed to be very wrong. T'was a series of portents and forebodings he was having, plain as flour.

When he got to his sixteenth birthday his mother admitted he wasn't adopted in any kind of official sense. Found by a couple of fishermen, wandering along the hydrangeas and azaleas of outer-edge Connemara, crying his lamps out. There was little or no legislation then. Finders being the keepers alright. The whole country driving drunk despite Middle Eastern petrol shortages and Mountbatten getting fried alive over there in Co. Sligo. They took him in anyway, thinking little of it. Fussed over him, made him their own. Bought him all the toys he could only have dreamed of. Donated a dozen handmade Hurley sticks to Scoil Einde in place of any kind of birth certificate. By the time a couple of summers had been and gone, the dreams had stopped clear and his quirky ways were on a par with any other GAA obsessed teenager. The best he could do for himself would be to think of them as his only family now and put away any notions of looking for the ragged lot that abandoned him.

'Your people, your clan, on your father's side, they owned shoe shops in Galway and Athenry from early times, is that correct?' He could see where they were going with this. I was watching him there, like. Up he jumps and heads to the kitchen to tear open a jumbo-size box of Barry's tae. 'We've a map here,' yer man shouts after him. 'It's a 1651 map, of Galway, shows the Shoemaker's Tower where Eyre Square Shopping Centre is today. Shoemaker's Lane, Bóithrín na Sudairí, the road of the shoemakers or the tanners, at Buttermilk Walk.'

Malalchi was only barely listening to the two boyos. He could've put an end to their delusions by telling them he was adopted. None of it applied. No, instead he decided that if they wanted a fucking leprechaun, he'd give them one. Danced in doing a sideways jig. Cracking circles around the coffee table, twisting his face up like a leather purse. I was trying to give him teachtaireachtaí on de telepathic. Me: Ó hÉalaighthe, dun-coloured world-mighty artistic bald plunderer, free from jealousy, a hound of the sea. But foremost a fire-sprung sprite and primogenitor of Malachi's for nigh on five hundred years. 'Hang in wee man! It be no bad thing to embrace your true nature, pull it back to basics. There's a lot to be said for a full moon on a dark night, and the road downhill all the way to your door.' But him being deaf as a haddock, he carried on losing the nelly regardless. Resorting to what any of our kind does under pressure, turning off his inner síceach, breaking his balls laughing. Singing away to himself the Soft Cell ditty 'Sex Dwarf' as Gaeilge. *Abhac gnéis, Abhac gnéis, you're my Abhac gnéis... isn't it nice, idir luibh is leigheas, dollies an dioscó, i ngreim an vice.* That's what Caoilainn called him her sex dwarf. Found nothing offensive in it though it made him squirm.

All of this could be just a superprank manufactured by his good friend Micheál O'Shaughnessy. His snake-begrimed dreadlocks in the high breeze at Spanish Arch, putting two randomers up to it for the price of a few gargles.

'Are you two plums for real, who sent yeas?!'

Did he notice an increase in blurred vision around electric streetlights? Was he plagued with heartburn? So many questions and forms to fill out and suggestions for what should happen next. Would he mind going public on it? Would he be up for more formal tests?

'We can see you're upset,' says one. 'It's hard to take in.'

'Any chance of some samples to make trebly sure?' asks the other.

They were pulling out tourniquets and antiseptic gauzes and the likes. Our Malachi had reached endgame, so he had. 'Feck off!' he tells them. He watched them screech off, feeling nothing but relief when they turned out of the estate and onto the sea road.

He headed off into the cupboard in the utility room where he often goes to rinse his head and scratch for a bit of peace away from her. What would happen when everyone got to hear about the likes of this? He'd be a proper celebrity about the place. Every eejit would be guffawing, taking the piss. Tourists queueing up to take snapshots for #insta, and all kinds of mná out of their bins pulling at his breeches. 'Short arse! Oi! Over here!' O'Shaughnessy would be roaring. A pint of craft glupe in one hand, copper-headed fraochún clinging to the other. A few other burly mallets in company too, waiting to see the real live modern-day Galway leprechaun.

The more he thought about Caoilainn, the more he wanted to scream the house down. She'd been bitching like mad about his wretched misery to the lads in the local. When he told her not to be telling virtual strangers their most personal of business, she called him 'paranoid'. But these fellas, they'd said too many things that he felt were beyond pertinent. He knew they considered her too good for the likes of him. He'd scored way above his station and should be eternally grateful. 'Watch your skull Malachi for Christ's sake, think of the good things ahead if you play your cards right.' What they were really saying was, 'Think of the baby, do what Caoilainn asks, she's the boss, you're lucky to have her.' The terrible mortification he suffered when they found out it wasn't her body that had the problems. Asking was there any chance he'd gotten chlamydia at some stage; her tests had come back normal. In and out of the gleaming clinic, leaflets rammed in their pockets. All manner of claptrap about follicle-stimulating hormones, the benefits of postcoital testing. Her making jokes to any aul ear about turning him into a sperm machine. Extracting juice at the exact hour needed to make it work. No concern at all about what it had done to his confidence.

The day came when he refused to take part in any more of it

at all. No more tests; leave it to fate like normal people. But she was having none of it. He could forget about sloppy burgers, jalfrezi from the new takeaway up at Spiddal, frozen dinners from Joyce's. The road ahead now was sunflower seeds, cow liver and cooked tomatoes. If he jacked in his job like he was threatening to do, he'd have to be the house husband fulltime, forever more. There'd be no going back. All the housework, the dinners, the scraping out of the fireplaces, the wallpapering and painting of walls. She wasn't falling for 'the voices' in his head stunt either. Too much of a burning coincidence. Too handy. The only voice allowed in his head was the same one she was experiencing on the hour every hour most days. How they'd manage to make the mortgage on one wage, the humiliation they'd have to go through borrowing more and more money off her father. 'Do you want that level of grief?' she'd shouted down from the bath. But sure when they'd captured their pot of gold at the end of the rainbow…when they were stood there staring into the cot at the perfectly formed tiny happy face grinning back up at them; it'd be worth it. It's no more than thousands go through every year all over the bloody globe to ensure it happens. It was her, after all, going through the painful daily injections, the crippling stomach cramps. Not him. It was her, all her, without complaint or a whimper.

All very different of course to the carefree days of early dating. When he'd spotted her outside Neachtain's in yellow high heels and a gorgeous black faux fur jacket, knocking back shots of whiskey, Kahlua and cream. O'Shaughnessy daring him to go over and ask her out, him being a good foot smaller than her. No one thinking she'd even bother with a sideways glance, never mind a resounding yes OKAY let's do it. Short strolls down The Long Walk followed by lingering lunches in Nimmos. Wrestling to make sense of the foraged herbs and unpronounceable grains she'd dared him to try. She'd opened a rake of new worlds for him, uncountable firsts. He'd sat through four hours of that godawful *Waiting for Godot* and even managed a plausible analysis afterwards to impress her.

Three nights in a row she'd come home and found him hiding out in the utility room, wishing with all his might for an end to her unyielding obsession. His first wish of getting her against all odds happened without a glitch, same for the second, which was nabbing the house in Barna, also against the odds. Massively over-priced and by all accounts they shouldn't have even passed the stress test. The navy suit from the bank said he'd learnt enough from the last round of booms to know they'd manage payments somehow. Malachi had tried everything to make the third wish happen, even growing a long beard to turn her off as he knew she detested them. 'If you want to look like a sad hipster, go ahead,' she said. 'As long as you get your trousers off when you're supposed to, I don't care what you look like.' If he'd said similar about her, how pasty she looked since she stopped wearing make-up, he'd be labelled a sexist pig.

She'd be back in an hour wanting the full lowdown on the two male nurses from the clinic. It took her weeks to organize and pin down a home visit. Did he answer their questions in full? Did he comply with the blood tests? Did he agree to the counselling sessions they'd discussed? Staying off the anti-psychotics? Talking through the option of fostering or adopting if the latest sperm samples proved just as rotten as the ones four months ago? 'Malachi,' I says. 'There's only one way out of this one: pack a bag and get yourself deep underground like the good people of the Tuatha Dé Danann had to do when they were banished for good, no turning back.'

He heard me alright cos he climbed out of the cupboard and shouted, 'That's not a bad idea, Tomás, all things considered.' Progress! I thought. However long the day turns out, the evening is still set to come, that's a pie man's certainty. 'You may also want to remember that forgetting a debt doesn't mean it's been paid,' I says to Malachi, always the man for the pause. 'I'll take the broccoli out of the fridge first,' he replied. 'She wants it steamed with the wild sea trout, done low in the oven, omega-3 fatty acids, motility and all that.

I'll see what the colour of her moods are like then, you know, take it from there?' Honest to God, the humble dragonfly would struggle to hear its own burp with the clatter of the world the way it's gone, and not even your own kind can be bothered to take decent advice anymore. 'The planet is fading,' I says. 'You're on your own boyo from here, my work is done.'

Conamara

The Conmacne were an early tribal group in the west of Ireland. The branch of the family who lived beside the sea were known as Conmacne Mara and this gradually evolved into the place name, Connemara. Others suggest the name may have derived from the indented coastline known as *Cuain na Mara*, The Harbours of the Sea, resulting in the name, Conamara.

Whichever way you spell it, it is a unique, magical, inspirational landscape, a rich tapestry of mountain, sea, peninsulas, lakes, rivers, wilderness and bogland. Because so much of the surface is under water, the constantly-moving light — much of which is reflected — keeps changing the colours of the surfaces. These effects create challenges for the visual artist and result in thousands of ways to interpret Conamara. Among the early artists to do so were Paul Henry, Charles Lamb, Kenneth Webb, Brian Bourke.

Countless musicians, songwriters and poets writing in Irish and English, such as Walter Macken, Richard Murphy, Éilís Dillon, Mary O'Malley, Pádraic Ó Conaire, Mairtín Ó Cadhain, Tim Robinson and John O'Donohue, have also been inspired by the area.

I remember picking up a young hitchhiker while driving from

Clifden to Galway one very wet December morning. As we crested a hill where the road ran around Glendalough, with the lake, the bog and the forest, a shaft of sunlight came through the clouds and lit up part of the landscape. It was a heart-stopping moment, as if thousands of multi-coloured neon lights had been switched on. My passenger said 'Wow! That is Conamara for you. That is nature saying, *Leave me alone boys, I have suits of many colours and I will change them if and when I want. I don't need you coming out here with your modern baubles, bungalows and poles. Leave me alone!*'

Pine Island.

The Conamara Giant in Recess.

Spiddal Promenade.

Micheál Ó Conghaile
(Translated by Frank Sewell with Úna Ní Chonchúir)

FATHER
(Conamara, 1996)

Once I had told him, how was I supposed to know what to do?
I had never seen my father crying before. Never. Even when
Mum died nine months ago in the accident he never cried, as far as
I know. I'm sure of it because it was me who brought him the bad
news. And I was there the whole time, right up to the funeral, and
afterwards. It was my job to stay with him. My uncles made all the
arrangements, shouldered the coffin. And the neighbours, instructed
by my sisters, kept the house in some order. But there was a sort of
an understanding — unspoken, mind you — that it was best if I stay
with Dad since I was the youngest, the only one still at home all year
round.

That's how I'm nearly sure that he never shed a tear. Not in broad
daylight anyway. He didn't even need his hanky, unless it was to blow
his nose. Sure, he was all over the place. You could hardly get a word

out of him. Long silences would go by while he just stared into the fire or out the kitchen window. But there were no tears. Maybe it was the shock. The terrible shock to his system. But then again, you wouldn't really associate tears or crying with someone like my father.

That's why I was so taken aback. Mortified. Not just the crying. But the way he cried. In fact, you couldn't really call it crying. It was more like something between a groan and a sob stuck deep in his throat. A muffled, pained sigh of revulsion, or so it sounded. It only lasted a few moments. And from the way he stopped so suddenly, you would think that he had swallowed it down like a big foul-tasting pill you have to take on doctor's orders. He didn't even look at me, except for a stray watery glance that skirred by when I told him. Afterwards, it was like he was trying to hide his face away, or half-away, from me. It should've been easier for him somehow, but not for me; there was no way I could look him in the face, for all I wanted to. So, while he dithered about, I sat there like a statue, with nothing left in me but my body heat. The breath was knocked out of both of us. Then I re-alised that even his smothered cry — if cry it was — was better than this silence. You could try to do something, maybe, about a cry, if it was out there. But a deadly silence was abstract and threatening. As long, drawn-out and painful as a birth. But of what? I just felt that, throughout the whole time, he couldn't bring himself to look at me, even when he had recovered enough to take two deep breaths one af-ter the other and, finally, to string two words together.

'So you are…' he said, as if the word stuck or swelled up in his throat until he didn't know if it was safe to release it, or else he hoped, perhaps, that I would say it — the word that had clogged his ears just now, a word he was never likely to form in his countryman's throat unless it was spat out in some smutty joke for the lads down the pub. A word there wasn't even a respectful word for in Irish, certainly not one that sprang to mind… Too busy trying to gauge his mind, I forgot that I hadn't answered him yet when suddenly he repeated:

'Are you telling me you're...'

'Yes,' I said, half-consciously interrupting him with a reticence similar to his, unsure whether he was going to finish his sentence this time, or not.

'Yes,' I repeated quickly, as though the word might run and hide from me, trying for a second to make up for the empty silence.

'God save us,' he said. 'Holy Son of God save us.' The words came out as though he'd had to drag them one by one from Mexico. It seemed for a moment like he would have said more, something at least, if there had been a ready-made answer or platitude handy, some string of words to pluck from the silence.

'See that now,' he groaned, taking a deep sniff of the kitchen air and blowing it out again with force. 'Do you see that now?'

He grabbed the coal bucket and opened the range to top up the fire. Then he lifted a couple of sods of turf out of the 10–10–20 plastic bag beside the range and, breaking the last two bits in half over his knee to build up his corner of the crammed space of the open range, shoved them in on top. It was a habit of his to combine the coal and turf like that. The coal was too hot—and too dear to use by itself anyway, he would say—plus it was hard to burn the turf sometimes, or to get much heat out of it, especially if it was still a bit soggy after a bad summer. He took the handbrush off the hook and swept any powdery bits of turf on the range into the fire. Then he slid the iron lid back into place with a clatter and took another deep breath, focusing on the range.

'And have you told your sisters about this?'

'Yes. When they were home this summer. The night before they went back to England.'

He stopped a moment, still half-stooped over the range. He opened his mouth, then closed it again, making no sound, like a gold-fish in a bowl. He tried again and, still choked with emotion, managed a broken sentence:

'And your mother—did she know?'

'Dunno,' I said. 'Mothers know a lot more than they get told.'

'Oh, they do, they do... God bless the souls of the dead.' He blessed himself, awkwardly. 'But fathers know nothing. Nothing until it's spelt out for them.'

He was standing at the table now, having poured a drop of well-water from the bucket into the kettle, which was already full. Then he placed the kettle back on the range as if he was boiling water for tea the way he did after milking-time. He always made tea with well-water, boiling it in the old kettle, instead of using tap-water and the electric kettle, unless it was early in the morning when he had no time. It would save on the electric, he always said. Even Mum couldn't get him to change. She wanted rid of the range altogether since the electric cooker was more reliable, more precise, as she used to say, for everything — boiling, baking, cooking dinners and heating up milk for the calves. 'But what if there's a power cut?' he used to say, 'due to a storm or lightning? If the electric runs out, that range will come in handy.' And any time it happened, he would turn to us, delighted, and say: 'Aren't you glad now of the old range?'

He lifted the poker, opened the top door of the range, and plunged the poker in to stir up the fire, trying to draw some flames from the depths. When the embers didn't respond very well, he turned the knob at the top of the range somewhat clumsily, making the chimney suck up the flame. He poked the fire another couple of times, a bit deeper, trying to let the air through. Soon there were flames dancing, blue and red, licking the dark sods and fizzing and flitting over the hard coal, shyly at first but growing in courage and strength. He closed the door with a deep thud, turning the knob firmly with his left hand, and put the poker back in the corner.

'And what about Jimí Beag's daughter Síle?' he asked suddenly, as if surprised he hadn't thought of this earlier. 'Weren't you going out with her a few years ago?' he said, a hint of hope rising in his voice.

'Yes... sort of,' I stammered. I knew it was no answer, but it was the best I could do just then.

'Sort of,' he repeated. 'What do you mean sort of? You either were or you weren't. Wasn't she coming round here for a year and God knows how long before that? Sure, she left Tomáisín Tom Mhary to go out with you, didn't she?' He stared at the bars over the range.

'But I was only—' changing my mind, I said, '—only eighteen back then. Nobody knows what they want at that age,' I added, 'or what's destined for them.'

'But they do at twenty-two, it seems! They think they know it all at twenty-two.'

'I'm afraid it's not that simple,' I said, surprising myself at going so far.

'Sure, it's not simple. Anything but!'

He pushed the kettle aside and opened the top of the range again as if he was checking to see the fire was still lit. It was.

'I went out with her, because I didn't know—I didn't know what to do, because all the other lads had a girl…'

'So you…'

'I asked her in the first place because I had to take somebody to the debs. Everyone was taking some girl or other. I couldn't go alone. And it would've been odd to bring one of my sisters with me. They wouldn't have gone anyway. And I couldn't stay at home because I would have been the only one in my class not there. What else could I do?' I said, amazed I had managed to get that much out.

'How do I know what you should have done? Couldn't you just be like everyone else… that, that or stay home?' There was something about the way he said 'home'.

'I couldn't,' I said, 'not forever. It's not that I didn't try…' I thought it best to go no further, afraid he wouldn't understand.

'So that's what brings you up to Dublin so much,' he said, glad to have worked that much out for himself.

'Yes. Yes, I suppose,' I answered. What else could I say?

'And we were all convinced you had a woman up there. People asking me if we'd met her yet… or when we'd get to see her. Auntie

Nora asking just the other day when we'd have the next wedding… thinking a year after your mother's death would be okay.'

'Auntie Nora doesn't have to worry about me. She never got married herself anyway, did she?' I said, blushing right away at the implication I was making.

'Up to Dublin! Huh.' He spoke to himself. 'Dublin's quare and dangerous,' he added, in a way that didn't require an answer.

He turned around, his back to the range, and shuffled over to the kitchen table. Then he tilted the milk-cooler with his two hands to pour some milk into the jug until it was nearly overflowing. Ready to get a damp cloth and clean it up if I had to, I was glad when he didn't spill so much as a drop. I felt awkward and ashamed sitting there watching him do this — my job, usually. He poured the milk that wouldn't go in the jug into the saucepan for the calves, and set it on the side of the range to heat it up until the cows were milked. After that, he would see to the calves themselves. He lifted the enamel milk-bucket that was always set on the table-rails once it was cleaned every morning after milking. Next, he gave it a good scalding with hot water from the kettle — water boiled so long that it had the kettle singing earlier. He set the kettle, with its mouth turned in, back down on the side of the range so that it wouldn't boil over with the heat. Then he swirled the scalding water around the bottom of the bucket and emptied it in one go into the calves' saucepan. He stretched over a bit to grab the dish-cloth off the rack above the range, then he dried the bucket and hung it up again rather carelessly, watching to see it didn't roll down on top of the range. It didn't.

All at once, he straightened up as if a thought had suddenly struck him. He turned round and looked at me for a second, our eyes meeting and taking each other in. The look he gave now was different from the earlier one — the sudden teary glance he gave me when I had first told him. Now I noticed the wrinkles across his forehead, some curled, some squared off, the short grey hair pulled down in a fringe, the eyebrows, the eyes. What eyes! They chased away whatever daydream was going through my mind just then. They made me want to run. Those eyes that could say so much without a word. I knew then that the only way to look at a man was right in the eyes, even if it was a casual side-glance, on the sly... I looked away, unable to take any more, grateful that he took it upon himself to speak. He had the bucket tucked up under his arm the way he did when he was going out milking.

'And what about your health?' he managed to say, nervously. 'Is your health all right?'

'Oh, I'm fine. Fine,' I replied quick as I could, more than glad to be able to give such a clear answer. I started tapping my fingers. Then it struck me just what he was asking.

'God preserve us from the like of that,' he said over his shoulder to me, facing the door. You could tell he was relieved.

'You don't have to worry,' I said, trying to build his trust, having got that far. 'I'm careful. Very careful. Always.'

'Can you be a hundred percent careful?' he added curiously, his voice more normal. 'I mean, if half what's in the Sunday papers and the week's television is true.'

I let him talk away, realising he probably knew much more than I thought. Wasn't the television always turned towards him, with all sorts of talk going on in some of the programmes while he sat there in the big chair with his eyes closed, dozing by the fire, it seemed, but probably taking it all in.

He took his coat down off the back of the door, set it over the chair.

'And did you have to tell me this secret of yours — at my age?'

'Yes, and no.' I had said it before I realised, but I continued. 'Well, I'm not saying I had to, but I was afraid you'd hear it from someone else, afraid someone would say something about me with you there.' I thought I was getting through. 'I thought you should know anyway. I thought you were ready.'

'Ready! I'm ready now, all right. And are you telling me people round here know?' he said sourly.

'Yes, as it happens. You can't hide anything. Especially in a remote place like this.'

'And you think you can stay around here?' he exclaimed in what sounded to me like horror. His words hit me so quickly I didn't know whether they were meant as a statement or a question. Did they require an answer? From me — or from him? I wondered. Sure, I was intending or rather, I should say, happy to stay. He was my father. And I was the youngest, the only son. My two sisters were married and living in London. So it was down to me. Even though my sisters had reassured me the night before they went back that there was always a place for me in London if I needed it.

Surely, he should have known I would want to stay. Who else would look out for him? Help with the few animals we had, look after the house, keep an eye on our tiny bit of a farm, see he was all right, take him to mass on Sunday, and keep him company? 'And you think you can stay around here...' I repeated, none the wiser, still trying to work out whether I was to take it as a question or a statement, and if he expected an answer or not.

He had dragged his Wellingtons over between the chair and the head of the table, and was bent down struggling to undo the laces of his hobnailed boots. He looked different that way. If I had to go... I said to myself. If he threw me out and told me he didn't want to see or have anything more to do with me...

I remembered at once some of my friends and acquaintances in Dublin. The ones who were kicked out by their families when they found out. Mark, whose father called him a dirty bastard and told him not to come near the house again as long as he lived. Keith, whose dad gave him a bad beating when he discovered he had a lover, and who kept him locked up at home for a month even though he was nearly twenty. Philip, who was under so much stress he had a nervous breakdown, who had no option but to leave his teaching job after one of his worst pupils saw him leaving a certain Sunday-night venue and the news spread by lunch-time the following Monday. The boys called him disgusting names right to his face, never mind the unconcealed whispers behind his back. Who could blame him for leaving, even if it meant the dole and finding a new flat across town? The dole didn't even come into it for Robin. His parents gave him twenty-four hours to clear out of the house and take all he had with him, telling him he wasn't their son anymore, that he had brought all this on himself, and that they never wanted to see him again as long as he lived. Which they didn't. They came home that night to find his body laid out on the bed in their room, empty pillboxes on his chest, half a glass of water under the mirror on the dressing table, a short crumpled note telling them that his only wish was to die where he was born, that he loved them and was sorry he hurt them but saw no other way.

The slow-rolling chimes of the clock interrupted my litany. He was still opposite me, struggling hard to get into his wellies, his trouser legs tucked down inside his thermal socks. If I had to go, I thought to myself, I would never see my father like this again. Never. The next time I would see him, he would be stone-cold dead in his coffin, his three children returning home together on the first plane from London after an urgent phone call telling us he was found slumped in the garden, or that they weren't sure if he fell in the fire or was dead before the fire burnt the house to the ground overnight, or maybe they would find him half-dressed in the bedroom after some of the neighbours had broken down the door... as they tried to work out when they had last seen him alive, no one able to work out the exact time of death.

He had got the better of his Wellingtons now and had straight-ened himself up. Wrapped in his greatcoat, with his cap in one hand, about to put it on, he stood there, for a moment, indecisively, with the enamel milk-bucket wedged under his arm.

Then he moved slowly, tottered almost, over to the front door.

My eyes followed his face, his side, his back, his awkward steps away from me while his last words of a moment ago kept going round and round in my head like an eel scooped out of a well on a hot summer day and set on a big flagstone.

He paused at the door, the way he always did on his way out, and dunked his finger in the holy-water font hung up on the door-jamb. It was an old wooden font with the Sacred Heart on it that my mother brought back from a pilgrimage to Knock the time the Pope was over. I could see him trying to bless himself, not even sure if it was the finger or thumb he had dipped in the holy water he was using.

He placed his hand on the latch, opened the door and pulled it towards him.

Then he turned round, headfirst, his body following slowly, and looked at me. His stare was so direct that my mind stopped racing and my thoughts recoiled at once to their dark corners.

'Will you stand by the braddy cow for me while I'm milking her?' he asked. 'She still has that sore teat.'

Micheál Ó Conghaile

ATHAIR
(Conamara, 1996)

Cén chaoi a mbeadh a fhios agamsa céard a dhéanfainn—th'éis dom é a inseacht dó—mar nach bhfaca mé m'athair ag caoineadh cheana ariamh. Ariamh! Fiú nuair a maraíodh mo mháthair sa timpiste naoi mí roimhe sin, deoir níor chaoin sé, go bhfios domsa. Táim cinnte nár chaoin mar ba mise a tharraing an drochscéal chuige. Is ba mé freisin a bhí ina fhochair i rith an ama ar fad: laethanta bacacha úd na sochraide. Níor leagadh aon chúram eile ormsa ach amháin fanacht leis. Ba iad a chuid deartháireacha agus deartháireacha mo mháthar—mo chuid uncaileachaí—a d'iompair an chónra agus a rinne na socruithe sochraide. Ba iad comharsana an bhaile, le treoir ó mo chuid deirfiúracha, a choinnigh stiúir eicínt ar chúrsaí timpeall an tí. Sórt tuiscint a bhí ann—cé nár dúradh amach díreach é, gur mise ab fhearr fanacht taobh le m'athair, óir ba mé ab óige: an t-aon duine a bhíodh sa mbaile ó cheann ceann na bliana.

Sin é an fáth a bhfuil mé beagnach cinnte nár shnigh oiread is deoir amháin cosán cam anuas ar a ghrua. Níor shnigh le linn solas feiceálach an lae cibé é. Níor úsáid sé a naipcín póca fiú murar shéid a shrón leis. Ó, bhí sé an-trína chéile siúráilte, é dodhéanta beagnach aon fhocal a bhaint as. D'imíodh tréimhsí fada tostacha thart gan tada á rá aige ach é ag breathnú uaidh — ag stánadh isteach díreach sa tine nó amach uaidh sa spás trí fhuinneog na cistine... Ach deoir ghoirt amháin níor tháinig lena ghrua. An seac ba chúis leis, b'fhéidir. An gheit dhamanta a bhain an seac as. Ansin aríst níorbh é m'athair an cineál duine a shamhlófá deora leis, ní áirím caoineadh...

Sin é an fáth ar baineadh geit chomh mór anois asam. Ní geit ach stangadh. Níorbh é an caoineadh féin ba mheasa ar chor ar bith ach an sórt caointe a rinne sé. Ní glanchaoineadh iomlán fírinneach—a bhféadfá a rá gan amhras go mba chaoineadh é— ach cineál pusaíle, sniogaíl nó seitreach bhacach... sea, seitreach phianmhar dhrogallach sheachantach a bhí ar leathchois. Níor mhair ach dhá mheandar nó trí. Cheapfá, nuair a stop sé go tobann gurb amhlaidh a shloig sé í—an tseitreach—le deacracht, ar nós táibléad mór a mbeadh blas gránna air a chaithfí a thógáil ar ordú dochtúra. Ní hé amháin nár bhreathnaigh sé orm—seachas leathamharc strae, a sciorr díom mar uisce tobair nuair a bhí mé á rá leis ach cheapfá gur ag iarraidh a éadan a choinneáil i bhfolach orm, nó ar a laghad leataobhach uaim, a bhí sé ina dhiaidh sin. B'fhurasta dó ar bhealach, is gan é ar mo chumas-sa breathnú díreach air, ainneoin m'fhiosrachta. É ag braiteoireacht thart. Shuigh mise ansin i mo dhealbh—gan fanta ionam ach teas mo choirp. Níor fhan smid aige: ag ceachtar againn. Is ansin a thuig mé gurbh fhearr an tseitreach de chaoineadh féin ach breith i gceart air, ná an tost. Seans go bhféadfaí iarracht rud eicínt a dhéanamh faoin gcaoineadh dá mairfeadh. Ach bhí an tost marfach éiginnte, dúshlánach: chomh mall fadálach pianmhar le breith. Bhraith mé i gcaitheamh an ama nach raibh sé ag breathnú i leith orm, fiú nuair a bhí uain aige ar anáil dhomhain nó dhó a shíneadh taobh le taobh agus cúpla focal a dhingeadh i dtoll a chéile...

'Agus tá tú...' a deir sé, ag stopadh mar a dhéanfadh an focal staic stobarnáilte ina scornach, at nó stad mar a bheadh an focal ag breathnú roimhe, féachaint an mbeadh sábháilte teacht amach—nó agus súil b'fhéidir go ndéarfainnse aríst é—an focal sin a rinne fuaim ghlugarnach ina chluasa tamaillín roimhe sin, focal nach móide a múnlaíodh as a scornach tuaithe féin ariamh. Focal strainséartha... Focal nach raibh fiú nath measúil Gaeilge ann dó nó má bhí, ní in aice láimhe... Níor rith sé liom nár fhreagair mé ar chor ar bith é, mise imithe amú thar teorainn, ag póirseáil istigh ina intinn, nó gur phreab a athrá mé.

'Agus deir tú liom go bhfuil tú...'

'Tá,' a deirimse, ag teacht roimhe leath i ngan fhios dom féin chomh focalsparálach céanna, gan tuairim agam an raibh seisean ag dul ag críochnú na habairte, ar an dara timpeall nó nach raibh.

'Táim,' a deirim aríst de sciotán, mar a rithfeadh an focal i bhfolach orm, ar feadh soicind, mé ag iarraidh aisíoc eicínt a íobairt as folúntas mo thosta.

'Go sábhála Dia sinn,' a deir sé. 'Go sábhála... mac dílis Dé... sinn,' a deir sé aríst agus é mar a bheadh ag tarraingt na bhfocal, ceann ar cheann, aniar as Meicsiceo. Bhraith mé gur mhaith leis dá bhféadfadh sé cur leo, dá mbeadh freagra nó—rud eicínt eile a rá— nó dá mbeadh caint shimplí réamhullmhaithe ann a d'fhéadfadh sé a tharraingt chuige. Rud ar bith a bhainfeadh slabhra focal as an gciúnas.

'An bhfeiceann tú sin anois,' a d'éagaoin sé agus é ag tarraingt anáil fhada d'aer na cistine isteach trína pholláirí agus á raideadh amach aríst le teannadh. 'An bhfeiceann tú sin anois?'

Rug sé ar an mbuicéad guail agus bhain an clár de dhroim an *range*, gur dhoirt carnáinín guail síos i mullach na tine. Thóg cúpla fód móna as an mála plaisteach 10-10-20 a bhí in aice an *range* gur shac síos i mbarr aríst iad—ag déanamh caoráin bhriste den phéire deireanach acu faoina ghlúin, lena gcúinne a shaothrú i gcúngacht phacáilte an *range* béal lán. Seo nós a chleacht sé i gcónaí, an gual agus an mhóin a mheascadh. Bheadh an gual róthe — agus ródhaor ar aon nós, a deireadh sé — agus ba dheacair an mhóin a dheargadh scaití, ná mórán teasa a fháscadh aisti, go háirithe as an gcuid de a bhí fós ina leathspairteach th'éis an drochshamhraidh… D'ardaigh sé an scuaibín láimhe den phionna gur scuab síos sa tine an smúdar seachránach móna a bhí tite ar bharr an *range*. Lig don chlár ciorclach iarainn sciorradh ar ais ina ghrua go torannach. Tharraing sé anáil dhomhain ard eile, é fós dírithe isteach ar an *range*.

'Agus ar inis tú do do chuid deirfiúrachaí faoi seo…'

'D'inis… nuair a bhí siad sa mbaile sa samhradh, an oíche sul má d'fhill siad ar Shasana.'

Stop sé soicind, agus é fós leathchromtha isteach os cionn an *range*. D'oscail sé a bhéal. Dhún aríst é gan tada a rá mar a dhéanfadh iasc órga a bheadh timpeallaithe ag uisce i mbabhla gloine. Ba ar an dara hoscailt dá bhéal a léim an abairt chainte amach ina dhá stráca thar an tocht plúchtach.

'Agus do mháthair… an raibh a fhios aicise?'

'Níl a fhios agam.' Agus dúirt mé ansin. 'Bíonn a fhios ag máithreacha i bhfad níos mó ná mar a insítear dóibh.'

'Ó bíonn a fhios, bíonn a fhios… Beannacht Dé le hanamacha na marbh.' Rinne sé leathchomhartha místuama na croise air féin. 'Ach ní bhíonn a fhios ag aithreacha tada — ní bhíonn a fhios ag aithreacha tada nó go mbíonn chuile fhocal *spell*eáilte amach dóibh.'

Bhí sé thuas ag an mbord faoi seo agus é th'éis braon beag d'uisce an tobair a bhí sa mbuicéad a chur sa gciteal, citeal a bhí sách lán cheana féin. Leag ar ais ar bharr an *range* é mar a mbeadh ag fiuchadh leis le haghaidh an tae, nuair a d'fhillfeadh ó bhleán. B'fhearr leis i gcónaí an tae a dhéanamh le huisce an tobair, fiuchta sa seanchiteal, ná a bheith i dtuilleamaí uisce an *tap* agus an chitil leictrigh, seachas moch ar maidin nó nuair nach mbíodh uain fanacht. Shábhálfadh *electric* freisin a deireadh sé. Níor bhain mo mháthair fiú as an gcleachtadh sin é. B'fhearr léise dá gcaithfí amach an *range* ar fad, arae bhí an sorn leictreach in ann chuile ní a dhéanamh, i bhfad níos rialta is níos staidéaraí a deireadh sí—dinnéar, cócaireacht, bruith, bácáil, bainne na laonta a théamh… Bheadh nó go mbeadh gearradh tobann cumhachta ann, a deireadh sé, le linn stoirme nó tintrí. Nuair ba ghéire a theastódh *electric*, b'fhéidir go mbeifeá dá uireasa. Chasfadh sé linne arís é ar bhealach ceanúil aon uair a bhíodh… 'Anois nach maith daoibh agaibh an sean*range*.'

Tharraing sé chuige an pócar. D'oscail comhla uachtarach an *range*. Shac isteach ann é go sáiteach ag iarraidh an tine a ghríosú le lasrachaí a tharraingt aníos óna broinn dá mb'fhéidir. Nuair nach raibh an ghríosach ag tabhairt mórán d'aisfhreagra air, chas go místuama an murlán ar uachtar an *range*, a spreag sórt tarraingt ón simléar. Shac an tine arís cúpla babhta—beagán níos doimhne an geábh seo, ag iarraidh pasáiste a dhéanamh isteach don aer. Ba ghearr go raibh lasrachaí damhsacha gormdhearga ag tabhairt líochán fada do na fóid dhubha agus ag sioscadh go léimneach ar dhromanna na gcloch crua guail—go cúthaileach ar dtús, ach ag bailiú misnigh is nirt. Dhún sé an chomhla de phlop buacach, ag casadh an mhurláin go daingean lena chiotóg. Chuir sé an pócar ar ais ina áit féin sa gcúinne.

'Agus céard faoi Shíle Mhicí Beag,' ar sé go tobann, mar a bheadh iontas air nár chuimhnigh sé fiafrú fúithi roimhe sin. 'Nach raibh tú ag dul amach le Síle cúpla bliain ó shin,' a raid sé, dóchas faiteach éiginnte ina ghlór.

'Bhí… sórt,' a d'fhreagair mé go stadach. Thuig mé nárbh aon fhreagra é sin, ach bhí sé ag cinnt orm tacú leis ag an nóiméad sin.

'Cén sórt, bhí sórt,' a dúirt sé arís. 'Bhí nó ní raibh. Nár chaith sí bliain ag tarraingt anseo, agus cibé cén fhad roimhe sin… Cén chúis gur fhág sí Tomáisín Tom Mhary, mura le dhul amach leatsa é?' Bhí sé ag stánadh ar an raca a bhí os cionn an *range*.

'Ach ní raibh mé ach… ní raibh mé ach ocht mbliana déag d'aois an t-am sin,' a dúirt mé, ag athrú m'intinne. 'Ní bhíonn a fhios ag duine ag an aois sin céard a bhíonn uaidh, ná cá mbíonn a thriall,' a chuir mé leis.

'Ach bíonn a fhios ag duine atá dhá bhliain is fiche, is dóigh! Bíonn a fhios ag duine chuile shórt faoin saol nuair a bhíonn sé dhá bhlian is fiche.'

'Níl sé baileach chomh simplí sin,' a dúirt mé, iontas orm liom féin gur tháinig mé leath roimhe.

'Ó cinnte níl sé simplí. Níl ná simplí!'

Bhrúigh sé an citeal go leataobh, agus chroch an clár de bharr an *range* aríst, mar chineál leithscéal go bhfeicfeadh sé an raibh an tine ag lasadh i gcónaí. Bhí.

'Bhí mé ag dul amach léi, mar nach raibh a fhios agam… mar nach raibh a fhios agam céard ba cheart dom a dhéanamh, mar go raibh chuile dhuine eile de na leaids ag dul amach le cailín eicínt…'

'Ó bhí…'

'D'iarr mé i dtosach í mar go raibh duine eicínt uaim le tabhairt chuig *social* na scoile. Ní fhéadfainn dul ann asam féin. Bheadh sé aisteach dá dtabharfainn Máirín nó Eilín liom. Ní thiocfaidís liom ar aon nós. Ní fhéadfainn fanacht sa mbaile, nó is mé an t-aon duine den rang a bheadh ar iarraidh… Céard eile a d'fhéadfainn a dhéanamh?' a deirim, iontas orm go raibh mé th'éis an méid sin cainte a chur díom.

'Cá bhfios domsa céard a d'fhéadfá a dhéanamh. Nach bhféadfá bheith ar nós chuile dhuine eile… sin, sin, nó fanacht sa mbaile.' Bhí cling ina ghuth nuair a dúirt sé an focal *baile*.

'Ní fhéadfainn,' a deir mé, 'ní fhéadfainn go deo… Ní hé nár thriail mé… 'Cheap mé go mb'fhearr dom gan dul isteach sa scéal níos faide ná níos mó a rá. Faitíos nach dtuigfeadh sé.

'Agus sin é anois a thugann suas go Bleá Cliath thú, chomh minic sin,' sástacht shiúráilte ina ghlór go raibh an méid sin oibrithe amach aige dó féin.

'Sé… 'sé, is dóigh.' Céard eile a d'fhéadfainn a rá, a smaoinigh mé.

'Agus muide ar fad cinnte gur bean a bhí thuas agat ann. Daoine ag fiafrú díomsa ar cuireadh in aithne dhúinn fós í… nó cá fhad eile go bhfeicfeadh muid í. Aintín Nóra ag fiafrú ar an bhfón an lá cheana cá fhad ó go mbeadh an chéad bhainis eile again... ag meabhrú nár mhór fanacht bliain ar a laghad th'éis bhás do mháthar.'

'Ní gá d'Aintín Nóra aon imní bheith uirthi fúmsa, breá nár phós sí féin ariamh más in é an chaoi é,' a deirimse, aiféal láithreach orm nuair a bhí sé ráite agam, faoin ngliceas a bhí i mo chuid cainte.

'Suas go Bleá Cliath! Huth.' Leis féin a bhí sé ag caint anois.

'Tá Bleá Cliath aisteach agus contúirteach,' a chuir sé leis, ar bhealach nár éiligh freagra.

D'iompaigh sé thart, ionas go raibh a chúl iomlán leis an *range*. Chrágáil a bhealach i dtreo bhord na cistine. Chroch mias an bhainne lena dhá lámh gur dhoirt braon amach as síos sa *jug* nó go raibh ar tí cur thar maoil. Bhí a rostaí ar crith, ag an gcritheán a thagadh ina lámha nuair a bhíodh faoi straidhn ar chlaonadh áirithe. Bhí mé buíoch nár shlabáil sé aon bhraon den bhainne ar an mbord: mé réidh le glantóir fliuch a fháil le glanadh suas ina dhiaidh dá mba ghá. Bhí sórt náire orm, i mo shuí síos ag breathnú air ag déanamh na hoibre seo—obair ba ghnách liom féin a dhéanamh... Dhoirt sé an fuílleach bainne nach rachadh sa *jug* síos i sáspan slab na laonta agus leag an sáspan ar ghrua an *range* le go mbeadh ag téamh leis nó go mbeadh na beithígh blite agus na laonta le réiteach. Tharraing sé chuige buicéad *enamel* an bhainne, a bhíodh leagtha i gcónaí ar ráillí an bhoird ón am a nglantaí gach maidin é th'éis an bhleáin. Scal le huisce te é ón gciteal—uisce fiuchta bruite a bhí ag pléascadh feadaíl aerach as an gciteal cheana féin. Leag an citeal, gob iompaithe isteach, ar ais ar ghrua an *range* le nach gcuirfeadh thar maoil leis an teas. Chiorclaigh timpeall an t-uisce scólta ar thóin an bhuicéid sul má d'fholmhaigh é de ráigín amháin i sáspan na laonta. Shearr beagán é féin, gur rug chuige éadach na soithí, a bhí ar an raca os cionn an *range*. Thriomaigh an buicéad leis. Chaith suas ar ais aríst é, go fústrach míchúramach, é á fhaire san am céanna faitíos go rollálfadh anuas ar bharr an *range*. Níor rolláil.

Go tobann, dhírigh sé é féin mar a theagmhódh splanc leis. D'iompaigh anall ormsa. D'fhéach ar feadh soicind, radharc ár súl ag beannú, ag dul thar a chéile. Bhí an fhéachaint a bhí ag silt óna éadan difriúil leis an gcéad fhéachaint—an fhéachaint thobann thais úd, a chaith sé liom mar a bheadh á caitheamh amach uaidh féin nuair a d'inis mé dó… Thug mé faoi deara na roicne ina éadan, na roicne crosacha leathchiorclacha leathchearnógacha, an ghruaig ghearr liath a bhí ag éirí aníos óna chlár éadain, na malaí: na súile. Súile! Is iad na súile a ruaig asam cibé brionglóidí cónaitheacha a bhí á n-atáirgeadh agam an ala sin. Is iad na súile a chuir cor coise ionam. Na súile a abraíonn an oiread sin amach díreach gan a mbéal a oscailt. Thuig mé ansin nárbh fhiú breathnú ar fhear choíchin, gan breathnú sna súile air, fiú mura mbíonn ann ach breathnú drogallach leataobhach, fuadaithe beagnach i ngan fhios… Bhreathnaigh mise uaim, gan mé in ann é a sheasamh níos faide, mé buíoch gur thogair seisean labhairt… Bhí an buicéad cuachta suas faoina ascaill aige, mar ba nós rialta leis nuair a bheadh ar tí dul amach ag bleán.

'Agus do shláinte!?' a d'fháisc sé aniar as a scornach go neirbhíseach. 'Cén chaoi 'bhfuil do shláinte, nó an bhfuil tú ceart go leor.'

'Ó tá mé togha, togha,' a d'fhreagair mé chomh sciobtha agus a d'fhéad mé, mé thar a bheith buíoch as bheith in ann freagra chomh dearfa sábháilte sin a thabhairt agus a fhanacht a chniogadh láithreach. Is ina dhiaidh sin a tháinig iontas orm go gcuirfeadh sé a leithéid de cheist…

'Cabhair ó Dhia chugainn as an méid sin féin,' a deir sé, a dhroim liom agus é ag coiscéimiú a bhealaigh siar go dtí an doras dúnta. Ba léir go raibh faoiseamh eicínt ina ghlór.

'Níl aon chall imní duit,' a dúirt mé, ag iarraidh tonn eile dóchais a fhadú, ó ba chosúil go raibh an méid sin faighte liom agam. 'Bímse cúramach. Bím an-chúramach i gcónaí.'

'Más féidir a bheith sách cúramach?' a chuir sé leis go ceisteach, a chaint níos nádúrtha. 'Más fíor leath dá mbíonn ar na páipéir Dé Domhnaigh, nó ar an *television* i gcaitheamh na seachtaine.'

Lig mé tharam an chaint sin. Chuimhnigh go bhféadfadh i bhfad níos mó eolais a bheith aige ná mar a cheap mé. Nach mbíodh an teilifís casta air sa teach againn síoraí seasta, chuile ábhar cainte faoin spéir tarraingthe anuas ar chuid de na cláracha, é féin caite siar sa gcathaoir mhór ansin, a shúile dúnta, é ag míogarnach chodlata ó theas na tine... ach é b'fhéidir ag sú isteach i bhfad níos mó ná mar a cheapfá...

Chroch sé a chóta mór anuas den tairne a bhí sa doras dúnta. Leag aniar é ar shlinneán na cathaoireach.

'Agus ar chaith tú do rún a scaoileadh liomsa... an aois ina bhfuil mé is uile.'

'Chaith agus níor chaith,' a bhí ráite agam, sul má thuig mé nárbh aon fhreagra é an méid sin. Lean mé orm. 'Bhuel, níl mé ag rá gur chaith mé é inseacht dhuit ach... ach ar fhaitíos go gcloisfeá ó aon duine eile é, ar fhaitíos go ndéarfadh aon duine tada fúm i do chomhluadar.' Cheap mé go raibh ag éirí liom mo phointe a chur trasna. 'B'fhearr liom go mbeadh a fhios agat ar aon nós, go mbeifeá réidh.'

'Réidh! Tá mé réidh anois ceart go leor... Is tá tú ag rá go bhfuil a fhios ag daoine thart anseo mar sin?' cineál múisce ina ghlór.

'Tharlódh go bhfuil. Is deacair tada a cheilt... go háirithe in áit iargúlta mar seo.'

'Agus an bhfuil tú ag ceapadh go bhfuil tú ag fanacht thart anseo?' ar sé de léim, noda imníoch scanrúil ina ghlór, dar liom. Bhuail an tsaighead thobann d'abairt leadóg sa leiceann orm, chomh tobann sin nár fhéadas idirdhealú comhuaineach a dhéanamh: ceist a dhealú ón ráiteas nó ráiteas a dhealú ón gceist. Ar impigh an chaint sin freagra: freagra uaimse nó uaidh féin... a d'fhiafraigh mé díom féin. Cinnte bhí mé ag iarraidh fanacht, nó ba cheart dom a rá—sásta fanacht. Ba é m'athair é. Mise ab óige sa gclann, an t-aon mhac... Mo bheirt deirfiúr pósta i Londain. Ba ar mo chrannsa a thit. Ach é áitithe ag na deirfiúracha orm, an oíche sul má d'imigh siad, go raibh Londain i gcónaí ann—go raibh áit ann dom dá dtiocfadh orm.

Nach gceapfá go mbeadh a fhios aige go maith go raibh mé

toilteanach fanacht. Cé eile a bhreathnódh amach dó? Lámh chúnta a thabhairt dó leis an gcúpla beithíoch, aire a thabhairt don teach, súil a choinneáil ar an ngiodán d'fheirm, freastal air féin, é a thabhairt chuig an Aifreann chuile Dhomhnach, comhluadar a sholáthar dó... 'An bhfuil tú ag ceapadh go bhfuil tú ag fanacht thart anseo,' a mheabhraigh mé dom féin arís, gan mé tada níos eolaí, fós ag iarraidh léas tuisceana ar cheist nó ráiteas a bhí mé in ainm is a dhealú ón gcaint sin. Ní raibh sé ag súil le freagra uaimse, nó an raibh?

Bhí a chuid *wellingtons* tarraingthe chuige aige, é buailte faoi ar chathaoir ag cloigeann an bhoird, é cromtha síos ag scaoileadh barriallacha a bhróga móra tairní le strus, a chruth cromtha ag breathnú difriúil. Dá mbeadh orm imeacht, a dúirt mé liom féin... Dá dtabharfadh sé bóthar dom, ag ordú nach raibh sé ag iarraidh mé a fheiceáil níos mó, ná baint ná páirt a bheith aige liom...

Chuimhníos láithreach ar chuid de mo chuid méiteanna agus lucht aitheantais i mBleá Cliath. An codán acu a fuair bóthar nó drochíde óna ngaolta nó óna muintir ar a nochtadh dóibh: Mark—ar dhúirt a athair leis de scread gur focar brocach a bhí ann agus gan an teach a thaobhachtáil lena bheo aríst: Keith—ar thug a athair griosáil dó nuair a fuair amach go raibh leannán aige, agus a choinnigh sáinnithe taobh istigh de bhallaí an tí ar feadh míosa é, agus é beagnach scór bliain d'aois: Philip—a raibh an brú chomh mór sin air gur chlis ar a néaróga, nach raibh de chríoch uile ann dó ach éirí as a phost múinteoireachta, th'éis do chladhaire dá chuid daltaí é a fheiceáil ag fágáil ceann de na beárannaí oíche Dhomhnaigh amháin—a thuairisc ar fud na scoile roimh am lóin an Luan dár gcionn. Leasainmneachaí maslacha gránna á nglaoch air ag na buachaillí suas lena bhéal... agus an chleatráil shioscach chúlchainteach. Cé a chuirfeadh milleán air, fiú mura raibh aige anois ach an dól agus aistriú chuig árasán ar ghualainn eile na cathrach. An dól féin ní raibh ag Robin... Ceithre huaire fichead a thug a thuismitheoirí dó le glanadh amach as an teach, agus gach ar bhain leis a bheith crochta leis aige, ag rá nach bhféadfadh sé go mba leo féin é, gurb é féin amháin a tharraing an cineál seo saoil sa mhullach air féin, nach raibh siad ag iarraidh é a fheiceáil lena mbeo go deo aríst. Is ní fhaca. Gan rompu ach a chorp nuair a d'fhilleadar abhaile an oíche sin. É sínte scartha ar an leaba ina seomra codlata féin… clúdaigh boscaí piollaí lena ucht, leathghloine uisce faoin scáthán ar an mboirdín gléasta, nóta giortach ag míniú nár theastaigh uaidh ach bás a fháil san áit ar gineadh é, go raibh grá aige dóibh, is go raibh aiféala air iad a ghortú ach nach bhfaca sé an dara rogha ag síneadh amach roimhe sa saol…

Thrasnaigh tonnbhuillí fadálacha aniar aduaidh an chloig mhóir ar mo liodán. Bhí sé féin thall os mo chomhair fós, ag rúpáil leis ag iarraidh a chuid *wellingtons* a tharraingt aníos ar a chosa le deacracht mhístuama — cosa a threabhsair fillte síos ina stocaí tiubha olla aige… Dá gcaithfinn greadadh, a smaoinigh mé, ní móide go bhfeicfinn m'athair mar seo aríst choíche. Go deo. An chéad uair eile a bhfeicfinn é, bheadh sé fuar marbh ina chónra. An triúr fiosrach againn tagtha abhaile le chéile ar an gcéad eitilt as Londain th'éis teachtaireacht báis de ghlaoch deifreach gutháin a fháil ón mbaile… gur tite amuigh sa ngarraí a fritheadh é, nó nach raibh a fhios cinnte an amhlaidh a thit sé sa tine nó an raibh sé básaithe ar aon nós sul má dhóigh an tine an teach go talamh domhain san oíche, nó b'fhéidir gur sa seomra leapa a gheofaí a chorp — faoi leath dá chuid éadaí — th'éis do chúpla comharsa doras an tí a réabadh isteach le lámh láidir… iad ag iarraidh comhaireamh siar cé mhéad lá ó facthas go deireanach é, gan ar chumas aon duine uain bharainneach a bháis a dhearbhú go cinnte…

Bhí a chuid *wellingtons* múnlaithe air. É dírithe suas ina sheasamh. A chóta mór fáiscthe timpeall air, caipín speiceach ina láimh, réidh le tarraingt anuas ar a mhullach. Buicéad *enamel* an bhainne uchtaithe faoina ascaill.

Ghluais sé go mall, stadach beagnach, trasna urlár an tí, i dtreo dhoras na sráide. Lean mo shúile a aghaidh… a thaobh… a dhroim, coisméig bhacach ar choisméig agus é ag éalú uaim — an abairt dheireanach a tháinig uaidh ar baillín beag á casadh féin timpeall athuair in mo chloigeann ar nós eascainne a gheofadh í féin caite tite ar leac the, th'éis a bheith taosctha aníos as tobar lá brothallach samhraidh.

Stop sé ag giall an dorais, mar ba nós leis i gcónaí ar a bhealach amach, gur thum a mhéar san umar uisce choisricthe a bhí crochta ar an ursain: seanumar adhmaid den Chroí Ró-Naofa a thug mo mháthair ar ais ó oilithireacht ar Chnoc Mhuire aimsir an Phápa. Chonaic mé é ag strácáil leathchomhartha na croise air féin go místuama, gan aon chinnteacht ann an í an ordóg nó an mhéar a tumadh san uisce coisricthe a bhí chun cinn ag déanamh an ghnaithe.

Chuir sé a lámh ar laiste an dorais. D'oscail é, á tharraingt isteach chuige.

Ansin a d'iompaigh sé timpeall gur fhéach orm, a chorp uile ag casadh thart go mall i ndiaidh a chinn. Bhí sé ag breathnú i leith díreach orm, ag baint an rásáil as mo chuid smaointe uile, is á ruaigeadh ar ais i gcúinní dorcha mo chinn.

'An seasfaidh tú roimh an mbó bhradach dom?' ar sé, 'fad a bheas mé á bleán… tá sine thinn i gcónaí aici…'

Rosscahill

Rosscahill is a townland just north of Moycullen. It derives its name from the Irish *Ros Cathail* or Cathal's Wood. At its centre is Ross Castle, which was built in 1539 by the O'Flaherty Family, known locally as the 'Ferocious O'Flahertys'. It was later taken over by the Martin family, who had strong literary connections, as the youngest daughter of James Martin was Violet Florence Martin, one of the famous Somerville and Ross writing partnership. The author J.M. Callwell was also connected to the family. The demesne is flanked by the beautiful tranquil Ross Lake.

A short distance away is Brigit's Garden, an enchanting eleven acres of native woodland and wildflower meadows, a nature trail and fairy ringfort that can take you on a magical journey into the heart of Celtic heritage and mythology.

Callownamuck, sometimes spelt Colinamuck, comes from the Irish *Caladh na Muc* or the Harbour of the Pigs, known as such because it was from here that the local farmers used to ferry pigs across the lake to the fair at Headford. This area has almost legendary status with lake fishermen, especially at that time of year when the mayfly appears.

Geraldine Mills

BY THE TIME THE THAW COMES

The buzzing woke Kevin. It sounded like it was coming from a jam-jar in the far corner of the room but when he looked, there was no bee, no jar. Pulling the curtains open he could see that the snow hadn't let up all night. The corrugated roof of the shed had been flattened into a blank sheet of paper. There was nothing for it but to ring Loper.

'You heard anything from Mam?' he asked. 'Been trying her phone a few days now and not a sausage.'

'Don't you know she only ever rings this place when she wants something off me. Probably gone to visit Delia or the Supple woman and didn't bring the phone with her,' his brother answered.

'They haven't heard from her either.' Looking out he couldn't tell field from field, all boundaries submerged.

'Then her mobile's down the side of the couch and she couldn't bother her fanny looking for it.'

His laugh pierced Kevin's eardrums. Why was he not surprised at his cruelty?

'No. It's more than that. You see, I woke up with a funny feeling. Like a bumblebee was trapped in a jar, buzzing away. Remember the...'

'Funny feelings, me arse. She's just pissed off with us,' Loper said, 'for not doing something we didn't know we were supposed to do in the first place.'

'Did you not listen to the forecast?' Kevin said, his voice rising. 'The newsman telling everyone to stay home. If it's even half as bad as they're saying, she'll be snowed in and if ...'

'That's the way with weather, isn't it?' Loper replied.

Typical. No care in him at all. 'But she'll need wood. The last lot I chopped for her'll be well gone by now.'

'Will you chill! Will you. No fear of her ringing to see if we're OK. Bet if we went up there, we'd find her warming her feet in the oven, the telly blaring, the cat up on the table, licking the butter. Since you're that worried about her, why don't you go up and find out for yourself. Betcha fifty notes I'm right.'

The person you have tried to reach is out of range or may be powered off. Please try again later.

Kevin put down his phone and sat looking at the telly. Inagh Valley blocked, Camus impassable, sheep buried in high drifts. Animal feed was already being airlifted beyond Maam. If the researchers had bothered their barney to come to Doon, they'd have seen that the roads around his place were as bad. He couldn't leave it any longer. He dialled his brother again.

'I don't care what you think. We've got to go up there, just to make sure.'

'What do you mean, we, paleface? Do you think I've nothing better to do than to head out into that blizzard? You're the one with time on your hands, after all.'

'If there was anyone else in the world, I can tell you I'd be asking them before I'd come begging to you.'

'Find someone so,' his brother barked into the phone.

By the time Loper relented, the last light was seeping out of the sky. Kevin braced himself in the passenger seat as the jeep inched its way onto the main road. The snow was a great leveller and looking around Kevin couldn't tell which were the fancy landscaped gardens and what was scutchy bog.

'If it's as bad here, imagine what'll it be like at the hill up at the house.'

'Will you stop fretting like a big woman's blouse? Didn't I say I'd get you there?'

The jeep turned off at the woods; the council had been out and gritted that part that led up the hill onto the Leitir road. They inched their way along through the tracks left by other vehicles but just beyond the houses where it began to rise again, the car engine stalled. Loper put his foot on the accelerator. The wheels spun on the ice. He tried again but all they did was whirr on the slope. Kevin could smell rubber burning.

'Jump out there and put your shoulder into it,' Loper said. 'If we get it over this hump we're laughing.'

Kevin did as he was told and put all his strength behind it, but the wheels just spun away, spitting sludge in every direction.

'Looks like there's nothing for it but to walk.'

'Mr Smart Fuckin' Ass.'

The air froze the nose off Kevin as he pulled on his high-viz jacket. Light jumped up from the snow. No one had come this way all day.

They were the only evidence as they walked away from their own prints. Ahead of them, he could make out the three-armed ghosts of giants beseeching the sky. The windfarm. Snow swishing around the blades in the night air. By now, icicles were piercing his face, melting into his eyes.

'You can see how it'd drive a person nuts.'

'What would?' Loper said.

'Swirling snow. All that coming down around you and you not being able to see anything else. The Eskimos have a word for it you know. They even have a word for…for big snow, little snow, snow that blows into houses, snow marked by wolves.'

'Well, aren't you the right little Wikipedia.'

When they stepped close to the house, the sensor picked up their presence and light sprang from the darkness, everywhere unsullied except for a flicker of paw prints that scurried through it earlier.

Kevin searched in the flowerpot on the windowsill and pulled out the key, turned it in the lock.

'Mam,' he called out as they stood in the back kitchen. There was the smell of damp, unused air. No one answered. On the floor was the chicken's basin, a slop of potato, bread crusts and orange peel. A blue fur was already growing on top.

Loper pushed open the sitting-room door and switched on the light. 'Mother, it's your two fine sons,' he called out. 'Don't be hiding on us now. Ah, look, there she is, on her precious chair, asleep like a little baby.'

'Go easy,' Kevin said, 'don't give her a fright, or it could set her heart off.'

But that wasn't Loper's style.

'Hey, Mother, hey there. Your favourite son's been driving me demented, thinking there was something wrong and here you are all the time having a little shut-eye for yourself.'

Kevin stood back. 'She's awful quiet, she's not, not…'

'Hmm.'

'Take her pulse, will you,' Kevin said, his voice beginning to grow thin. 'See can you get a pulse?' He could feel his sphincter loosen. He tightened it, watched as his brother put his ear down to her chest. Then stood up.

'No. Not a meg out of her. She's gone.'

Kevin tried to hold his composure. 'She can't be. She can't…'

'Check for yourself if you don't believe me.'

Kevin shook her shoulder gently. 'Mam, Mam, come on, wake up, please.'

'I'm telling you, you're wasting your time.'

'But, but, she… she looks like she's just having one of her little naps before she goes off to Mass or… or bingo with Delia and the Supple woman. Building up her energy before she…'

Loper took out a packet of cigarettes, released one, tapped it off the edge of the box and lit up. He blew a guppy O of smoke into the room.

'She wouldn't go just like that on us, would she?' Kevin asked, holding his two hands together to stop them from shaking.

'Nothing to keep her now, was there?'

He should have come sooner, Kevin thought, as soon as he heard the buzz. 'How long would you say since…?'

Loper put his hand to her forehead. 'Probably going downhill for a few days, if the chicken slops are anything to go by, then a couple of hours before she finally kicked the bucket.'

That buzz was the sign. If he hadn't been faffing around all day, maybe he could have caught her in time. He went to the cupboard and searched out the bottle. He poured two glasses. Loper knocked it back, lifted the bottle and topped it up. Kevin felt the cold whiskey hitting his teeth. 'This place is freezing. We'd better turn the heat on, light the fire, at least.'

'Don't be an eejit. Do that and, as sure as eggs, she'll start smelling before our very noses.'

'What will we do, so?' Panic was finding a clear path and rising up right through him. 'There's no way a hearse'll get up that hill; no way we'll get her down any time soon, either.'

Loper topped up his drink. 'Looks like there's nothing for it but take her out into the shed. Quick freeze. Every bit as good as the mortuary,' he said. 'Otherwise, she'll have maggots crawling out of her by the time the thaw comes.'

'We can't...'

'You got a better idea? Wait until everything inside starts to explode, enough to blow a cork out her nose, her ears, her backside?'

Kevin put his hands over his ears. 'Stop it! Stop it!'

'She's dead. It doesn't matter a fuck what I say.'

'God, but you're cold enough to freeze her right through. For all your talk, isn't it funny how you still have to fill yourself up with that crap, so you can block any feelings inside you?'

'Sticks and stones and all that,' Loper replied, filling the glass even higher.

'I'm getting something to wrap her in. And you cut out that language. She might still have her hearing left. I don't want her listening to your filthy mouth.'

'Block her ears, so.'

Kevin went to the hot press in the hall, pulling out a sheet from between the towels and the bedclothes, brought it back and laid it down on the floor beside his dead mother.

'Would you ever leave down that glass and give me a hand?' He lifted her legs and eased them off the chair while Loper caught her shoulders and swung her down onto the sheet. Then, securing each end of it, they shuffled her through the scullery where the smell of rotting food filled the air. 'Easy, easy, don't hit her off the wall. She's not one of your old bumpers.'

'I'd be more careful if it was.'

The weather whipped them as they manoeuvred her out the door and across the yard in the sudden blaze of the outside light. They headed towards the lean-to, a three-sided affair they had jumbled together for her to keep the rain off the wood. A bag of kindling was waiting to be brought into the house. The saw-horse was stabled by its side.

'Ease her down gently, will you, onto the spot. The love of God, don't drop her like that.'

'For a small woman, she's a dead weight.'

Kevin looked at her lying on the ground. 'Oh, no, no, no!'

'What are you on about now? Her weight?'

'No! We can't just leave her on the dirt like that. It's not right with rats scuttling around, chickens doing their business.'

'Lay her out on the sawhorse, so, if you're that fussy,' Loper said and dragged the log holder over beside them.

'What? Our own mother? Have you no screed of decency in you at all?'

'Well, it's better than leaving her on the ground. On the count of three: One; two; three; lift.' Soon she was stretched across the double V of the contraption.

Kevin shook his head. 'She, she…'

'She looks like she's part of a magician's act about to be sawn in half,' Loper said, putting another cigarette in his mouth, the lighter a tiny comet of flame in the woodpile. 'Ladies and gentlemen, roll up, roll up.'

Kevin shouted at him. 'No, no. I'm, I'm… I'm not having her waked like that. If we're going to leave her out here, she might as well be laid out properly.'

'She's dead. Do you not get it? D.E.A.D. It doesn't matter a frigging iota where we leave her.'

Kevin turned to his brother. 'Even so, she should be in her recliner at least.'

'What the fuck are you talking about, now? I always knew you were a three-quarters eejit, but this takes the biscuit.'

'In her favourite chair. That'd be the most fitting thing to lay her out in. It's the way we should remember her. And it'll take two to carry it, so come on.'

Kevin looked at his brother, waiting for him to refuse.

To his surprise, he didn't.

'What did she have to buy such a bloody big yoke for, anyway?' Loper said as they stood in the sitting-room, sizing it up. 'It's not going to fit through the scullery door.'

All Kevin could think of was how much she loved that chair and the whole palaver of how she got to buy it. Taking lamb chops out of the freezer after their father's funeral, hadn't she found a wodge of old money — punts — in among the garden peas and the Donegal Catch. Rushing into the kitchen with the frozen twenties and fifties, she had spread them out all over the table, pegged them on the clothesline above the range and when there was no more space left, laid them on the floor, Yeats and the blind harpist thawing out all over the place.

'I'd say it was the first time in her whole life she had a bit of money to herself,' he said to his brother, 'the smile on her face when she pulled the plastic off that chair.'

Their father was barely settled in his grave when the workmen came and hammered through the gable-end to put in the new double doors that opened out onto a small patio of Chinese tiles, cluttered with pots of begonias and geraniums that were now smothered by the weight of snow.

'Well, said chair's not going to go through the kitchen door,' Loper said, 'so it'll have to be through her fancy doubles.'

But the snow had shored up against them so tightly on the outside they weren't going to budge without major clearing. A shovel with half a handle and a coal scuttle that they found in the scullery got them going.

It took time.

'That should do it, now,' Loper said. 'Go back in and see if a push from the far side'll knock back the remaining bit.'

Kevin put his shoulder to the door. It gave way just enough for them to have a passage through. They folded up the footrest and taking an arm each, they carried the chair through the open space, once again, out into the freezing air, flakes landing on the brown tweed, so that by the time they got to the lean-to, the chair was reupholstered in white.

Kevin shook off the snow and they stretched their mother out on her seat. He was grateful they didn't have to break her legs, but they could do nothing with her mouth. Even when they put a rolled-up towel under her chin, it refused to close, the teeth not quite meeting.

He straightened her hat on her head, settled the jacket so it wouldn't get crushed. Then he fixed her hands in a prayerful pose.

'What are you doing that for?' Loper said.

'So that when they come to pick her up, they'll think she was at peace.'

'Well, she wasn't. She never was, so what does it matter?'

'It does to me,' Kevin said. There was a part of him inside breaking. Across the white land the giant arms of the turbines were swishing power into rotors to feed milking machines, juicers and electric toothbrushes.

'We had to suffer her cruelty, too late now for her to make it up to us.'

'She wasn't the worst.'

'You didn't know the half of it.'

'What do you mean?'

'Give over, will you?' Loper said.

Kevin couldn't let it go now. 'She could have gone off and left us, had us fostered or something. But she didn't.'

'Maybe we'd have been better off if she had. Someone else would have given us a proper home.'

'Who'd have put up with us? Answer me that. No one would, so we wouldn't have been better off. I'll say it again, she didn't. She didn't leave us,' Kevin said.

'Well, she has now, and without telling.'

'She didn't do that on purpose.'

'I wouldn't put it past her.'

Looking back, Kevin knew he should have done something that time when she went grey in the face and she had to hold onto the table for support. He should have seen the change in her. But he hadn't wanted to; he had been too afraid.

'Ah, don't be saying that. She was just a bit bothered, that's all.'

'Bothered is it? Do you know what bothered her? Wanting to be somewhere else, not lumbered with two lads that spancelled her to that waster that was our father. She should never have had us.'

'Well, she did, and now they're both gone and it's just yourself and meself.' Kevin said. Loper didn't reply. They stood like that until the sound of the match struck the silence and he lit up another cigarette. He passed the box to his brother.

'Why are you scourging me when you know I haven't had a puff in years?'

'Listen, Saint Kevin, for old times' sake.'

Something in his brother's voice had him reach out. 'OK, so.' He took a drag from the cigarette. 'God, I'd forgotten how good they taste.'

They sat on the pile of logs, two little red fireflies glowing in the dark. Beyond them were the shadow arms of the turbines pleading with the sky. Swish, swish they went.

'Isn't it a pity her bit of land wasn't on the right side of the road for the windfarm. With the money they pay, we'd be rolling in it now,' Loper said.

'That's if she even put us in her will. She could have left it to the dogs' home for all we know.'

'True, I suppose, we'll find out soon enough.'

'Remember the time we stole her packet of Gold Flake and she went half-demented looking for them everywhere?' Kevin couldn't help but laugh.

'And I put the empty box in the paws of the dog, what was his name again?' Loper blew rings into the air.

'Rusty, his name was Rusty, he was a grand dog.'

'She cared more for that dog than she did for us.'

'She didn't even punish him, just brought him in by the fire in case he'd get sick.'

'Rusty thinking all his birthdays had come together.' Kevin dropped the butt on the ground and heeled it into the dirt. It was so damn cold, he could smell it, the chickens clucking night-dreams in the henhouse nearby. He'd feed them as soon as it was light.

'Remember I said to you this morning about hearing the bumblebee?'

'Yea?'

'God, but she was like a demon that day. Her arm in a sling after she fell off the chair. Shouting at us to go out and catch the bee for her.'

'She didn't fall.'

Kevin felt something crumble inside him.

'She did, she said she did.'

'For Jesus' sake, grow up. After all those years, you can't still be denying...'

'Don't say that...'

'...that he wasn't beating the lard out of her, gone for days into Galway, flittering away all his wages in the bookies; only coming back when one of his buddies found him in Woodquay and brought him home.'

'But she never... I never...' Kevin said, plucking a grey hair from the sleeve of her jacket. He knew his father could be rough with Loper, but, no, not this. 'You're saying that just to rise me.'

Loper said nothing.

All those years when their father stumbled out the door, across the fields raving, trying to catch white horses, his mother would send Kevin to his room and he'd hear her shouting at Loper. 'And you went every time, bringing him back, getting a thumping from him, a tongue-lashing from her, me thinking it served you right for the something terrible you'd done.'

'It is what it is.'

'What you're not saying is that she sent you to do her dirty work, and all of that was kept hidden from me. Letting it all go over my head.' As long as he could remember they had been bashing against one another and it had never crossed Kevin's mind. 'You were protecting me.'

'Younger brother, after all,' Loper said.

'You're right, I am a three-quarters eejit. Always thinking you brought it on yourself...'

'Don't be making heavy weather of it. You'd talk the cross off the back of a donkey.'

'Wish I'd known that; I could have...'

He thought he heard humming. Bees or wind blades, he wasn't sure.

'Doesn't matter now. And don't be going soft on me, either,' Loper said. 'Anyway, see here, she's beginning to freeze, like the bumblebee.'

The look on her face now was just like that day. How they had to wait ages to catch one, because it was wet and windy, and the bees weren't inclined to be out. When one finally landed on a dandelion, they clamped the jar over it and brought it back into her.

'Will you ever forget the buzzing of it when she put it in the fridge?'

'Waiting till the cold had frizzled the poor little bastard down so slow it could barely move.'

She had them tying a skinny bit of white thread around its chest because she hadn't the use of one hand. Then like a pet on its lead, she took it for a slow fly around the kitchen. The bee doing a whisper of a...

'...buzz... buzz... buzz...'

'... its frozen wings just about holding the little striped body in the air while around and around she went with it. Finally, it began to defrost.'

'... and bit by bit it upped its speed ...'

'... until it warmed itself fully and became a bee again.'

'Then she opened the window and it flew back to wherever it came from.'

'It was like the bee thawed something inside her for a while after that.'

'Pity it didn't last a bit longer. But I guess it doesn't matter now, the bee is getting its own back at last,' Loper said. 'Just feel it here.'

Kevin touched the pink sleeve of her jacket. It was already stiff. In the sensor's light, he could see the glisten of frost on her hair that peeked from underneath her hat, the eyelids beginning to ice over. Crystals were forming on her old grey lashes, on the septum of her nose, on the fine hairs standing up each side of her disappointed mouth.

Killary

Killary, *An Caoláire Rua*, is a deep fjord formed by a massive glacier carving its way from the land to the Atlantic. The border between Counties Galway and Mayo runs through the centre of this dramatic natural harbour with its spectacular scenery and wonderful panoramas. On the Mayo side you have the cliffs of Mweelrea Mountain and the Ben Gorm range, and on the Galway side, the Maam Turks and the Twelve Bens.

This area was very badly hit by the Famine, as you can see by the ruined houses and the lazy beds along the Famine road, which was built in 1856, the labourers working in return for food. Today this area of contrasts attracts huge numbers of tourists in the form of naturalists, walkers and climbers, marine zoologists, birdwatchers and artists. The stunning Aasleagh Falls must be one of the most painted scenes in Ireland.

Writers came too, attracted by the inspirational surroundings and the chance of solitude. Notable among them were Ted Hughes, the English poet who stayed in Doonreagan; Antonin Artaud, the French Dramatist; and Ludwig Wittgenstein, the Austrian philosopher who stayed in Rosroe.

Not every village has the luxury of a one-of-a-kind expanse of visually distinctive landscape at its disposal but the village of Leenane does. Its landforms and vistas are alive with colour and made it the ideal location for the making of the now-famous film *The Field*.

Aoife Casby

JOHN

John.
 Water.
 Research.
 Wombs.
 History.
 Voice.
 Sex.
 Love.
 Pigeons.
 Grief.
 Killary.
 Home.
 Knowledge.
 Ludicrous.
 Myth.

Immaculate.

Corridors.

Fire.

Prayer.

Dream.

Water

The thing about water is this: it is where we started. All that womby fluid. It is without doubt where John started; where he may have ended too.

'At room temperature it's like us, tasteless, but its colour is blue—this is some cosmic joke,' John says.

'Blue?' I say, letting the tasteless comment go by.

'Tell me,' he says, 'when you think of blue, what do you see?'

'Sky,' I say.

'Heathen,' he says.

'The Virgin,' I say.

'Bingo,' he says. 'The Immaculate Virgin.'

'John,' I say.

'Atlantis,' he says, 'I'm going to find it. It's hell, the real hell. People think it's all heat and brimstone but no, hell, it's an undertow, it's underwater, a place that pulls you down and takes your breath away. Back to where we came from. Dust, my arse.'

I suppose I always loved John.

Research

So I did all this research. Freedom of Information. Trying to locate my birth, the record of it, pinpoint the day and its disasters. I was dragged into this world in Tuam; it says it on the certificate in spindly inky curls, but there's no record of the birth. No record? What do you mean? I'm in the register, look, birth cert, see; but there's no record of me in the hospital?

I wanted to know the minutiae: the time of the day (before noon, afternoon, around the gloaming), the weight, the name of the doctor, the preciseness of the gloves, the aloofness of the forceps, the exquisite nature of the drugs, all the hostile details. It was important.

There were patterns I'd be able to detect and classify. I felt sure of it. An attitude towards time or a specific paranoia, or a laying down of my willingness to let other people decide things for me. That sort of thing.

The over-worked man on the phone suggests I may have been a home birth. But my birth cert says Bon Secours. He tells me he checked my name, my mother's name, father's, all of us on dates within five years either side of the date I gave him, says he checked spelling and whatnot, but there was no baby girl born that was me. I think he is silently grateful that all the signatories to this particular piece of paper are deceased, no longer inconveniently with us. Registrar, parents. The lovely expediency of history.

Wombs

'But water is a threesome,' he said. 'What do you think about that? H_2O. Those two little hydrogens, and that odd oxygen. It's a threesome.'

And I was thinking about this, about Mam and Da and me and how water was the slippery root of everything, even us, and I told him this, partly to see that smile on his face.

'Especially us,' he said, 'but really. Oh no. Water is two with the big old spirit that makes it one. Do you see?' he said.

'I don't,' I said.

'I didn't think you would,' he said.

'Say oxygen is God. And us. We're the hydrogen. We're greatly combustible, alone. We need something to hold us together. Marriage is such a thing, the introduction of God into the equation.'

'John,' I said, 'I don't think...'

'You don't,' he said, 'that's right.'

'Do you know what hydrogen means?' he said.

'No, John, I don't, but I feel sure that you're going to tell me.'

'I am,' he said. 'I am.'

'Well?'

'Water former. It's the water former,' he said, 'I know that there's a connection and it all ties up somehow. I just can't figure it out.'

We were friends.

I would have married him.

I didn't get the chance.

He should have married me.

History

John and I met at a choral recital or performance or whatever in St Nicholas'. My boyfriend at the time, Chad (an awkward name), was a singer and brought me along one dreary winter evening in the hope of sparking something in me, or more really, into us. The initial mutual attraction had worn itself out and we were realising there was nothing left. I tried to hear, to listen, but I wasn't that interested in the music. I loved the light, the heat, the colours and the dizzy respect that people seemed to have for one another. There was a class of a smile that I have never been able to achieve, a facial movement that doesn't reveal the teeth but arms the eyes. On me, it never developed beyond a grimace. And the man, John, in the seat beside me had a very lovely smell which he later told me was *Zino Davidoff,* sampled in Brown Thomas, a very male fragrance, he said.

It's hard to get a handle on people you don't know from the beginning and there is no one around now that I know from near my beginnings. I'm an only child. The only child of only children. Orphaned. I like the word. There are no grandparents to send me cards or to expect a Christmas visit from me; no aunts and uncles so therefore no cousins. I am alone. There is no blood relation as far as I know. I think my Grandfather on my mother's side had a sister and a brother who embraced bachelorhood and spinsterhood like it was a badge. I imagine this because I never had a conversation with my parents about their parents. I assume these unknown Grand Aunt and Uncle are dead. My parents died when I was eighteen. Together. In a car crash. Simple. Everyone's parents die. Everyone dies. This is what John said.

John also asked me why my birth and its details were important.

'My entrance into the world,' I said. 'I won't know about my exit, but I can know about this.'

'Why won't you know about the exit?' he asked.

'Afterlife?' I said. 'Not likely.'

'Hmmmm,' he said.

Voice

John was an actor and a hydrologist. At least that's what he was when he started out. Well, actually, he was originally training to be a vet and then got involved in drama soc and left studies, became an actor, back to college, degree in some aspect of science, then did voiceovers for commercials. In fairness, he had a lovely voice. You couldn't talk about it as if it were just a sound because it was much more than that. It was a feeling. His voice was comfort. At other times it was that thing that happens when you have a sudden sharp insight into your mortality. He did audiobooks too. I always thought that this would put him in the great conversationalist area, but no, it didn't.

He seemed convincing enough when he did the radio plays, but the understanding wasn't there. He was no more interested in talking about the merits of the relevant literature than the man on the moon.

Music, though.

Different story.

Sex

Later.

'Amphoteric,' he says.

'Am fo what?'

'Teric,' he says. 'Water. Can be acid or base. I'm simplifying it. But you know, there's something in the water. It makes sense. It's simple. I think it's part of what I was missing. It can give a proton or take a proton. You know. Almost it's like it's male or female for sexual purposes.'

John and I never had sex. It is one of my big regrets. I have an idea that it would have been beautiful, the dimension our togetherness needed.

I imagine.

And then.

What?

I have a polaroid photograph of my mother when she was about twenty. I like to believe I am there in her belly. She stands in a doorway on a terrace. There is no way of knowing who she's looking at, who she's thinking about, or if there is someone behind her. She looks startled; in black and white. I imagine she wants to go back inside but she is stuck there forever half-way in or out the opening or closing door.

The threshold. We, John and I, were on the threshold of never, a place where life stagnates.

Love

So I woke up one morning in my threshold time, thinking that yeah, I needed to write a short story. Love triangle, drugs, that sort of thing. The way the common man couldn't care less about politics. I told John my idea. He laughed. That's people. Said I should just write myself. That's a line I can't hang on to. How do I know who self is if I can't even find my beginning.

'Have you ever smelled a rock?'

'Rocks don't have a smell, John.'

He ignored me.

'The smell of a rock that had recently, say 1000 years ago in rock-time, pre-Cambrian or so, been in water. Not just water, but water in which a God swam, or where a man in need of love pissed. I mean, any day of the week in the nineties you could walk down along the canal and invariably find someone pissing into it, usually a man, students or the homeless or those pissant can-drinkers and occasionally a woman, you know, squatted, knickers at the ankles in an awkward-looking statue pose,' (like this, he hunkered down in front of me, his sandy hair covering his eyes, then stood again). 'Can you see them, piss spraying between the shoes, golden there between the lovely Irish white arse cheeks. Pissing didn't seem to matter in those days. Now we're freaked by it all. We're all so into hermetics, so clean and phobic and then the cryptosporidium, have you seen a picture of it?'

'No, John.'

'Little sausagey creature. Freaky.'

'What does that rock smell like, John?'

He looked at me with pity, baffled by inability to see.

'It smells like water, Mac. Like water.'

Pigeons

1989 may have had the fall of the Wall, Tiananmen Square, but it also had The Bangles, Donny Osmond (that comeback soldier of love), Belle Stars — the awful music of the nineties was on the way; it was difficult, John said. The fizz and wheeze of coffee machines muffled all of the unsaid in the cafés we met in. It was impossible to hear yourself in places like that. We sat, not talking much, me and John, in comfortable gloom, and outside it was sunny. Pigeons on the footpath. I don't know about city birds and their territorial nature. Those lads looked really well fed. John joked that they had a look about them like they had just eaten in top-class restaurants before coming out to strut and discuss the concepts of space and time. It wasn't funny. The pigeons cooed.

'These are the lads you want about after the flood,' he said.

'You mean doves.'

'Same thing.'

John told me I was the perfect woman, gave me a list of my attributes. One of them was my ability to cook a steak just the way he wanted it.

I walked up Shop Street wondering did all those strangers know that about me. That I could cook a perfect steak.

Grief

And I remember myself reading Enid Blyton and that sort of thing. But none of these are the real memory, are the sort of thing that you cannot take back, that change the way the years of your life have been up to that point. John got an eye infection. Bloodshot eyes. Inflamed iris. A halo of pink around the blue-green like the blood of several sea creatures disappearing into a cold, calm sea. He started to lose his sight. At the time I thought that at least it wasn't me. I liked to read. He liked to listen to stuff, to talk. It would have been worse if it had been his ears.

Killary

In Killary, now, I see clenched fists all along the changeling aspect of the briny inlet and the ripped valley and how clouds or the weak sun bewilder the light and almost make you believe in the red skin of the hills, in the reality of the animal that Galway is, this close to the ocean. Now and again I walk the little fist of hills that John dragged me up.

'You won't believe it,' he said the first time, a ragged map in hand, 'the view from the Devil's Testicles.'

'Testicles?' I said.

'Yeah, or mother, the Devil's Mother. It's enough to make you believe in something the way the land is named around here.'

The steep grassy slopes with the hopeful cairns always made me a little sad. Those badly structured mounds of rocks built by strangers who would never meet one another atop the ball of these hills and the path that glacier took as it ripped its way to the sea leaving the deep fjord in its wake is almost too much for me. But each sparse February since he left, I go to that edge of the Atlantic, to where he may have killed himself, or went missing, or died, was last seen, disappeared from. Whatever. A fucking fjord in Ireland, he used to say. A fjord. Killary. (Out of the red-blue brine. And in the red-blue too. He was never found. He could walk back in the door. Any minute now. Couldn't he?)

So February I go there. Just in case he remembers that he needs to come back. The weather is slightly different at the edge of the water. The moon is too. It's best a clear night. All silvery and broken in the fjordy waves. This year I had to visit a few times in February. To get that clear night. The full moons for each month of the year have their own names. John told me this. They are, in chronological order, named Wolf, Snow, Worm, Pink, Flower, Strawberry, Buck, Sturgeon, Harvest, Hunter, Beaver and Cold. I see the moon as hungry. The hunger of the moon in February, it hurts. And when I taste the rain I imagine bits of him there. I dip my fingers into dark

Killary and imagine him in the water like a homeopathic remedy (I don't dwell too long on all the other people that would conceivably be there too. I think there is something in my thoughts or in my cells that would recognise only John). It wasn't too hard to imagine him drowning. Taking all that water into his lungs. I couldn't help it, but I tried to imagine his drowning second by second, detail by detail—his thoughts, the open unseeing eyes, the cold, the tightening, the distance, the filling ears and the sound of his own heart slowing, the fish, perhaps a scared newt, the whole thing. I also see him walk away.

I see him walk away.

I see him walk away.

Home

It is hard to get a handle on people you haven't known from the beginning. John tried to fill in the details for me and some I continue to fill in myself.

Like this: He used to collect newts when he was young. In mucky backyards in a cool, alert shadow of those scratchy, twisted Maumturks. Dragonfly infested bogholes. Damp places. He'd keep each little newt a day or two in a homemade terrarium: cardboard box, bowl of unfriendly water stolen from a marble rill, jewelly seamed rocks, twigs, whatever. And then, when the thing began to tire, he let it back to its reality.

I bet that some of those precious newts died.

He spoke of them as if they were little gods. And *sooo* fast, *sooo* damn fast in water, he'd say, his voice like a magnet for soul. 'I'm not sure if anyone knows what a newt is today.'

'Do kids learn about that sort of thing?'

The thought of classrooms is comforting. Full of eagerness and astonishment. I try to remember my mother bringing me to school that first day, but all I see is her face from the polaroid.

The things I do for John are a list of oddness. I bring him newspapers. I unhurriedly iron shirts. I cook a steak now and again, spend hours listening to and under-appreciating Mozart. And Abba. Just to please him. He had a record player and we bought loads of really cheap LPs at a stall in the market where the pigeons may have shopped. I liked the way his shoulders drooped and the man of him came into the room when he heard that hissy music. The torture of its history all over his awkward body that was unfit for dancing.

His mother died when he was fifteen. 'An old fifteen,' he used to say. He reckoned she died of neglect. Neglect by herself, by home, by doctors, by family, by God. She died of TB.

'You can't blame yourself, you were only fifteen,' I'd say to him. And all to myself, silently, I'd hug that teenage boy, my hot snotty tears falling onto his hair, even though I didn't know him then.

Knowledge

There are lots of 'used tos'. We used to know a Scottish lad called Hamish. Missha, we called him; but he died, killed by a crane.

We used to meet up more often in the early years.

We used to talk about how the land is our mirror.

We used to talk about our dreams.

The future is full of meaningless stuff. All we need is here in the present.

I can't not want to know about my birth.

'My sister had a nice smile,' he'd say.

'My mother had a nice smile,' I told him, showed him the photo (again).

'She's not smiling in this,' he pointed out.

'No. No, she's not, but the potential is there. You can see that.'

John smiled at me.

Ludicrous

The movie we watched together on Christmas Day. I didn't like it much, all that family stuff and losing babies and having babies and being happy and mothers and I couldn't really see where the dog fitted in. Like, what was the point? But John loved it. Although what about it he loved I could never quite figure out.

'You know the only reason for *Marley and Me* is to make you cry,' he said. 'How much of the movie did they really need? I mean, could it have just been a two-minute short of a dog going to sleep on the vet's table?'

This is what John wanted to make movies about.

'Don't show their faces,' he'd say. I mean, he actually rang around vets in the city and asked could he film the end of dogs. Well, that's what he said to me. His face used to shine when he talked about it. 'It's such a *verboten* thing,' he'd say (his enthusiasm often produced continental European accents, words). I heard him on the phone. '*Hmmm. Yes. Yes. I understand.* But tasteful,' he'd say. 'It will be tasteful. I only want to film the dog's face and the owner's hands.' The sincerity in his voice startled me. It was like a person inside him was speaking, someone I didn't know.

He was indignant when the vets always said that none of the clients would agree. 'But it's art,' he'd say. 'I have a soundtrack made.'

'What about the dog shelter?' I said.

'Same response,' he said, 'it can be upsetting.'

Ludicrous.

Myth

Getting back to water. It's what we're all at. Trying to get back to water — our bodies are at it even if we don't know about it ourselves in a conscious way. Our amphibian brain or something like that. I mean, have you ever met someone who can't swim, apart from fishermen and older people who wouldn't dream of removing their outer layers of clothing in front of someone else (it has always bothered me, elderly people and hospital gowns. There is no way you can get training for that and what it must do to the soul). But water.

It's true.

Water is true.

I think the details of my birth involved water somehow, water beyond the breaking; water beyond the womb. I have thought that it may be that she was thirsty, that the waters broke too early; that I was thirsty. That it rained. Someone was late. Someone stepped in a puddle. They put me in a bath. I didn't like the cold. Did I cry? Did she cry? Was thirst involved?

I'll never know. I think about my mother a lot. The birth cert is so tatty now. I am going to get a copy.

I'm trying to *write* John since he died, write him really accurate so that my when my imagination begins to conjure faded visions of him, the words are there and there's always water somewhere in the account, like the lakes, rivers, coast of this county. Someone's drowning or fishing or nearly drowning or spending far too much time washing their face or thinking about the water in some way. John did a lot of learning for me about water. It obsessed him for a while (my birth), until it didn't. He told me that most cultures on this planet have a myth where something or someone is being born out of water, think Aphrodite he said, and I swear, I can't see the scum that washes up along the edges of Aasleagh Falls when I go to look for him and not think that it could be big reefs of divine cum. John can still make me smile, even when I don't want to.

Immaculate

'Do you know what immaculacy is?' he said.

And there was that excitement in his eyes that he used to

have when he'd meet me after coming out of the chemistry lab and a particularly explosive lab tutorial. 'It's being free from stain, immaculacy, hmmm, and in one of its forms, it rhymes with ejaculate.'

What this has to do with water I don't know.

We were standing on the weir bridge and he tells me to look, see, the water has a twinkle. The Corrib, it was considering him and he knew it. There was a shine on his forehead and he'd a kind of unfriendly reptilian aspect under the bridge lights. I didn't like the look of him then. I don't like to be reminded of a vicious lizard.

'I know,' he said, interrupting his own thoughts because I was saying absolutely nothing. 'Immaculacy. It's water. That's the connection. Wash away the stain. Clean the thing. Immaculate it and Bob's your uncle. Off you go and reward yourself with a bit of ejaculate.'

'I dunno, John,' I said. 'It's a little bit weird. Non-syllogistic you might say.'

He looked at me and made one of those whole body sighs, the sort within which you detected resignation and an acceptance of the impossibility of interpersonal communication.

He was then a Chemical Engineer working in Water Treatment. Never did a man and a job seem so right or so wrong.

'We're all fucked,' he said.

I knew John. I knew what he meant.

This world is very sad.

Mary, the Virgin, is supposed to have appeared in Mayo. John believed she did. For a man who could divine water, his devotion to her surprised me. It wasn't faith in God. It was her. The woman. The mother. The poor put-upon teenage girl who got all the responsibility in the world and no one asked her how she felt about it. He never tired of telling me that it didn't rain underneath her feet when she appeared. The grass stayed dry even though the heavens themselves were unloading on the vision.

Corridors

Water charges bugged him. He didn't think any of us understood the whole thing really, said it was a distraction from ourselves, that we needed something to be angry about and that the water charge was the last straw. He'd been at it since the 80s. Hating the charges, having feelings towards them, says he remembered sitting with his mother in a damp corridor on plastic chairs waiting to have an uninterested civil servant stamp a waiver and dinner being cold and scummy because they were talking about court cases for non-payment and whatnot. He used to get a kick out of watching the lads putting down the meters, watching the indignation and the anger and the ordinary voter people surprised at themselves learning new ways to use words they didn't know they knew.

John made a list of all the little, big and lost loughs about the fjord and surrounding hills. Water returning to the sea and water that wants to return to the sea. Water that understands all the nuance of blue, green and grey he'd say. Water we walked towards, looked at, were silent in front of, together. Water he grew up around. Muck, Dernasliggaun, Doolough, Loch na Fuaiche, Tully, Inagh, Nadirkmore, Glencullin, Kylemore, Doolough, Nacarrigeen, Derrintin, Fee, Fin, Cunnel, Killary, Lugloughaun, Tawnyard, Nambrackkeagh. Water that sounded like prayer. Water he met.

Fire

I arrived at his flat and there was a fire brigade.

'What were you trying to do, John?'

'I was trying to burn water, Mac. I was trying to burn water.'

And he told me too about an old man, Pake, on the neighbouring farm who had spent the wartime trying to get water to combust, slaving away for hours in a huge hayshed on a slowly disintegrating David Brown VAK1. Such was John's way. He remembered the details.

He said the tractor was still in the shed, all rusted to shit but all its story breathing away around it.

I think he'd started to become himself in that shed, on the neighbour's farm. I really wish I had known John when he was little. Before the need got into him, if there was such a time.

Prayer

If I remembered how to pray, I might ask Mary for a favour.

I sometimes imagine.

And then.

The fact of him gone.

The fact of me maybe being the only one remembering him. Unless there were the random people he came across and he sometimes flashes into their minds. Like my birth, I'll never know.

When someone like John goes, you think you'll never love again.

When someone like John goes, you discover you were in love.

Dream

In the dream he was tall, his body familiar but with unspeakable disjuncture about it, about the way he held it, as though himself were no longer whole. It left a discomfort in the room. He wore a faded t-shirt, snug-fitted shorts. Dying. He was afraid and made his own death (and dying, like I said). His limbs, his hands, began to shake as if what remained of his flimsy soul was being winnowed from his flesh. That withdrawal was dire. He knew it. I held him. He began to lose intimacy with his animal self, with his tired limbs, his well-used and tattooed skin, the haunted bones beneath. Becoming familiar with how we never touched was ugly. Beginning in his feet. I held him. Put one hand on his head and with the palm of my left, felt the warmth of his lower back. It was a gentle touch just saying I am here. I held his body firm, wide as I could splay my fingers, in a vain attempt to trap his leaky spirit in. Sadness was unoriginal and we waited for that moment when all experience became history. The instant where the universe is laid bare by the disappearing. We were waiting for the moment he would wake, become cold, waiting for long moments in between, for guidance. His stomach flesh was youthful, up and down with needy breath. I kissed him. A frightened act. Suddenly he said he wanted to have a child and asked if I would be the vessel of his wish to stop his death. Then how absurd. It was like the end of *Lost* and how they could not explain the polar bear and that was the least of all the problems; or the end of all those series, all those hours of *Battlestar Galactica* where against all reason I had hoped the screenwriters knew the meaning of life, knew where we came from, where we should belong. I had almost been satisfied with the fact that I could comfort, love and understand. I become useless. Reduced to womb. The room is garish. Other people shout. Events occur too fast and John is dead. I whisper to him that I want to walk with him into a lake. That I want to feel his body against mine in the water.

The wine on the table is undrunk, unwashed clothes sculpt space along the edges of the room. Dust collects in the sulk beneath the bed.

Inisbofin

Situated off the coast of north Conamara is a magical island, Inisbofin, The Island of the White Cow, inhabited since at least 4,000 B.C. Legend has it that it was a floating place until some fishermen, who landed there in a fog, lit a fire, which dispelled the magic, fixing the island in place. They saw an old woman driving a white cow and when she struck it, it turned into a rock, hence the name. St Colman built a monastery there in the 7th century and 1,000 years later, Oliver Cromwell built a prison there to incarcerate and torture Catholic priests.

'Bofin, it is a very relaxed, timeless place with a population of about one hundred and sixty people. A former parish priest told me that when he first arrived, there was a welcoming committee to make him feel at home, including an eight-year-old boy. The priest asked the boy what he did on the island during the winter. 'Oh, I help my father, Father,' the boy answered. 'That's nice, what does he do?' The priest asked. 'Nothing.' And the priest thanked the Lord for sending him to a very special place.

Inisbofin is one of the few places in Ireland where you can still hear the corncrake. The last time I heard one, it was about 5am. It sounded like he was on the sill of my bedroom window in Day's Hotel making that very distinctive sound of his, very loudly, and, if the truth be known, I wanted to murder the bastard.

Elaine Feeney

SOJOURN

I'm familiar with the sea. Throughout my girl summers I'd walk into her wet coughs, up to my knees, shiver, the cold water shocking my thighs, shiver, salting my darkened navel and over my nipples until it pooled in front of my sternum, shiver, shoulders dry, like a dipped portrait one now sees in a gallery, top of the head obscured with a cover of sorts, a masking tape or oily ebony paint that has been applied to obscure something, breasts or sternum, clavicle perhaps? Something bony and sharp.

Artists are inclined to obscure human portraits and it must be dependent on their mood or the mood of the weather, for the latter does furiously interact with one's spirits. But we can never quite get to root intentions of the artist, for I notice artists with brushes don't answer questions on motivation in the same way I must, in the way I constantly defend my work, especially to myself.

I had often entered the dank sea off the coast of England since my moving there, but lately, since the birthing of the two tiny humans, the sea was inducing a most unsettling sickness, which in turn unsettled me, the constant up and down of it, the back and forth, and moreover the thought of vomiting up in public without due warning, which would absolutely mortify me. The sea had begun to feel much like the mess under the stairs or the cramped scarlet bus I rode, though I ride it far less so now, as cadging around the two children is awfully bothersome. And the sea was inducing a movement that made no progress, much like the cooking a woman must do when she doesn't choose to.

And to that end, the motivation of artists who obscure a portion of their canvas must be surmised. I imagine they dip the canvas into paint to upset their subject long after they have finished it; perhaps the portrait preys on their mind, like humans do, all the insecurities of portraying someone other than oneself. I remain in constant obsession about this level of obscuration that comes from one's art, one's mistakes.

It was autumn, and decided that Husband and I would holiday on the West coast of Ireland for a brief sojourn and to visit a small island off the town of Cleggan, and the park where Yeats has a tree with names etched into it, of writers and dreamers. We were to be the guests of the poet, Richard. Husband said that I'd decided it, to get away from the squalling babies. I seem to remember it differently. But this is the way of us. Whatever the rationale, the trip was beginning to cause me much anxiety, after all that had been and gone, for now we had different abodes, Husband and I, and the unsettling came at me as a pulsing, not as sounds, but the accumulation of tiny vibrations, like the children's early vowels or cutting a beef tomato and the knife pulsing off the wooden plinth. I fear the power of knives, so I threw away the soft red tomato slice in the trash and left the knife down. Out of reach of the children.

Also, I do not like packing, especially for this particular trip, where I wasn't entirely sure in what capacity I was joining Husband, or even Richard, of whom we would be guests, given my letters with him. Perhaps it was indeed that Husband would accompany me in some guesthouse, but even this detail was uncertain. I berated myself, compared myself with my mother, who would have asked such questions, been quite certain of her rank and the order of things, before her departure.

I knew the island, Inisbofin, was sea-locked, without a bridge of any kind, and that set me to fretting about the water and if I would ever rediscover my sea legs. I found this alarming, another thing to add to an over-cluttered *to do list*, as though packing my suitcases and dressing myself accordingly weren't enough of an ordeal, now one must go and actually find something that isn't in the least tangible, *sea legs*. I grew increasingly concerned about the boat, a hooker named the Ave Maria, and so that by the time we arrived in Cleggan, I had indeed forgotten my physical self entirely.

Husband chatted about class on the trip, himself, Richard, the islanders; everywhere we went were long and rude conversations about the idiocy of people, ordinary people, women, writers. I always find the English, or the Anglo-Irish / English so obsessed about class and the mores of people. This must come from shallowness about oneself, for I am quite sure that Husband is mostly concerned about the ignorance of his broad tongue. Yet, despite the conversations, I don't know how the native Irish class determine themselves from the Anglo-Irish class, but I can easily spot the difference. Clothes on first encounter, or shoulders, and of course the broadened beautiful vowels.

Richard didn't have the appeal of an Irish voice that I liked, the timbre of which could excite me. His was rather slim and nasally.

After some time at Cleggan, awaiting Richard and the hooker to moor at Nimmo's Pier and take us off to Bofin, Husband, tiring of waiting and seeming unimportant in reflection of the vastness of the

Atlantic Ocean, suggested we go get a drink in a public house with the locals, because this was an Irish custom before boarding a boat, and he was ever so polite with customs that were manly and existed in a bar. Also, they'd asked for his signature in their guestbook and I thought it might lift his spirits were he to leave his mark somewhere.

The pub was pleasant, if a little dark, and immediately upon stooping under the door, Husband went and signed their book, like one does in a boarding house, and I noted, to my upset, that he didn't use our address, the one we share with our children, and I was conflicted. I wanted to both fuck him and kill him that very moment, but this was our way, and for now, I thought rather haughtily, he could stay in Halifax and let Halifax mind him, for he needed so much minding, giving so much away to people we had never met, who would pore over his signature in the weeks to come and ask all sorts of questions. Of course, this village seemed far too real for the wants and whims of poets; perhaps they would think we had a holiday home and a fixed abode, and this settled me somewhat.

The strangers in the bar didn't seem happy with our being there, darting glances and quizzical wiry faces, and who could blame them? They dragged their tulip glasses full of black porter into themselves, as though they were cradling a baby, and guffawed at Husband, not that he'd care, for he was louder than anyone in the world when he wanted to be, and then he could be completely silent, and that presence was all-encompassing, like the shadows of rooks; it would come on him without any warning. He would go deadly quiet and contorted in his physical body, put his head down and stoop into his coat collars, and then, after some hiatus, rise out of it like a wise tortoise and talk and talk and talk, usually about other people, the way of them and less about their work, which infuriated me. But sometimes it was enjoyable, particularly if I was feeling low, or envious.

I said so much to him in the bar as I drank the warmest glass of Guinness, the black eel making his warm way up through the yellow froth. I found it hard to understand how a nation had built so much myth on this drink that tasted oddly like my own blood. Husband hardly looked up from his pint, for I was not in the least agreeable, all tense and fluttery, and though I nudged him hard so he might look at me in the eye, he only lifted his finger to the barmaid. I knew then it would have been best if I hadn't favourably recommended Richard's poetry, it drove Husband into himself, but the Cleggan Disaster was such a sad affair, and I liked him, Richard, and his poem about the sinking boat, well it blew me away in that way you get blown away when you're not expecting it, your mind is astray about beaches or money or a flower you saw once but never saw again, a deep violet one.

Husband lifted his finger to call the bar for another pint.

After we finished our drinks, we took our tentative leave. Husband ran his hand over the guestbook upon exit, perhaps to take some luck out with him. His face was ruddy now, and he was somewhat more jovial and in better spirits. But I was ever so flat-footed as we walked along down the street to the pier.

Nimmo's Pier was named after an adventure, though I find it difficult to figure out how anyone could decide to start an adventure here. That said, I imagine the situation was one where a boat simply crashed into the coast, for that's about the size of how most adventures begin, with a crash or by an accident. Even explorers just happen upon lands by fate, whichever way one sees it, though they pretend it's all been arranged prior; that's the way of the male, everything is planned, metre, form, rhyme, nothing is a stray word, or action, but of course it is, and we know it and keep it to ourselves, all the magic accidents that were planned as though Husband's work were like that of creating a bridge or laying rail track.

Of course it's not, it's not nearly that important.

The boat arrived with her big buffeting white sails and looked unsteady. The West of Ireland was billowing in a muted buffet of bleak colour, not in a Constable way, but in a different way, like how smoke might leave a gentleman's pipe and fingers yellow, and his eyes and cap grey, a grey tweed herringbone, I imagine, though the style of tweed was of no concern to the locals, who favoured oiled skins and fisherman's hats. I think they must be entirely practical rather than taking flights of fancy like we do. I cannot particularly remember the weather with any sort of decent specifics; it had that awfully grey hue, suffice to say, the mock-up of the day was a grey that matched the rock and the sea and the sky and Husband.

Back in Devon, the children aren't sleeping at night; they resemble Irish weather, grumbly. They're ever so unsettled since Husband took leave, and they miss his physicality about the place, and squawk at me all day long, no matter what I seem to do with them. I bring them out and they cry as it is so very cold, or perhaps that's just a freezing memory from last winter and all that entailed. Tiredness fuels empty thoughts, shiver, but not the same intense grey that the West coast of Ireland seems to have burled up in my face, and in Devon we stay in for a considerable amount of day, as long as I can bear without tearing out my eyelashes with boredom.

pluck, pluck, pluck . . .

I find my rearing of them does not resemble my mother's, and this is somewhat a tragedy. For one thing, my kitchen is so different to Mother's. One always assumes they'll follow their mother in some way, particularly in the way of her kitchen. Once or twice I tried, but it is difficult to settle yourself on domestic chores when words constantly reel inside your head, observations to be recorded. She had a terrifically big kitchen, which would scare me now. She would slice mangos on hot days, and prepare fish; it would all appear to be perfectly normal, these scenes, until I began to think more about it, Mother and the house and the sea and Father and the great man he was, and I can make out the husk of my memory shell, but little else besides. It's empty, and when I try to see it, it floats upwards, so furiously unreliable, like what happens to the dead when they're dead, and to bring it back to mind, I have to imagine myself walking upstairs, with my feet on the steps, and I count them out in German, but then I can't remember his face at all, it just ups and disappears from my memory . . .

eins zwei drei

But it doesn't matter, for in my dreams I cannot walk straight up a staircase. Firstly, I cannot seem to put my foot flat on the mahogany boards and then I lift upwards and outwards over the bannister and I must hold on very tight to it; and secondly, for I'm not a ferociously strong woman, but in a dream and especially a day-dream, I try to convince myself that of course I have power. But it is hard to be louder than Husband.

Richard stood on deck, skinny and hollow like a sailboat, and I remarked on it, as a woman remarks to make everyone feel a lot more comfortable and at ease, though I had made little else except to unsettle the whole darn lot, yet I said, rather unfortunately, that Richard looked a lot like Husband. I wasn't sure if it was a rugged handsomeness or that he looked out of place and kind of useless; if there was a storm on the way from Cleggan to Inisbofin, we would have to Mayday an islander or a man from the town of Cleggan and he'd have to come out and do something, as useless as these men looked.

The crossing had been uneventful, as I locked myself inwards and lay prone down on the floor of the boat, but nobody passed remarks. Richard and Husband were busy criticizing the work of other poets, mostly letters, and nonsense about publishers. We docked at the pier at Inisbofin; it was slippy as I alighted, and I remember some old rusty tin and the like, but the action hummed in such a way I thought I could most certainly die here, and that calmed me, although the thought was fleeting, and Richard took my hand as I walked from the boat. Husband had already begun walking off, up the pier with his hands behind his back—in that way a man walks and thinks at the same time.

I would have liked to have asked Husband to wait up, but I thought that I'd catch up later, and in any case, it wasn't worth making a fuss in a strange place before one had even settled into their lodgings and unpacked their clothes and toiletries and bits of ends, and asking a man to wait up when they hadn't remembered you in the first instance was *needy*, and I knew enough to know that now wasn't the time to be needy. No, now was the time to be needed and I had to figure this out, how to be needed. It was something I had never fully come to grips with, not in the way Mother had. I would think about it on the island, if we managed to remain solid and not succumb to our usual habit of becoming horny and self-destructive, as we did after wine and talk of beautiful phrases and things we had seen during our days.

I was hot and bothered by the time I arrived at the guesthouse. In the lodgings I was shown to my room, along a dark narrow corridor. The locker was ever so near the bed and the bed was covered in an eiderdown of plain cream. I noticed a jug and a bowl and became startled, for I'm never quite sure what to do when one finds oneself face to face with the past. But I asked the woman of the house for a little warmish water and she filled some into the jug, in that way a woman can predict another woman's needs, though might not always meet them. I was ever so grateful for it and poured it into the bowl and began to wash my face and neck with a cloth, the water soothing, in the way I had hoped, but I was terribly conscious of the fact that I'd have to redo my face make-up. I rationalised this with myself and agreed the soothing was worth a possible reapplication. I had been so face-flushed on the boat and Richard kept on about it and in turn on about how he'd bought the hooker boat named as the Ave Maria off this man who loved it more than a woman, and I thought that's about right, because from everything I know of how a man loves a woman, this made the most sense. I lay down for a while and shoved my face into the cream eiderdown. I may have cried.

I slept. Upon my stirring, the woman of the house knocked gently and advised me of the hour and suggested I had a little time to myself, a polite way of putting my abandonment, before meeting up with my charges later that evening. She suggested a swim, and I agreed, that after the awful motion of the boat, being in the water may recalibrate the way I feel. She began to chatter about the disaster of that boat that had gone out and not returned and had left the fishermen to the sea, but then immediately she started fretting that she shouldn't have told me, as I gathered my swimming costume into myself and pawed it with my hands. But it was part of the reason I wanted to come here. I kept this to myself.

I left the house and walked out as far as the East Beach. I so wanted to go in for a swim, shiver, but I should like to test the water in advance, and all I could think of was the disaster; there was something about giving someone part of a story which was worse than not telling them at all, and far worse than giving the entire account. I have noticed that about the Irish, particularly the men — they talk a long time about very little, as though the topic is somewhere around the chatter, and it's your puzzle to find out.

I held my costume close into me and thought of the fishermen drowning and crying out, and I could hear Husband's voice, saying things to me, suggestions and chatter, but I couldn't concentrate on anything at all, especially recently what he was going on about. He didn't seem to want to be there, with me, in the same place as me, in the dark kitchen with me, or a garden, or walking along the street, and I wasn't entirely sure that us both leaving for another country was going to help us one bit; but men are far less concerned with long games anyhow, and are all far more impulsive.

I changed, feeling awkward as a couple ran a kite on the beach while their children played in the sand, one digging, the other building. The water was like a friend, helping, and it did what cold water does, made me feel awake. And for the first time in a long time, vibrant.

Later that evening, I returned to the lodging and fixed myself. I twisted my hair after braiding it, and my neck was tingling from the saltwater. I was giddy and unreliable.

The Bar was dark, and I was disappointed I hadn't bumped into Husband along the walk back from the East Beach. I didn't hassle the woman of the house as to his whereabouts, as women often do to each other, holding them accountable for the disappearance of a man.

The men were there, and I joined them. We started with a bottle of white wine and Richard tasted it and then looked like he had bitten into a lemon, though I found it quite pleasant, but a little too warm, like the earlier Guinness. I drank it very quickly until the flush rose on my breasts and up to my face and Husband shot me a look. I smiled at him. Richard was quoting Yeats and I wished they'd give over about apples.

I sat among them, blessed, and thought I'd like to light a long cigarette at this moment and escape. But I had none, so I poured myself another glass of wine and there was a moment of silence, but then all the men laughed, and I felt instantly angry.

I drank the wine and was feeling giddy, noting that Husband hadn't looked me in the eye since I sat down. The server woman came and smiled at me and stood at our table for some time and I asked after her family and she after mine, which brought them to the surface like boiling oil.

Of course something happened with Husband and I, in the way it always does with us, hidden and secret. Maybe I was inclined towards Richard. I think back on this and I am never certain or trustworthy of my recollection, of who touched who, but of course initiation is a futile mulling, for it's the aftermath that's always the more dramatic, and how inane it is to meet a man's leg under a table, and though I berated myself—please note I am also quite long-legged like a moorhen, as is Richard—sometimes I think that I was caressing the calf of Husband, and it was willing, hard, warm, so welcome, and I like this memory best. But then I think of *her*, with her dark hair and large lips, and I know it must be Richard I was seeking, or perhaps they were all seeking me, angrily, in the way men compete with each other. I had better stay on the sea like a portrait, remain there, dip myself down in the rainbow colours of the kites, bury myself alive in the child's bucket on the East Beach. I was self-destructive and seeking attention in the way I sometimes do, like Husband. Husband, noting my flirtation, or rouge, rose from the table, most irritated, and muttered about indigestion or a sharp pain in the bowels, lifted his collar up and over his chin.

I followed out into the night, after him, shiver, gathering my skin up and together, but couldn't catch up, shiver, and my shoes were now so tight they were melted on my hot feet, which began to swell. I took rest on the damp ditch, the dew falling as it did, without warning, more liquid than expected, enough to dampen me entirely, the back of my dress and my pants. I took off my shoes and curled my feet over the grass and the cold water began to bring the swelling down, faster than usual, and I could see the sinews in my feet, each bone that protruded into a toe, the baby toe, like the crowing heads of the children, and I rubbed them.

A dying corncrake cried out in the field behind the dry stone-wall that was precariously laid on the grass, bravely or stupidly, and I watched the corncrake move into the corner, like a rook returning back. I sat there to sing to it at first and to cool the toes, shiver, but I couldn't remember the words of any song.

I thought of the drowning men and the paintings with the faces dipped and I thought if I were to be a painting, I'd rather the face was covered in the blackest rook-black, and not in the cerise or the lemon sherbets, and that the painting should hang in the corner of a gallery, so no one sees it, like this dying corncrake, and its swalking swalking swalking, that I couldn't shut the damned thing out. Oh fuck, but so make me a rook in a gallery, blackened with only my breasts on show, although it's most unlikely I'd get any attention.

I hummed a little. I think it was Brahms, with the hard pianoforte banging after the violins, but the corncrake cawed out, louder and louder, my new friend, and I pulled my skirt down around my legs, taking my hair down and rubbing my arms fast with my hands. I took long deep breaths and watched the men bolt from the bar in his wake. In search of Husband, I went, but he was gone, far up the road as the corncrake cried out again, squalling, squalling, against the sea.

Clifden

Sky Road.

Clifden, the largest town in Conamara, is beautifully situated where the Owenglin River meets the sea at Clifden Bay. It was a planned town, built by the local landlord John D'Arcy at the beginning of the 19th century. It grew rapidly but the population was almost decimated during the Famine.

The town benefitted greatly from the opening of the railway line to Galway in 1895 and, at the turn of the century, from the construction of the Marconi Radio station in Derrygimlagh. The most famous visitors to the area were Captain John Alcock and Lieutenant Arthur Whitten Brown, two English airmen who, in June 1919, were the first people to fly non-stop across the Atlantic. They crash-landed in a bog near the Marconi Radio Station and are thus much celebrated in the town.

In the mid-nineteen-seventies, a local teacher, Brendan Flynn, decided to set up an annual Arts Festival in the Community School, a week-long celebration of the arts, which he hoped would help develop artistic and social skills in his pupils and provide them with a means of self-expression and creativity. It succeeded beyond his wildest dreams and became so successful that the community helped expand the festival throughout the town and surrounding area, transforming Clifden into a year-round cultural hub.

Siobhán Mannion

LEMONADE

She pedals hard, already late. A driver raises his hand in greeting and Audrey waves back. The sun does its usual dance, picking out the pink bells of fuchsia and the flaming montbretia. The sea spits salt into the air. Arriving in Clifden, she balances on tiptoe, the crossbar of the bicycle a little too high.

It is another busy morning in the café, a prolonged downpour keeping the stragglers in. 'Cat altogether,' says her grandmother, setting down pots of tea and triangles of cake, while locals and visitors shake out their anoraks, hanging them on the backs of tall, wooden chairs.

Mary, the woman who appears for a few hours each day, crouches at the oven, empties and reloads the dishwasher, tips warm bread onto a rack. Audrey slices oranges and cucumbers for the water jugs, and whips up metal bowls of cream. In the dining room, she clears the tables and greets the customers.

'So, you're Linda's girl,' says an expensively-dressed lady, handing her twenty euro at the till. Audrey nods, slipping the note into its drawer, counting out the change. 'I knew your mother when we were about your age.'

'Oh,' says Audrey politely. The woman studies her for a moment, and gives her a quick, tight smile before dropping her coins into the tips. A burst of laughter travels over to them: her grandmother joking with a party of locals. 'Would any of ye be heading into Galway this week?' she asks them. Audrey sighs and escapes to the kitchen.

*

They do not speak to each other for a full half hour, choreographing their tasks to avoid eye contact. Eventually, the lunchtime rush dissipates. A large pot of blackberry jam sits on the worktop. It will not open, no matter where Audrey presses on it. She swears at it under her breath.

'Come on, love. It's not so bad, is it?' Her grandmother sidles over, gently nudging her above the elbow.

'I keep telling you. I can get the bus. I'm not a child.'

'Sure aren't you better off getting a seat all the way in?'

Audrey does not reply. Silently, Mary takes the jam jar and runs it under the hot tap. She twists it open, and it gives a tiny *pop*. 'Thank you,' says Audrey, and busies herself spooning big shiny blobs into small white pots.

'Okay, okay,' says her grandmother. 'If you take the lift tomorrow, I'll talk to your Dad about next week.'

*

In the afternoon the weather lifts, the sun blazing inside the bay window. A young couple relocates to a more shaded table.

Through the hatch, Audrey watches a French family: a woman and a man consulting a map, a teenage boy in a green t-shirt emblazoned with a word she cannot make out. She has seen them before: once in the supermarket, once outside the bike shop, and three times at the foot of her grandmother's lane, near their rented house. She carries over their coffee and sparkling water, leaving the imprint of her fingers on the chilled glass. The boy checks his mobile without looking up.

'Hello,' says a tall man, stooping slightly as he comes in the door. 'Table for one?'

He smiles at her, his blue eyes younger than his face. 'I'll just say hello to Eily.'

Her grandmother slips out from the kitchen, her cheeks flushed. 'How are you keeping?' she asks, her voice light. Audrey folds a pile of napkins, observing them.

'Grand. I'm grand. How is she doing this week?' he says.

'Oh, hard to know. A bit better, maybe.'

They talk quietly, standing close. Briefly, the man touches her grandmother's shoulder. He gives Audrey a small wave on his way out.

*

At three o'clock, her grandmother lines up the ingredients for the last of the day's scones. Audrey makes tea, pressing the same bag against the inside of two mugs.

'Do you remember what *you* were doing the summer you were fifteen?' she asks, taking the milk from the fridge. Her grandmother does not respond, shaking flour through a sieve. Audrey thinks she has not heard the question over the music on the radio. But then she begins to move her hips, in time with the song.

'Ah, I couldn't be sure, love.' She smiles. 'It's so long ago.' She throws a pinch of salt into the bowl.

'What about Dad?'

'Same as you now.'

Audrey slides the butter and the raisins across the steel worktop, and sips at her tea. 'What's the story with Mary?'

'What do you mean?'

'I mean, does she ever speak?'

'She does, if she has something to say.'

*

The last hour is always the longest. Audrey sticks her head out the back door for a blast of sunlight. Warm air hangs in the familiar whitewashed yard. She steps over an oily puddle streaked with tiny rainbows. A ginger cat ambles along the top of a wall.

'Go on. Find your friends.' Her grandmother is holding up a brown paper bag.

'What about the coffee machine?'

'I'll do it.'

'And the cake tins?'

'Those too. Go on.'

*

Back on the borrowed bicycle, she races out of town, into the second beginning of the day. At the house, she changes into her swimsuit, pulls on a t-shirt and her favourite cut-off jeans. Carefully, she gathers up all the photographs spread across her duvet, making a neat pile beside the computer. She perches at the end of the high bed to tie her shoelaces.

Downstairs, she refills her water bottle, zipping it into her backpack with her jacket and a rolled up towel. Outside, she grabs the bodyboard, fixing it awkwardly behind the seat of the bike. Along the narrow road, she veers unsteadily, close to the low stone walls, slowing at the sound of every passing car on the short ride to the ocean.

The beach lies deserted. She takes her place on the big speckled rock that looks like a humpback whale, ancient and grey, half-buried in the sand. A wave breaks a few metres away. She waited more than an hour, that first evening, for the group of local teenagers to show, finally taking to the water on her own. They have yet to reappear since her grandmother got chatting to them, almost two months ago.

The bag reveals a peanut butter sandwich and one of the scones spliced with a generous, slippery dollop of jam. She devours everything, scrunching the paper into the front pocket of the rucksack, and then strips off, pushing her clothes into the bottom of the bag. She carries her board down to the shoreline, attaches its leash to her wrist, and paddles out on her belly, ignoring the cold.

When she is far enough into the sea, she turns to face land, wriggling into position, grabbing a top corner of the board with one hand. At the approach of a wave, she kicks her legs until she is carried by the water, arching her back to pick up speed. A calm delight surges through her. Again and again she wades out through the breakers; she has found the hidden hours in the day.

Audrey keeps going until her limbs are trembling. Paddling out for the final time into the sunshine, a memory floats back, from a summer far away. Standing at the edge of a swimming pool, her mother tall beside her. Bright streaks of turquoise and silver, the heavy scent of strange, trailing flowers. *You can do it, love. Go on.* How all it took was to stop thinking about it; to let herself fall into the arc of the dive, and enjoy the easy glide of it.

*

The figure on the rocks has one arm outstretched, wielding the pole of a fishing net. She shields her eyes, and recognises the pale green t-shirt. It rides up the French boy's back when he crouches to lay down his net. He takes something from the pocket of his shorts, and tightens the jumper tied around his waist.

She watches as he raises his mobile to take a photograph, angling and re-angling the shot, adjusting the kink of his elbow, the tilt of his head. She wonders what he is trying to capture in the background; there is only sky behind his face. Carefully composed images of her schoolfriends have been pulsing into her own phone all summer long.

'Do you want me to take your picture?' she says, climbing out of the sea.

'I'm not in the picture. It's the rocks,' he says in his foreign voice.

'Oh,' she says. 'Okay. Catch anything?' She nods at the fishing net. He smiles and shakes his head. Briskly, she rubs her towel across herself, and drags on her clothes over the damp swimsuit.

*

It is an evening of strong light, mimicking the break of day. Their conversation evolves into a walk in the direction of both their houses. He carries her board under his arm, fishing net in hand. She wheels the bicycle between them. Seawater drips down the back of her neck, and her ankle brushes against the thistles and daisies poking out of the hedges.

'Comment tu t'appelles?' she says, shyly.

'Oscar.'

'Audrey,' she says, pointing to herself unnecessarily.

Oscar has cycled the Sky Road, explored the beaches of Ballyconneely, been to the National Park and climbed the Diamond. Oscar has three days left in Ireland. His free arm swings with the rhythm of his stride; she admires the smooth tan of his skin. The word on the front of his t-shirt is still illegible. She decides she will ask him about it at the first lull in conversation.

'What does that mean?' He touches the back of her hand clutching the handlebar, the letter 'i' written in blue biro.

'To remind me,' she says. 'To buy more ink for the printer.'

'Oh,' he says. 'Me, I just remember things.'

They pass his family's rented house without acknowledging it.

He tells her he wants to be a geologist. He gestures ahead, and she finds herself glancing in that direction, as if his future is tangible, shimmering right in front of them. Oscar takes out his mobile to show Audrey something, and discovers that the battery has died. He mentions a day trip to Inishbofin. Would she like to join him, in the morning? She nods, as if she might really be free, and not stuck in a car with strangers for the hour and twenty minutes it will take to transport her to the hospital, another hour and twenty back in the evening.

'There's a rock on the beach that looks like a whale,' she says.

'Yes,' he smiles. 'I've seen it.'

*

It had been another difficult visit last week.

Audrey found her mother in the corridor, caressing the skinny leaves of a large spider plant. Gently, she took her by the elbow, and guided her back to her room. 'Is it time?' she asked vaguely, leaning on her daughter's arm. She was wearing her favourite yellow cardigan. 'Yes. Time to sit down for a while. Look. I've brought you something.'

Audrey took out the latest printouts and laid them across the table. Her mother examined them — sunny days, outdoor days, holidays — saying nothing. Audrey pulled her chair a little closer, watchful for any gleam of recognition.

Later, arriving at the house with bags of takeaway, Audrey found her father at the bottom of the garden. Silently, she put her arm around him. The two of them stood looking at the weeds that had sprung up in the wild, rampant months between Easter and late summer. She closed her eyes, flinching once more at the thought of the absurd, unlikely moment that had landed them here: her mother tripping on a paving stone, cracking her head on the corner of a wall, on the short walk into town.

'Dad, can I come home now?' she asked.

He sighed. 'Not yet, love. Not until you're back in school. Not when I'm so rarely here.'

*

Nine-thirty and still daylight; half an hour since she texted her early-to-bed grandmother with a second update on her whereabouts. They have made it as far as the white painted bench at the side of the house. Audrey reaches into her bag for the water bottle, takes a drink and offers Oscar a sip. He puts it to his lips and finishes it. The talking stops. She looks down and covers his nearer hand with her own. A flare of anticipation travels through her. He smiles and puts his fingertips to her collarbone. They kiss without hesitation. She licks his tongue and his warm, salty skin. He opens his mouth wide enough to take in her nose, her lips, her chin.

During the second kiss, he clasps one hand to the back of her neck, the other unzipping her jacket. She runs her hands around his waist, and he has his hand under her top, sliding up. His fingers move inside her swimsuit, underneath her left breast. *This.* This is what she will wake up tomorrow thinking about. Gently, she pulls away, and immediately he retreats. When she shakes off her hoodie and pulls her t-shirt over her head, he takes in an audible breath. 'Audrey,' he says, her name a new word in his accent.

She lets her hands fall, and waits. Slowly, he lowers the shoulder straps, rolling the material down to her hips. They kiss again. She considers what it would be to bring him into her bed, and manoeuvres herself to lie along the bench. Oscar climbs onto her, stretching out one leg. A loud crash jolts them apart, one wheel left whirring on the upturned bicycle. He sits up, gripping the armrest behind her head.

'I must go,' he says.

'Now?' she says.

'Mes parents. It is late.' Awkwardly, he brings himself to standing. 'Demain?' he asks.

'The day after?'

'The day after is good,' he says, grabbing his fishing net and running off.

The moon is out, although the night is yet to fully take hold. Audrey spots Oscar's jumper at her feet and slips it on, the soft wool brushing lightly against her nakedness. She hugs her knees to her chest, and hears the quiet plick plick of his footsteps evaporate. A mild sea breeze picks up, but she will not move for a while yet. She listens closely for the sound of the ocean, but all she can make out is the rustle of the wild grass.

ACKNOWLEDGEMENTS

Acknowledgements are due to the following publications in which versions of some of the stories included in this anthology first appeared: 'DeeDee and the Sorrows' by Celeste Augé was first published in *Fireproof and other Stories* (Doire Press, 2012); 'Athair' and 'Father' by Micheál Ó Conghaile were first published in *An Fear a Phléasc* and *The Colours of Man* (Cló Iar-Chonnacht, 1997 and 2012, respectively); 'Futuretense*' by Nuala O'Connor was first published in *Joyride to Jupiter* (New Island, 2017); and 'Poetic Justice' by Moya Roddy was first published in *Crannóg* (2008).

The editors would like to give a tremendous thanks to each of the twenty writers included in this anthology for generously allowing us to share their stories of Galway.

A big thank you to Sarah Bannan and the Arts Council of Ireland for their support.

Another big thank you to Marilyn Gaughn, Liz Kelly and Galway 2020 for their support.

Thanks also to Tom Kenny for his brilliant one-of-a-kind antecdotal neighbourhood bits; to Róisín Flaherty for jaunting all over Galway city and county to capture her extraordinary photographs; to Tríona Walsh for her amazing maps and icons; and to John Walsh for helping out along the way to make this book the best it can be.

Final thank yous to Mary Costello for her good words and to Anne-gret Walsh for her clever ideas.

ABOUT THE EDITORS

ALAN MCMONAGLE is a writer based in Galway, Ireland. In 2015, he signed a two-book deal with Picador, and his debut novel, *Ithaca*, was published in March, 2017 and nominated for the Desmond Elliott Award for first novels, a Bord Gáis Irish Book Award and the Dublin Literary Award. He has received awards for his work from the Professional Artists' Retreat in Yaddo (New York), the Fundación Valparaiso (Spain), the Banff Centre for Creativity (Canada) and the Arts Council of Ireland. He has published two collections of short stories, *Psychotic Episodes* (Arlen House, 2013) and *Liar Liar* (Wordsonthestreet, 2008), both of which were nominated for the Frank O'Connor Short Story Award. His stories have appeared in many journals in Ireland and North America, and he has read from his work at many festivals at home and abroad. He also writes for radio and three radio plays (*Oscar Night, People Walking on Water* and more recently, *Shirley Temple Killer Queen*) have been produced and broadcast as part of RTE's *Drama on One* season. His second novel, *Laura Cassidy's Walk of Fame*, is due from Picador in March, 2020.

LISA FRANK was born and raised in Los Angeles but lived in the Pacific Northwest for several years before moving to Ireland in 2007. She received her MFA in Creative Writing from Eastern Washington University and has published fiction, poetry, creative non-fiction and screenplays. In 2016 she won second place in the Francis MacManus Short Story Competition and in both 2015 and 2020 she was a joint-winner of the Irish Writers' Centre Novel Fair Competition. Her very first publication, 'The Seven Deadly Sins: From God to the Simpsons', was reprinted in *Common Culture*, an American university text book on writing. She is the editor of *Galway Stories* (2013) and co-editor of *Belfast Stories* (2019). Having taught creative writing in a variety of settings, including a mens' prison, she now lives in Conamara with her fiancé and is co-director of Doire Press.

CONTRIBUTORS' NOTES

CELESTE AUGÉ is the author of *Skip Diving* (Salmon Poetry, 2014), *The Essential Guide to Flight* (Salmon Poetry, 2009) and the short fiction collection, *Fireproof and Other Stories* (Doire Press, 2012). *World Literature Today* wrote that 'In her debut collection of short fiction, Augé creates poignant and accurate outlines of women and their places in the world'. Her writing has been widely published in literary journals and she has given readings at festivals, libraries and pubs, as well as chairing literary events. Celeste's poetry was shortlisted for a Hennessy Award and in 2011, she won the Cúirt New Writing Prize for Fiction. She lives in Connemara in the west of Ireland.

NAIMH BOYCE won the Hennessy XO New Irish Writer of The Year in 2012. Her debut novel *The Herbalist* was a critically-acclaimed bestseller, won the Sunday Independent Debut of the Year at the Irish Book Awards and was nominated for an IMPAC Award. *Inside the Wolf*, her debut poetry collection, was released in 2018. Her fiction and poetry have been broadcast, adapted for stage and anthologised, most recently in *The Long Gaze Back*, *The Hennessy Anthology* and *Hallelujah for 50 Foot Women*. Her second novel, *Her Kind*, is based on the Kilkenny Witchcraft Trial of Alice Kytler.

ALAN CADEN is from Galway, where he lives with his wife and two children. He teaches English and Spanish. In a former life he worked in Taylor's Bar, before it closed in 2004. He is a once and future member of the Atlantis Collective, a group of writers who have published three short story collections; *Town of Fiction*, *Faceless Monsters* and *Eat the Swans*. Other stories have appeared in *Ropes* and *Galway Noir*. He is currently engaging in the Galway past-time of writing a novel.

JUNE CALDWELL's short story collection *Room Little Darker* was published in 2017 by New Island Books and in 2018 by Head of Zeus. Her novel *Little Town Moone* is forthcoming from John Murray. In 2019 she wrote the introduction for *Still Worlds Turning*, published by No Alibis Press, and in 2018 for the new edition of Nuala O'Faolain's *Are you Somebody?* She is a prize-winner of The Moth International Short Story Prize and lives in Dublin.

AOIFE CASBY lives on the west coast of Ireland, where she swims and grows potatoes. She works as a writer, editor and visual artist. Her short fiction has been published in *The Dublin Review*, *The Stinging Fly*, *Banshee*, *Noir by Noir-West* (Arlen House), *Ropes*, *The Cúirt Annual*, and *The Cork Literary Review*, among others. She was the winner of The 2017 Doolin Short Story Prize and has been longlisted for the Seán Ó Faoláin Short Story Award and the Fish Short Story Prize. Aoife has also been awarded literature bursaries from the Arts Council of Ireland and Galway County Council. She is currently working on a novel and is completing a PhD at Goldsmith's University, London.

DANNY DENTON is a writer from Cork with an MA in Writing from NUI Galway. His first novel, *The Earlie King & The Kid in Yellow*, was published by Granta Books in 2018. Among other publications, his work has appeared in *The Stinging Fly*, *Southword*, *Granta*, *Winter Papers*, *The Dublin Review*, *Banshee*, *Tate Etc*, *The Guardian*, *The Irish Times*, *Architecture Ireland* and *The Big Issue*. He is also the editor of *The Stinging Fly* magazine.

ELAINE FEENEY has published three collections of poetry, *Where's Katie?*, *The Radio was Gospel* and *Rise*, as well as a drama, *WRoNGHEADED*, commissioned by the Liz Roche Company. She teaches at The National University of Ireland, Galway, and St Jarlath's College. Her work has been widely published and anthologised in *The Poetry Review*, *The Stinging Fly*, *The Irish Times*, *Copper Nickel*, *Stonecutter Journal* and others. *As You Were*, her fiction debut, will be published in June 2020 by Penguin Random House (Harvill Secker).

ÓRLA FOYLE'S first novel *Belios* was published by The Lilliput Press. *Red Riding Hood's Dilemma* (poetry) was published by Arlen House and shortlisted for the Rupert and Eithne Strong Award in 2011. Arlen House published *Somewhere in Minnesota*, her debut short fiction collection in 2011, and her second short fiction collection *Clemency Browne Dreams of Gin* in 2015. Her work has been previously published in *The Wales Arts Review*, *The Lonely Crowd*, *The Dublin Review*, *The Manchester Review* and anthologized in *Faber and Faber's New Irish Short Stories*, 2011, edited by Joseph O'Connor. Órla's novel *The Sawdust Dictator* is forthcoming.

CAOILINN HUGHES was born in Galway and studied at the Queen's University of Belfast and later at Victoria University of Wellington, New Zealand. Her first novel, *Orchid & the Wasp* (Oneworld 2018) won the 2019 Collyer Bristow Prize, was a finalist for the Hearst Big Book Awards and the Butler Literary Award, and was longlisted for the Authors' Club Best First Novel Award. For short fiction, she won The 2018 Moth Short Story Prize and an O. Henry Award in 2019. Her poetry collection, *Gathering Evidence* (Carcanet, 2014) won the Irish Times Shine/Strong Award 2015. Her second novel, *The Wild Laughter*, is forthcoming in May, 2020.

JAMES MARTYN JOYCE lives in Galway. His work has appeared in *The Cúirt Journal, Books Ireland, The Sunday Tribune, The Stinging Fly* and *The Shop*. He was shortlisted for a Hennessy Award, the Francis McManus award and The William Trevor International Short Story Competition. He has had work broadcast on RTE and BBC and won the Listowel Writers' Week Originals Short Story Competition in 1997 and the Doolin Writers Prize in 2014, as well as being a joint-winner of the Greenbean Novel Fair in 2016. He is the author of *What's Not Said* (short stories, 2012) and the editor of *Noir by Noir West* (2014), both with Arlen House, as well as the author of two poetry collections, including his most recent, *Furey* (Doire Press, 2018).

HUGO KELLY has won many awards for his short fiction, including the Cúirt New Writing Award and the Brian Moore Short Story Competition. He has twice been shortlisted for the Hennessy Literary Awards in Emerging Fiction and the Fish International Short Story Competition. His work has appeared in many publications and anthologies, including recently in *The Stinging Fly* and *Counterparts: A Synergy of Law and Literature* anthology. BBC Radio 4 and RTE Radio 1 have broadcast his short stories. He also writes for younger readers and won the inaugural Children's Writers' and Artists' Yearbook Short Story Award in the UK. Hugo works as a librarian in NUI, Galway.

SIOBHÁN MANNION was born in Ireland and grew up in Cambridge, England. Both her parents were from Connemara: her mother came from Ballyconneely and her father was from Clifden. Her work has appeared in Irish and international publications, including *Granta, Winter Papers, Banshee, Eighteen Bridges, Stand, The Moth* and *The Long Gaze Back: An Anthology of Irish Women Writers*. She is a recipient of an Arts Council Literature Bursary, a MacDowell Colony fellowship and the Hennessy Award. She lives in Dublin, where she worked for many years as a radio producer in RTÉ and is now completing a collection of stories.

UNA MANNION lives in County Sligo. She has won numerous prizes for her work, including the Hennessy Emerging Poetry Award and the Doolin, Cúirt, Allingham and Ambit short story prizes. Her work has been published in *The Irish Times*, *The Lonely Crowd*, *Crannóg* and *Bare Fiction*. She edits *The Cormorant*, a broadsheet of prose and poetry. Her debut novel will be published by Faber and Faber in 2021.

PATRICK MCCABE was born in Clones, County Monaghan in 1955. He's had many novels published, including *The Dead School*, *The Butcher Boy*, *Winterwood* and most recently, *The Big Yaroo*. He is married with two grown-up children.

AOIBHEANN MCCANN Aoibheann McCann is originally from Donegal. She lives in Galway where she writes fiction, non-fiction and the occasional poem. Her work has been published in literary journals in Ireland, UK, Italy and the USA. Her work has been anthologised by Pankhurst Press (UK), New Binary Press, Arlen House and Prospero (Italy). Her short stories have been longlisted for the 2019 Colm Toibin Award, shortlisted for the 2015 Words on Waves, the 2018 Sunday Business Post/ Penguin Ireland, the 2019 Cúirt New Writing, and placed second in the 2019 Maria Edgeworth. In 2018 Aiobheann was awarded the Tyrone Guthrie Residency by Galway City Council. Her first novel *Marina* was published by Wordsonthestreet in 2018. She is currently working on her first collection of short fiction.

GERALDINE MILLS is a native of Galway, growing up in Ballyfoyle when it was still country. She is the author of three short fiction collections, a children's novel and five collections of poetry, her most recent *Bone Road* (Arlen House). She has won a Hennessy New Irish Writer Award, a Katherine Kavanagh Fellowship and has been awarded two Arts Council bursaries. Her story 'Pretty Bird, Why You So Sad?', which was published in *Galway Stories* (Doire Press, 2013), was winner of the inaugural RTÉ/Penguin Short Story Competition. Her short stories and poetry are taught in several US universities. She is a fiction mentor with NUI, Galway and a member of Poetry Ireland Writers in Schools' Scheme. She lives in Rosscahill with her husband, Peter Moore.

MICHEÁL Ó CONGHAILE was born in 1962 in Conamara. He established the publishing company Cló Iar-Chonnacht (CIC) in 1985. He has published poetry, short stories, a novel, plays, novellas and translation work. In 1997 the Irish American Cultural Institute awarded him The Butler Literary Award. In 1997 he won the Hennessy Literary Award and the Hennessy Irish Writer of the Year Award. In 1998 he was elected to Aosdána. His works have been translated into various languages, including Romanian, Croatian, Albanian, Slovenian, German, Bengali, Polish, Macedonian, Arabic and English. He was writer in Residence at Queen's University, Belfast and at the University of Ulster, Coleraine, and received an honorary degree from the National University of Ireland, Galway in 2013. *Colourful Irish Phrases* was published by Mercier Press in 2018.

NUALA O'CONNOR lives in Ballinasloe, County Galway. In 2019 she won the James Joyce Quarterly competition to write the missing story from Dubliners, 'Ulysses'. Her fourth novel, *Becoming Belle,* was published in 2018 to critical acclaim in the US, Ireland and the UK. Her forthcoming novel is about Nora Barnacle, wife and muse to James Joyce. Nuala is editor at new flash e-zine *Splonk*. www.nualaoconnor. com.

ELIZABETH (E.M.) REAPY is a writer from Mayo. Her debut novel *Red Dirt* was published in 2016. It won an Irish Book Award and the 2017 Rooney Prize for Irish Literature. In 2018, she was a Dublin UNESCO City of Literature Writer-in-Residence. *Skin*, her second novel, was released in 2019. She lives and writes in Galway.

MOYA RODDY has been living and working in Galway for over twenty-five years. A 'Jackie' of all trades, she's been commissioned to write for television, film, radio and stage, including RTE, Channel 4 and Scottish Television. She's published a novel, *The Long Way Home* (Attic Press), described in the *Irish Times* as 'simply brilliant', as well as *Other People* (Wordsonthestreet), a collection of short-stories that was nominated for the Frank O'Connor Award. In 2018 she published her debut collection of poetry, *Out of the Ordinary* (Salmon), which was shortlisted for the Shine/Strong Award. In 2017 she was shortlisted for the Hennessy Award.

ABOUT THE PHOTOGRAPHER

RÓISÍN FLAHERTY is a photographer/artist from Conamara. She also works as a vision engineer for TG4's Irish language soap, *Ros na Rún*. After graduating from National Fisheries College as Ireland's first female chief marine engineer, she spent years on fishing vessels, which started a life-long love of light, sea and landscape. Her experiences as both a lighting technician and a vision engineer in film and television work laid a foundation towards fine art photography. You can find her work on Facebook (www.facebook.com/roisinflahertyphotography) and on Instagram (www.instagram.com/roisinflaherty).

ABOUT THE RESEARCHER

TOM KENNY was born in Galway and educated in Scoil Fhursa, Coláiste Iognáid and UCG. He has worked in the family business, Kennys Bookshop and Art Gallery, since leaving college. For most of that time, he has been involved with the art end of the business and has hosted several hundred exhibitions by Irish and international artists, and organised many such shows in different parts of the country. He has published a number of books and written and lectured on local Galway history for many years.

ABOUT THE GRAPHIC ARTIST

TRÍONA WALSH is a Graphic Designer / Illustrator from Dublin. She works on a wide variety of projects from advertising and promotional work to book illustrations and covers. Her traditional/digital hybrid collage art has been part of a number of group exhibitions and been sold into private collection globally. She is also a writer and was the winner of the Molly Keane short story competition, the Jonathan Swift short story competition and was a joint winner of the Irish Writers Centre Novel Fair, as well as being shortlisted for the Francis MacManus short story competition in 2019. www.trionawalsh.com / www.chromaticatticdesign.com.

NEIGHBOURHOOD LISTINGS

BALLINASLOE

An Tàin Bar
5 St Michael's Square, Townparks
090 9645157

Clooncummer B&B
Beagh, Creagh
090 9643983

Kariba's Restaurant
7 Society Street, Townparks
090 9644830
www.karibas.ie

Moycarn Lodge
Shannonbridge Road, Creagh
090 9645050
www.moycarnlodge.ie

Venezia Restaurant
Dunlo Street, Townparks
090 9646483
www.veneziaballinasloe.com

BARNA

Abbeyville B&B
Freeport
091 592430
www.abbeyvillebarna.com

Galway Coast Cottages
Forramoyle East
091 592784
www.galwaycoastcottages.com

Hooked Fish & Chips Restaurant
Unit 20, Barna Village Centre
091 596623

O'Gradys on the Pier Restaurant
Seapoint
091 592223
www.ogradysonthepier.ie

The Twelve Hotel
Barna Road, Freeport
091 597000
www.thetwelvehotel.ie

CITY CENTRE

Balcony House B&B
27 College Road
091 563438
www.balconyhouse.ie

Caprice Café
1 Church Lane
091 564781
www.caprice.ie

Charlie Byrne's Bookshop
The Cornstore, Middle Street
091 561766
www.charliebyrne.ie

The Crane Bar
2 Sea Road
091 587419
www.thecranebar.com

The Dough Bros
1 Middle Street
091 395238
www.thedoughbros.ie

Dubray Bookshop
4 Shop Street
091 569070
www.dubraybooks.ie

Eyre Square Townhouse
35 Eyre Street
091 568444
www.eyresquaretownhouse.com

The Galway Arms Inn
65 Dominick Street Lower
091 564555
www.galwayarmsinn.com

Harbour Hotel
New Dock Street
091 894800
www.harbour.ie

The Hardiman
Eyre Square
091 564041
www.thehardiman.ie

The House Hotel
Spanish Parade, Latin Quarter
091 538900
www.thehousehotel.ie

Il Vicolo
The Bridge Mills, Dominick Street Lower
091 530515
www.ilvicolo.ie

Judy Greene's Giftshop
Kirwan's Lane
091 561753
www.judygreenepottery.com

Kashmir Restaurant
10 Fairhill Road Lower
091 589900
www.kashmir.ie

Kenny's Bookshop
Liosban Business Park, Tuam Road
091 709350
www.kennys.ie

Monroe's Tavern
14 Dominick Street Upper
091 583397
www.monroes.ie

Róisín Dubh Bar and Club
9 Dominick Street Upper
091 586540
www.roisindubh.net

Taylor's Bar and Beer Garden
7 Dominick Street Upper
091 450475
www.taylorsgalway.ie

Tigh Neachtain Pub
17 Cross Street
091 568820
www.tighneachtain.com

CLIFDEN

Abbeyglen Castle Hotel
Sky Road
095 21201
www.abbeyglen.ie

The Clifden Bookshop
Main Street
095 22020

Lowry's Irish Music and Whiskey Bar
Market Street
095 21347
www.lowrysbar.ie

Mannions Seafood Bar and Restaurant
1 Market Street
095 21780
www.mannionsbarclifden.com

Sea Mist House B&B
Seaview, Beach Road
095 21441
www.seamisthouse.com

CONAMARA

An Caladh Gearr B&B
Knock South, Inverin
091 593124

Ballynahinch Castle Hotel
Recess
095 31006
www.ballynahinch-castle.com

Pádraicins Bar and Restaurant
Furbo
091 592444
www.padraicinsrestraurant.com

Renvyle House Hotel and Restaurant
Renvyle
095 46100
www.renvyle.com

Standún Giftshop
Spiddal
091 553108
www.standun.com

White Gables Restaurant
Ballycuirke West, Moycullen
091 555744
www.whitegables.com

INISBOFIN

The Beach Day's Bar & Restaurant
Middlequarter
095 45829
www.thebeach.ie

Dolphin Hotel and Restaurant
Knock
095 45991
www.dolphinhotel.ie

Doonmore Hotel, Bar and Restaurant
Fawnmore
095 45804
www.doonmorehotel.com

Harbour Lights Bookstore
Harbour Lights

KILLARY

Blackberry Restaurant
Letterbrickaun, Leenane
095 42240
blackberryrestaurant.ie

Gaynor's Bar
Letterbrickaun, Leenane
095 42261

Leenane Hotel
Clifden Road
Letterbrickaun, Leenane
095 42249
www.leenanhotel.com

Le Fjord House B&B
Letterbrickaun, Leenane
095 42325

KNOCKNACARRA

Capone's Restaurant
Kingston Hall, Kingston Road
091 520060
www.capones.ie

Clybaun Hotel
Clybaun Road
091 588088
www.clybaunhotel.ie

Tom Sheridan's Pub and Restaurant
14 Glenvale Court, Clybaun Road
091 525315
www.tomsheridans.ie

ROSSCAHILL

Brigit's Garden Café
Pollagh
091 550905
www.brigitsgarden.ie

Kinnevey's Pub
Clifden Road, Ross Demesne
091 550112

Ross Lake House Hotel
091 550109
www.rosslakehotel.com

SALTHILL

Black Cat Restaurant
179 Upper Salthill
091 501007
www.blackcat.ie

Galway Bay Hotel
The Promenade
091 514645
www.galwaybayhotel.net

Gourmet Tart Co Restaurant
Upper Salthill
091 861667
www.gourmettartco.com

Lonergan's Bar
258 Upper Salthill
091 522049

Oslo Bar
226 Upper Salthill
091 448390
www.galwaybaybrewery.com/oslo

Salthill Hotel
The Promenade
091 522711
www.salthillhotel.com

The Wave B&B
12 Ocean Wave
087 9254702

About Galway 2020

Galway is the European Capital of Culture in 2020. As one of the largest cultural events in the world, Galway 2020 promises to deliver a year of thrilling, life-enhancing experiences through culture and the arts. The exciting pan-European programme for the year will see events in unexpected venues and locations throughout the region, on the islands, in remote villages, in fields, mountains and on beaches. From food, music, dance, literature and visual arts to poetry, theatre, sport and largescale spectacle, everyone will get the opportunity to enjoy a fun-filled, once-in-a-lifetime experience.

Visit galway2020.ie to view the full programme.

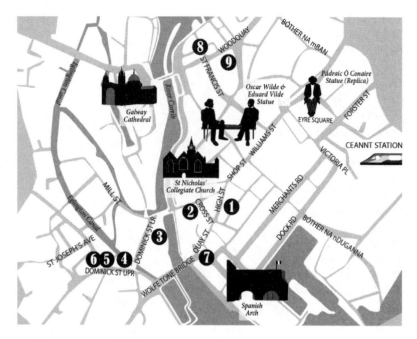

Story Locations

1. *The Blow-In's Guide to Galway* by Aoibheann McCann
2. *Angel Hands* by James Martyn Joyce
3. *I Ate it All and I Really Thought I Wouldn't* by Caoilinn Hughes
4. *DeeDee and the Sorrows* by Celeste Augé
5. *Socrates, in His Later Years* by Alan Caden
6. *The Galway Spike* by Patrick McCabe
7. *The Doteen* by Niamh Boyce
8. *Poetic Justice* by Moya Roddy
9. *Rainwords* by E.M. Reapy
10. *In Between Days* by Una Mannion
11. *Statistics are Against Us* by Hugo Kelly
12. *Motorbike Accident, Roscam* by Danny Denton
13. *Futuretense®* by Nuala O'Connor
14. *It Can Be Good* by Órla Foyle
15. *Malachi Dreams in a Cupboard* by June Caldwell
16. *Father / Athair* by Micheál Ó Conghaile
17. *By the Time the Thaw Comes* by Geraldine Mills
18. *John* by Aoife Casby
19. *Sojourn* by Elaine Feeney
20. *Lemonade* by Siobhán Mannion

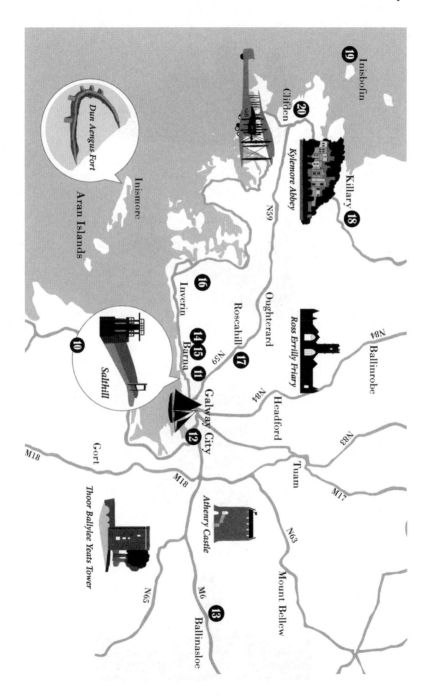

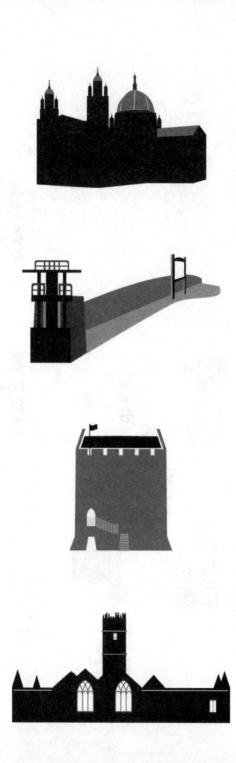